Hannie Bennet's Winter Marriage

Kerry Hardie was born in 1951, grew up in Bangor, Northern Ireland and read English literature at York University. On returning to Ireland she worked for the BBC in Belfast and for the Arts Council. She has published two books of poetry with the Gallery Press and is the winner of the Friends Provident National Poetry Prize [Ireland]. She now lives in Co Kilkenny with her husband, the writer Sean Hardie. This is her first novel.

ALSO BY KERRY HARDIE

POETRY

A Furious Place (Gallery Press)
Cry for the Hot Belly (Gallery Press)

Hannie Bennet's Winter Marriage

KERRY HARDIE

HarperCollinsPublishers

HarperCollins*Publishers*
77–85 Fulham Palace Road,
Hammersmith, London W6 8JB

www.**fire**and**water**.com

A Paperback Original 2000
1 3 5 7 9 8 6 4 2

A catalogue record for this book
is available from the British Library

ISBN 0 00 651342 5

Set in Stempel Garamond by
Rowland Phototypesetting Ltd,
Bury St Edmunds, Suffolk

Printed and bound in Great Britain by
Clays Ltd, St Ives plc

For Sean
Without whom there'd be no book

❧ *Acknowledgements* ❧

*M*y grateful thanks to all the following, who helped or read or advised:

Carmel Cummins, Olivia Goodwillie, Paddy and Dorothy Jolley, Barbara and Irene Kelly, Kieran Lineen, Val and Marian Lonergan, Pat Murphy, Helen Parry-Jones, Helen O'Brien, Paddy and Fintan Ryan, and all those at the Butler House.

The author also wishes to thank the Tyrone Guthrie Centre at Annaghmakerrig.

✎ *Chapter 1* ✎

She met him at a wedding she had gone to only because she needed a husband and a wedding wasn't a bad place to begin looking.

She didn't try to hide much from him, which was sound judgement because he didn't know much about women and he couldn't have talked to a woman who wasn't straight with him. But more than judgement, Hannie had luck. She met Ned when he was looking anyway, so most of the work was done for her. And he took to her, he liked her crooked straightness from the start.

She came from nowhere, had no family, no country and no background. None of that would have mattered only she had no money either so she needed somewhere to live, something to live on. She was fifty-two, she made no secret of it, nor of the fact that her need for a husband was overwhelmingly financial.

That didn't put Ned off. Nor did the fourteen-year-old son she'd left in Africa while she came prospecting for their futures.

Ned didn't know what he wanted when he met her, he'd only just admitted to himself that he wanted anything at all, so her directness eased things for him. He didn't know it, but he couldn't have coped with a woman of delicacy who left him to do the running, and he couldn't have coped with a woman who wasn't an outsider.

So the way of it was she decided Ned might do and she got round Tom and Beth so they helped her, and Ned went along with it not because he was trapped by her as his friends thought, but because she was what he wanted all along.

Social situations were what she needed, and introductions to the right sort of men: men who didn't know her history or reputation, who might be charmed and cajoled into taking her on. By luck a widow this time not a divorcée, she still had a few respectable connections to exploit, so when she decided on taking this trip to England she phoned the Grenvilles from Kenya and asked Beth for a bed.

'For the wedding,' she said. 'Maybe a day or two after, I'm not sure of my movements. So much to be taken care of – Andrew's English estate – London – Andrew's solicitors . . .' She left it vague.

Strictly speaking, she hadn't asked, she'd just said her piece and then waited, knowing that Beth wouldn't be able to let the silence run on. Beth was soft, everyone knew that, most of all Hannie, who was anything but soft. There were other people she could have asked, but she didn't. If you were going to use someone, best choose someone trustworthy who assumed that you were the same until they were reminded that you weren't. It wasn't long before Beth was reminded, but by then it was too late.

The wedding invitation was more luck. The bride had been Andrew's god-daughter, the embossed invitation had come in the post a bare six weeks before he died. Andrew had answered at once: congratulations to his little Sophie (not so little any more, it seemed); he and Hannie would most certainly be there to see her married. Between this acceptance and his death a few weeks later he had issued his ultimatum and Hannie had left.

But Sophie didn't know this and neither did Sophie's parents, who wrote their commiserations when the death-notice appeared in the London *Times*. The letter was addressed to Andrew's widow, Hannie Bennet.

Hannie wrote back that she would be in England on

business matters and she very much looked forward to this meeting with Andrew's old friends and his god-daughter at her wedding. Andrew had spoken of them so often, she felt it only right to be there as his representative.

She sealed the letter, trusting they wouldn't yet have heard the gossip. Even if they had, they'd hardly write and tell her so. Or make a scene when she turned up at the church.

She was still an attractive woman, Beth thought, watching Hannie sitting at a table on the lawn. There was the usual wedding marquee but the day was fine and dry, the tables had all been moved outside.

Very attractive, whatever Tom might say. Tom liked more grooming: nice hair, a little make-up, something finished in the look. Yet he woke up when Hannie was around, he pretended he didn't, but he did.

Any fool could see she was trouble, Tom used to say; there were always nods and murmurs of agreement from his listeners. Beth thought men saw the trouble and they liked it, even Tom. They liked the aloofness, the lack of involvement, the way she walked by herself.

Hannie had kicked off her shoes under the table, her hair was sun-bleached and she wore a not-new dress in faded grey. Beth pulled the floral frock she'd thought she liked so much down over her stomach. She wished she'd tried for elegance not prettiness. She wished she didn't care that her waist had broadened and her stomach bulged. She wished that, like Hannie, she didn't try to hide it.

Funny how it looked all right if you didn't care. Except it probably wouldn't on her. She resolved to eat less, walk more. She knew she wouldn't. She resolved to stop worrying so much about what she looked like, to 'accept' herself (that curious language that her children spoke). Hannie had just done that thing she did when she stopped being interested by whoever it was she had been being interested by. Switched off the light and gone out. Beth had almost forgotten that trick, the way she could not-be-there, like an abandoned puppet, a rag-doll left out in the rain. Men always fell for it, they suddenly got frantic that she wasn't listening any more, wasn't interested when she had been, so intensely. Funny how easy it was for some people.

It didn't feel easy to Hannie. It was all smooth and smart and understated, all grooming and opinions. She had to wrench herself up to the mark, make herself perform, not give up and go under. She felt blunt and shabby and old. And tired, really tired.

She met Ned through a young woman called Jessica who'd sought her out and introduced herself.

'My mother knew your husband. She said you might be here. I'm to offer you her sympathies.'

Hannie hovered for a moment on the edge of paranoia. She dismissed it. This Jessica would neither know nor care about the marital gossip of another generation on another continent.

'She knew the family. Years ago in Oxfordshire. She had a thing about the oldest brother.'

'Edward,' Hannie said.

'Edward,' Jessica agreed. 'You must tell me how he is. She'll want to know in detail –'

'He's dead. Died before I ever met him.'

'Really?' Jessica sounded quite interested. 'My father will be relieved. Edward was her untravelled road. She does rather tend to let herself regret him out loud when she's cross.'

Jessica was tall and slender with grey eyes and perfect skin and perfect self-possession. A woman, not a girl, nearer thirty-five than twenty, her voice was clear and well-bred and she wore a loose green linen dress which showed off her wavy, fair hair. She was like daylight, Hannie thought, not liking her.

She had a man with her, following a few paces after like a dragged anchor, so that he didn't seem to be with her though he was. He caught up with her and stood almost beside her and she introduced him. Ned Renvyle.

Hannie shook hands. He was very tall and bony, with a full head of fine grey hair. The hair was much younger than the face, which was tanned and folded into long broken creases like the wandering courses of wadis in the dry season. The eyes were withdrawn and almost invisible between deep lines and puckers.

Jessica had finished with Hannie, she had enquired about her mother's old flame and was ready to move on, but a sudden eddy of people pressed into them and the space for retreat closed. Resignedly the two women began again. Ned Renvyle stood and listened.

Jessica worked in broadcasting, a producer not a secretary, Hannie's assumptions smoothly corrected. She spoke briefly of a series she was executive-producing, throwing in a couple of observations that were meaningless to Hannie but made Ned Renvyle nod appreciatively. It was all gracefully done: self-aware, modest, informative. Hannie glanced at the hands. Jessica wore no rings.

'What do *you* do?' she asked Hannie. Her tone was pleasant, conversational. Your turn, it said, I've done my bit.

What you don't do, Hannie thought. Live off men. When I get the chance.

'Marry,' she said starkly.

Jessica looked startled. Hannie was startled herself, she probably hadn't intended to say it aloud, she wasn't entirely sure. The bony old man twitched slightly, the wine jumped in his glass. He had been watching Hannie closely while seeming not to.

Jessica laughed. She lifted her glass as though to drink to Hannie but it was empty. Ned Renvyle automatically held out his hand for it. 'Perrier water,' Jessica said. He held out his hand for Hannie's glass. 'Red,' she said. He turned and bored his way through the crowd.

'So you're currently out of a job?' Jessica asked lightly.

Hannie nodded. 'I am looking for a new position.'

'Oh?' Jessica said. 'That must be tedious. Wouldn't you rather a break?'

'Economic necessity,' Hannie said.

Jessica looked at her curiously. It seemed to occur to her that Hannie was serious. Her interest was almost caught – it was the tastelessness of Hannie's remarks. She seemed about to speak but a tall, impeccably dressed man with a thatch of straight brown hair was shoving his way furiously through the crowd.

'That was Ned Renvyle,' he accused as soon as he reached her. 'I saw you talking to him, couldn't get near you … Honestly Jessica, why didn't you hold on to him? You knew perfectly well I wanted to meet him.'

This was not a boyfriend, Hannie realised, nor a lover awaiting divorce. This was a consort or a partner or whatever these things were called now; a husband she hadn't yet bothered to marry. Jessica introduced Hannie, but the man hardly glanced at her.

'He didn't want to meet anyone,' Jessica continued calmly. 'He wanted to hang on to someone so he didn't have to. I can't think what he's doing here. He's terribly shy –'

'Shy? You're talking about a man who marches up to headhunters and invites himself round for a year or two. He's not shy, Jessica, explorers aren't shy, for a halfway intelligent woman you do talk a load of crap.'

'Shy in this sort of company. Stop making such a fuss and go and find him yourself. He's gone to get us drinks, but he's probably forgotten by now. Mine's Perrier water, Hannie's is red wine.' She spoke like a mother ignoring a child's petulance.

He glared at her and headed off after Renvyle. Then he stopped, turned on his heel and came back. He addressed Hannie.

'Sorry,' he said. 'Very rude of me. Bit of an obsession.'

He wheeled and stomped off again, ignoring Jessica.

'It's true,' Jessica said. 'The obsession bit. He read the books when he was a boy and just completely fell for them.'

'What sort of books?'

'Travel. The Gentleman Adventurer. More Thesiger than Fleming, but slightly later and not so well connected. Quite obviously incredibly brave, only never ever written like that. Touching, really.' She paused, her eyes on a woman who seemed anxious to shepherd them towards the lunch tables.

'Of course, they're hopelessly out-of-fashion and out-of-print and cluttering-up-the-second-hand-bookshelves. I shouldn't think Ned Renvyle's royalty cheques are exactly keeping the mice from his door.'

'Where is his door?'

'Oh, Ireland somewhere.' Jessica spoke in a neutral voice. 'Old family. You know the sort of thing. Nettles and decay.'

Hannie didn't, and it didn't sound very promising. Still, she wasn't exactly being bombarded with opportunities; she might follow it up for want of anything better.

She scanned the tables, found her name on a bit of card and picked up the one from the place-setting next to it. Three tables up, she found Ned Renvyle's name-card. People were beginning to take their seats but she ignored them, leaned over and changed his card for the one in her hand. She went back to her table, sat down, and put Ned's card on the setting beside her.

Jessica was right, Ned Renvyle lived in Ireland. Hannie had listened for an estate but heard only a house, a farm.

A family farm?

No, not a family farm but the next best thing. A farm near the places and people he'd known in his childhood. He'd bought it when he left off roaming around the place and came home.

Home? He was an Irishman?

His family had lived there for generations, he said, not answering her question.

But he wasn't a farmer?

He was now. Before that, he told her, he'd mostly travelled, written the odd book, given lectures, that sort of thing. There'd been some rooms in London where he'd lived when he wasn't away. Now he farmed a few acres. Nothing much, but it kept him occupied. He lived alone. Been married once, his wife had died. He was over for this wedding. And to see his publisher, visit friends.

They were snarled in a long line of traffic with no visible reason for the hold-up. Hannie sat in the back of the car, staring absently out of the window while Tom and Beth bickered about Beth's choice of route.

Ireland. She hadn't thought of Ireland, had never been there. It might be the answer. He was on the look-out, she knew that, just from the things he'd said this afternoon. And he'd taken to her, she knew that too.

She'd have to find things out, she decided: how much land, if there was money to go with it, if there were any commitments.

You couldn't rely on family any more, Andrew had said. Or schools. A chap could sound right and have nothing. These days, there was more likely to be money if he sounded wrong.

Ned Renvyle would definitely have sounded right in Andrew's book. Hannie didn't care what a chap sounded like as long as he wasn't flat broke.

She could probably hook him if she played him right, she thought, and he might be the start she needed. She could always leave him if she couldn't stand him, but he must be pushing seventy, he couldn't live for ever, she might just stick it out till he died. With a bit of luck he'd leave her somewhere to live or enough to live on. With a lot of luck he'd leave her both.

If he turned out to have anything at all.

8

But she'd have to let him do the next bit. She wondered how fast he would move if he made up his mind to it. She wondered how fast she could move in her turn. If he did as he'd told her he planned to do and went up to London, she'd have to follow him, invite herself on someone. She couldn't afford a hotel, couldn't put all her eggs in one basket at this stage when nothing might come of it.

But he might not go to London, he might stay on. And if he did, she'd stay on too. She'd tell Beth the truth, or a version of it, ask for her help. Beth would understand. Not like that blonde bitch at the wedding with her career and her salary and her future.

She would explain about the separation which she hadn't so far mentioned. She would tell Beth there'd be no money coming, even after the will was settled, Andrew's children would inherit; she was broke and needed to marry again.

They'd hear it all anyway, and there was no predicting when. Africa gossip, it might take a while, but it would permeate through in the end. Tell Beth, but ask her not to pass it on to Tom. She would of course. So if they heard before she was ready, she'd be covered.

But she wouldn't tell her about Joss or the reasons for the separation.

The traffic began to move. Tom stopped telling Beth she'd chosen the wrong route and started complaining about the cold supper she was planning. All that fidgety food they pushed at you at weddings. You needed a decent dinner to settle you down, he said. He was quite drunk.

For once Beth stood her ground and stuck to her cold meats and salad. She was tired, they'd eaten a massive lunch, and the help had the evening off. It wasn't like Africa, she said over her shoulder at Hannie. Africa, where everyone had servants. There was nostalgia in her voice.

Hannie said nothing . Where everyone like *you* had servants, she thought, remembering days when she hadn't had enough to feed herself and Joss, much less a servant.

9

Ned Renvyle. Only if she was desperate. Maybe not even then. The next move was his, anyway.

'Oh, the Woodburns,' Beth said. 'Minster Lovell, beautiful house, Jacobean, been in the family for generations. Jessica's the youngest. Nice, isn't she?'

Hannie said nothing.

'And terribly successful.'

More silence from Hannie. Beth began to waver.

'It must be wonderful,' she said, 'to be like her.'

Hannie looked at her.

'Oh, you know . . .' Beth flapped her hand around vaguely. 'Not having to wait for the right moment. A job. Confidence. Beautiful clothes . . .'

'Career.' Hannie corrected her.

'Career?'

'She has a *career*, not a job. She told me so.'

The two women sat outside in the sunshine, helping the help. And Hannie was working on Beth, she was re-establishing herself and gathering information.

'I never liked stringing beans,' Beth said. 'I always slice my fingers as well as the beans. Shelling peas is different, I like shelling peas. The little bump-bump-bump noise in the bowl. Mummy made us volunteer but we never minded.' She picked up the next runner bean from the pile on the table and looked at it balefully. 'I bet Jessica Woodburn *never* strings beans.'

'Are there many like her?' Hannie asked. Her voice was neutral.

Beth sighed and leaned back in her deckchair. 'It's the way things are now,' she said carefully. 'Women like us . . .'

Hannie waited.

'Anyway, I like my life,' Beth continued, 'I don't really want to be like that. Except sometimes. Sometimes it's hard – feeling you haven't done anything. You have to *do* something, you know. Not just marry and have children and run a house. Sara says I'm a bad role-model. That means an example for her to base herself on. She says it won't be her fault if she turns out just like me.'

Hannie laughed. Then she remembered herself. 'What does Tom say?' she asked tactfully.

Beth cheered up. She sat forward, waving a runner bean around as she talked. 'Tom? He just wants things to go on as they've always done. His home the way he likes it, food the way he likes it, me here to look after him. To "service him", as Sara says. Even the boys talk like that since they went to Cambridge. And they're right, of course they're right, and I wish I was different, I'd so like them to be proud of me, especially Sara.'

'These Jessica Woodburns,' Hannie said, 'do they have children?'

'Oh, yes. One or two. Late. It's all wonderful. Then they get a nanny and go back to work. Just like our mothers, my dear, only they went back to their social lives. Which is what work is to them anyway, as far as I can see. Still, it gives the lie to the men laying down the law about the sacrifice they make for us, slaving away in the office all their lives. These women simply can't wait to get back there.'

Beth stopped suddenly. Hannie was looking across the lawn, that still, empty expression on her face. Beth heard herself and blushed to her hairline. So stupid, she'd forgotten for a moment about Hannie. She was always so poised, her English almost flawless, she had been so very much at home in Andrew's world where they had met her.

And it might not have been true, it could have been just spiteful gossip. She tried desperately to think of something to say but nothing came.

Hannie rescued her. 'What do the men think?' she asked lightly.

'I don't know. They don't seem to have much choice. They're not really allowed to say anything, whatever they may think. Which is about time, really,' she finished, brightening. 'But *we're* not allowed to say anything either. Not even discuss. We've wasted our lives and we're jealous. But I'm not jealous, really I'm not, and I don't mind if that's what they want to do, I just don't want to have to start doing it myself . . .'

Sara appeared in the doorway behind them.

'There was a man on the phone for Hannie. I said I'd get her but he got in a panic, said he'd ring back in an hour.'

Beth swivelled round in the deckchair. She addressed her daughter. 'What was his name, darling?'

'I don't know, Ren-something,' the fifteen-year-old replied. 'First he wanted her and then he didn't. Couldn't make up his mind.'

Hannie couldn't, either.

ᴥ *Chapter 2* ᴥ

*N*ed Renvyle sat on a bench by the river in the late afternoon sunshine. He hadn't gone to London as he'd first planned. Instead he'd left his friends the Langtons and their hospitality for a timbered pub one village away from Hannie. He knew Jean and Alasdair Langton were perfectly aware of what he was about, knew this attempt at concealment was both foolish and futile, but he felt, at least, less overlooked.

Courting was never a dignified business. Women might thrive on it, but it made men look like fools. A bit late to start worrying about that now, he decided. The river was narrow with dirty, thick-looking water and mown banks, the grass worn thin by picnickers and courting couples. There were litter bins and benches and lifebelts on stands. Fishermen stood in line all day and threw back what they'd caught when they'd caught it. Hard to see what they got out of it. A travesty of a river. He should be grateful for the benches, he supposed; saved his piles.

He shut his eyes and a warm orange glow of sunny darkness closed over him. He dozed or dreamed, saw the small rushy meadows of home, the ragwort and the dampness, the cattle wandering about in them. He heard their quiet trampling and chomping and the harsh cry of a heron in the reedbeds.

He felt miserable, weary and old. He wanted her all right, but almost as badly he just wanted to get finished up here and go home. Suddenly he hardly cared about the outcome. With or without her, he'd go back to the farm and the fields and the river.

Yet at the same time he had wanted her badly enough to

have sat it through this far, he had to remind himself of this in his dejection. Why he wanted her, he hardly knew. It wasn't for anything he could put into words and say aloud to someone else.

He had a picture that was really more of a vision at the edges of his mind. Sometimes he called it up deliberately, but more often it came when he wasn't thinking and floated in front of his eyes. He saw a hallway with dark wood, sun-shafts, dust-motes. And flowers leaning out of shadow into light.

With the picture came a jumble of sense-impressions: morning and a garden, dew and dewy grass in the early sun, the swish of skirts. Then a china jug pulled from a wooden press and water gushing in till it ran over.

The sense-impressions settled and stilled. The scent of flowers, the quiet drop of petals on old furniture.

Then a feeling of simplicity. Of his life inhabiting his body. Of his body sitting simply wherever he was when the picture came. Of this being enough.

He knew that this yearning vision of flowers was a yearning for home. Not the house he had now, but the home he had left fifty years ago to sit on the bare ground beneath unknown stars with strangers, with unfamiliar tongues and smells and sounds about him, and a peace in his blood more intense than fire or wine.

And nothing would do him then but to have those stars, that peace, and no price to be paid was too high. And nothing would persuade him that his life lived in Ireland wouldn't be narrow and diminished beyond endurance.

There'd been flowers too, in his wilderness places: carpets after rain, a white bloom clenched in a rock.

Only now he wanted what he'd left behind him all those years ago. Or the ghost of it. He was neither so old nor such a fool as to imagine that anything could be again as it once was.

He'd spent too many years in search of himself, confronting

himself, till it was like living in a high altitude where the visibility is always intense and clear. Now, an old man, he found that he could not altogether bear this. Nor the losses time brought: that intense sweet peace only a memory now.

The truth was he was lonely, as simple as that, he told himself. Finally, after almost a lifetime away, he'd decided to come home. He had bought a house in the place he'd known in his childhood and now, five years later, he was still waiting for it to turn into his home.

Somehow he'd got it into his head that a woman might make the difference, and he couldn't get it out of his head, though he knew that acquiring one would solve nothing, the yearning would simply transfer itself to something else, he'd be led by the nose to follow another dream. That had been the way of it all his life. In the meantime he wanted a wife, so there was nothing to be done but to go and find one. But Hannie? The woman was a nomad, not a homemaker. Had he taken leave of his senses altogether?

The sun had left the bench where he sat and the coolness of the evening was upon him. It wouldn't be much longer now, he thought. He'd ask her. She might have him or she might refuse him. Either way, at sixty-nine, he'd look a bloody fool.

And he'd look a worse fool, bringing her back with him, than leaving her here and no one any the wiser. Fortunately his few close friends were scattered. If she said yes he would write to them, tell them his news by letter. Then they could let off steam, calm down, write him a civil note. No need to tell anyone at home, might as well just turn up with her. They'd know soon enough, probably before he knew himself.

Well, if he'd minded men's opinions he'd have lived a different life. Let them think him a fool, he supposed that he could bear it one more time.

And when he was with her, he didn't care. She had that effect on him. Caution left him. It was her attitude. *Why not?* she said, as others might say, *Why?*

She had a lopsided walk. He liked that, he didn't know why. He'd asked her about it and she'd laughed. No, no injury, she'd said. Just the way she was. Didn't seem offended.

He liked her, that was all he could say. Liked her untidy hair and the way she took her shoes off under the table and went fishing around for them when it was time to go. Liked the hearty way she ate and the way that she laughed with her head back and her mouth open. She got under his guard.

Oh, he knew she was untrustworthy, unsound, knew she was running, though he didn't know from what. If pushed he'd have said she was a selfish woman of loose morals and bad habits. But also courageous, strong-minded, energetic. She didn't try to cover or apologise. He recognised her as he would have recognised a man.

And he might have befriended such a man, but he'd never have let him come too close.

Then why was he letting *her*? Holding the door open, inviting her in?

He thought about this one for a long time and the answer he came up with confused him with its simplicity. He felt warmer in her company.

He'd cut his London plans. No point. He had no desire to sit in his club and talk to the other old fogeys. The London part of his trip had only ever been an excuse to go looking for a woman. The whole thing was, if he was honest. But he'd taken her up for the day when he went to see his publishers.

Publishers. Hadn't published anything for years and then there was a letter out of the blue.

Backlists. Something might be done about backlists. Perhaps lunch? Next time he was in London?

As though he was in and out of London every second week. As though he lived that sort of life.

She'd worn her good dress, the same one she wore for the wedding. He'd liked that, that she'd thought enough of a day out with him to wear it. Not that he liked dressed-up women, he didn't. But he liked her in that dress, and he was flattered.

She impressed the publisher fellow, that was clear enough, though he'd been a bit put out when Ned first introduced her, had muttered something about business, and not knowing they'd have company . . . Ned had ignored him, he'd reached the age when he didn't hear if he didn't want to.

Anyway, the petulance didn't last long. When the publisher fellow was doing his stuff she sat quietly and listened in and when he'd finished she joined easily in the small-talk. He asked her about Africa and she told him. When he started asking her what she read, she said she read nothing, she used to read, but she hadn't for years. He started dropping names then – people he knew, people they published. She should read this, read that. He wrote the names down for her and she laughed and folded them into her handbag. She said she probably wouldn't read them, but she might. If she did she would write and let him know what she thought.

Ned liked it that she was honest, that she didn't need to seem to be what she wasn't. He hadn't any time for people who said with pride that they never read, but she didn't say it with pride, she just said that she had once, but she didn't now. She didn't explain why.

Ned smiled to himself. Publisher fellow wanting her to himself, trying to work out what it was about her, was she with him, what was going on? Chap half his age, too. Hannie with a good few years on him and not pretending that she hadn't.

He didn't think anything would come of this backlist business. Still, it was a decent place, she'd enjoyed it, and he'd enjoyed having somewhere to take her.

Afterwards he couldn't keep it to himself. He fancied you, he'd said and, I know, she'd said, and laughed as though it was a good joke and made him buy her an ice-cream to eat in the sun outside the National Gallery though she'd just eaten two puddings off the trolley.

She'd never been to the National before, knew nothing about pictures and never had. He said he'd write her a list to go in her handbag and she smiled. He had planned to take her to the English section, to the Turners and the portraits, show her the things he liked, but he couldn't remember the way and he couldn't get her to walk past anything that caught her eye. She spotted the Monet water lilies through the arch from the room before and once she was there he didn't want to move her away. She didn't say anything, just stood looking. He told himself he could see how she'd have looked when she was a girl, and it wasn't so different. He wondered why she'd never seen pictures when it was plain that she liked them.

She didn't bother to look at anything that didn't attract her right away. There was a Holbein she went for, a woman full-length in a black dress on a dark-green ground, a fine painting.

Christina of Denmark, he told her. Painted for Henry the Eighth to see if he liked the look of her. Lucky for her, he didn't.

But Hannie didn't know about Henry the Eighth and his six wives. He was taken aback. You didn't learn British history in Dutch schools, she said, especially when the schools were in obscure Dutch colonies.

She might not know much about history or pictures, but she didn't miss much.

When he asked her why she liked the picture she said because the woman owned herself. And then she said wasn't it funny she should go on owning herself even hundreds of years later when she was long dead. He knew what she meant if he didn't think about it.

When they came out and they hadn't looked at what he had wanted to show her, she said she was sorry but she'd been excited and had forgotten.

He didn't mind. He had enjoyed watching her excitement. She had taken his arm walking down the street. He was pleased. The expedition was a success.

He smiled to himself now, remembering. The picture of

Hannie in London faded. He saw again the river bank in the evening light. People strolling, a loiter of dogs and children. A little cloud of midges danced by his left ear. He scratched, reached down for his hat, got up and set off up the path to the village pub where he was staying.

'Been enjoying the sunshine?' The landlord was cheerful in his polished bar parlour. Ned thought of Keoghs, its wooden shelves and stacks of untipped Carrol's cigarettes and dusty bottles of Guinness. Mrs Keogh coming through from the back, drying her hands on a dirty cloth. Serving him in silence, leaving when it was done.

He thought of the wide Blackwater, its wooded banks and hidden farms and windy skies.

He'd ask her, get it over with. Then he could go home.

Chapter 3

*H*annie had made her move as soon as it looked as though Ned Renvyle might come through. She'd told Beth she wanted to take her into her confidence, put all her cards on the table. Then she'd told her about the separation and the will.

She might get something in the end, she said, but then again, she might not. That was all in the future anyway. For now she was broke and she needed to remarry. She asked Beth for help.

Beth couldn't let a kitten drown, much less a scrawny old cat like Hannie, and anyway she knew the facts of life for women of their generation. Or rather she knew that she didn't. She had always lived in comfort, was terrified as to her future should Tom ever decide to abandon her, she had an acute imaginative sympathy for Hannie's dreadful position.

Tom didn't, but Tom let it run on because that was what Beth wanted and anyway he didn't mind having Hannie around for a bit, she livened things up, added spice to the daily fare, though that wasn't what he told his wife.

Tom was a dull man; he'd been dull in Kenya, and he was duller here. If she hadn't been at such a low ebb, Hannie thought, she couldn't have stood it for two hours, much less two weeks.

'Invite them,' Andrew had said to Hannie years ago in Kenya. 'He's a bore but he might be useful.' Andrew had had an eye for useful men.

So she had. A little racing and a lot of booze – Tom and Beth, letting their hair come unpinned for a year or two, far from the Home Counties. Well, now they could pay for their fun.

'He's too old,' Beth said. 'They'll say you're marrying him for his money.'

'Who'll say? I don't know anyone any more. Besides, he hasn't got any money, or none that you'd notice. If he had, I wouldn't be dithering around like this, would I?'

'Oh, Hannie,' Beth wailed, 'I wish you wouldn't do that! You know how slow I am. I always think you're serious.'

'I am. Totally.' She got up, took out her cigarettes, remembered and put them back. She walked round the room to calm herself. Ned had been to the house for a drink. Now Beth was having second thoughts.

'He might die,' Hannie said. 'He's pushing seventy. At least then I'd have a house.'

Beth shot her a swift look. She stabbed at the needlepoint she was working. 'I do hate this cat,' she said passionately. 'All these marmalades and browns. I have such a lovely one waiting for when I've finished this.' She gazed at Hannie, her eyes wistful and large.

'Roses and honeysuckle on a green ground,' she went on. 'Beautiful colours, all shading into each other. Andrew died, Hannie. It won't necessarily help –'

'True,' Hannie said, ignoring the tapestry. 'Andrew died. And no house. Not so slow, my dear Beth.'

Beth flushed with pleasure.

'And it's not true that you don't know anyone, Hannie,' she said, taking courage. 'It's never true. One always knows someone, no matter where one goes. It's one of those laws.'

Hannie said nothing. Beth retreated.

'Well, at least you wouldn't have to cope with sex.' She had the air of one trying to look on the bright side.

Hannie stared. Then she roared: 'Oh Beth, you great booby, how can you be such an innocent?'

It was Beth's turn to stare. 'At his age?' she said weakly. 'Oh no, Hannie, surely not?'

'At his age, either he can't or he'll rut like a baboon. At least till the novelty wears off. He won't be any good, though –' she stopped abruptly. She'd gone too far, had offended Beth's sensibilities.

But it seemed not. 'Won't you mind?' Beth asked, concern in her voice.

'Why should I? That's not what I want him for.'

'I don't mean that. I mean if he wants to do it all the time.'

'I know that's what you mean. It won't make any difference either way. It's not what I want him for. Sex isn't the problem.'

Her voice was indifferent. She glanced at Beth. Now she *had* gone too far. Too bad. She'd asked Beth for help, not counselling.

But Beth hadn't finished. 'I couldn't bear it.' She shuddered. 'Someone one didn't know. At our age . . .'

Hannie looked at her. 'How married you are, my dear Beth,' she said lightly. 'Only to have sex with someone one's known for twenty years . . .'

Beth blushed. She picked up her needlepoint. Hannie could be quite cruel.

'If you hate that cat so much, why are you sitting there martyring yourself over it? Why don't you just dump it, start a new one?'

'Sara,' Beth said hopelessly. 'Sara gave it to me for my birthday. Tom helped her choose. He said he thought I'd *like* cats with pansies in the border.'

'Let me see.'

Beth handed her the frame. Hannie carried it over to the window and studied it briefly. 'Horrible,' she said. 'Why don't you have an accident?'

'Oh, Hannie, I couldn't.'

'Why ever not? Spill something. So disappointing. But Sara would forgive you. You could console yourself with the other one. Would you like me to do it for you?'

'Oh no, Hannie, no. Please give it back. I don't mind it, really I don't.'

Hannie shrugged. She handed it over.

Beth bundled the wools up together and pushed the whole lot out of sight.

In case I make a grab for them, Hannie thought.

Beth gathered herself. 'Where is this house, anyway?' she asked, determinedly.

'Somewhere on a river called the Blackwater,' Hannie said. 'Near a town pronounced *Yawl* and spelt Y–o–u–g–h–a–l. It's where Sir Walter Raleigh planted his American potatoes. He seems to think that's important. But it's a farm, not a house. A farmhouse.'

When Tom came in from the office looking for attention and a drink he found the two women on their hands and knees on the floor, pouring over an atlas. Beth scrambled to her feet, talking about the time and how she hadn't noticed. Hannie stayed where she was, elbows on the rug, bottom sticking out, chin cupped in her hands, staring down at the opened book. When she'd finished staring she shifted her gaze up to Tom and regarded him balefully.

'We were just looking for somewhere,' Beth was explaining vaguely. 'The children had the atlas out – some argument they were trying to settle.'

'We're trying to find where Ned Renvyle lives,' Hannie said. She straightened up and sat back on her heels. 'With a view to deciding whether or not I should marry him.'

'Has he asked you?'

Hannie grinned. 'Not yet,' she said. 'But he will, and I want to be ready with my answer. We're just adding up the pros and cons, working out his assets. If he's got any, that is. Or at least enough to make it worth my while. You couldn't help, could you, Tom? All your contacts? The Langtons? Somebody must know?'

'No, I couldn't,' Tom said. 'And I'd stay well clear of the Langtons. They're fond of Renvyle by all accounts, won't want to see him taken advantage of. Any more than I do,' he added pompously. 'It's not decent, what you're doing, Hannie, you should lay off him. I've a good mind to ring him up and tell.'

'But you won't,' Hannie said, getting to her feet and giving Tom an affectionate pat on the arm on her way to the drinks tray. 'You're much too English to go interfering. Besides, if you do that you'll never get rid of me.' She handed him a drink. She poured herself a refill and fished out the glass that Beth had quietly pushed behind a vase out of Tom's sight. She poured a large gin into that, too, and held it out to Beth. Beth flushed and took it, not looking at Tom.

'I could throw you out.'

Hannie shook her head. 'You'd upset Beth. The house would be unsettled for at least a week. You'd hate that. Better marry me off to Ned.'

Beth gaped at her when she said such things, but Hannie knew it earned her keep with Tom.

'Anyway,' she went on, 'I can't see what you're taking such a high moral tone about. Ascertaining assets is all I'm doing. Perfectly sensible and respectable and it's always gone on. I bet Beth's father wanted to know exactly what *you* proposed to keep her on. And if he didn't it was only because *her* mother had it all off your mother long before you even knew you liked her.' Hannie sat herself down on a leather pouf. She looked intently up at Tom.

'Well, I haven't got a mother and I'm not thinking of marrying Ned for reasons of altruism. He'd understand. He'd probably show me his bank statements if I asked him. And he's quite mediaeval enough to believe in dowries and exchange of lands.'

'Neither of which you happen to have.'

'True, but if I had I wouldn't be thinking of marrying him at all, would I?' she said shrugging. 'He's no catch, Tom. He's nearly twenty years older than I am and he wants a wife. He can't have it all ways, he'll have to deal.'

'My God, Hannie, I'm glad I'm safely married to Beth. Is this what you did to poor old Andrew?'

'I didn't have to with Poor Old Andrew,' she said. 'Poor Old Andrew liked my terms. I married him in the nick of time to stop that Clayton woman he was screwing from leaving her husband and landing in on him. Remember her? Janine Clayton? Looked like Zelda Fitzgerald with a temperament to match? Poor Old Andrew was just begging to be saved from Janine. Anyway, it was a straight deal. A wife in his house and a mother for his children. Someone to tidy away his women. I needed a home for Joss.'

'Andrew and Janine Clayton?' Tom was caught irresistibly. 'But didn't she kill herself around . . . ?'

'Around that time? Two weeks after Andrew and I were married. Booze and pills. Got out of that one by the skin of his teeth, didn't he? And it nearly came out. Husband hysterical, wanting to tell the world, show Andrew up for what he was. Poor bastard loved her, you see. Under a lot of financial pressure, though. Got leaned on by the Powers-That-Be. Tell, and we won't lift a finger keeping off the vultures –'

'And did they?' Tom was unwilling to let the story go.

'Indeed they did. Helped him sell up, ship himself home.' Hannie shrugged her shoulders, took a mouthful of gin. 'Didn't you know all this? It wasn't so long after you left –'

'Who killed herself?' Sara stood in the doorway, her face young, blank, deceptively innocent. A strand of dark hair lay over her shoulder. She picked it up and chewed at it absently, her eyes intent.

Hannie swivelled lazily round on her stool. 'A woman we knew once,' she said.

'Because of your husband?'

'Partly. Partly because she was a mess.' She swivelled lazily back, catching Beth's tightened mouth in the turn of her eye. The little bitch didn't like her. The little bitch was the apple of her mother's eye. Beth was shooing her out now, a good sheepdog, careful of its charge, firing darts of reproach at Hannie as she went.

Sod, Hannie thought. Now Beth would go all prim and

proper on her again, remember she'd said she'd help Hannie find a husband but only if Tom didn't know. But she had to feed Tom the odd titbit, keep him diverted, stop herself from dying of boredom. This way he'd forget to grouse at her living in his house and drinking his gin and leading his wife astray.

❧ *Chapter 4* ❧

*N*ed took her for dinner that night, to a place someone had recommended. It offended him – the thick carpets, the starched damask, the fancy words in the menu. And he didn't like the prices.

She watched him, his crotchety reaction. She saw his age, the setness of his ways and opinions. She refrained from soothing him or playing up to him. No sense in bringing him to the point, if she wasn't going to be able to live with him.

He studied the menu while the waiter hovered. He looked up, caught her eye, flushed.

'We could go somewhere else,' she said neutrally.

'And have you think me a cheapskate?' He made an effort, smiled self-consciously.

She raised an eyebrow, not returning the smile.

'What do you want, Hannie?' Ned asked her. The waiter was approaching.

She picked up the menu. 'Whatever's most expensive.'

'Is it a test?'

She nodded, not looking up. The waiter was standing there, silently waiting. She ordered the lobster. Ned did the same. The waiter wrote it down.

'Did I flinch?' Ned asked when he'd gone.

'Hardly at all,' she said. 'Call him back and we'll change it.'

'No we won't.'

'Yes we will. Try and hide your relief, Ned. The waiter will despise you.'

'Do you?'

'Hardly at all. And I don't like lobster.'

The food was better than the surroundings. Afterwards, they sat on over the coffee. Ned had offered her information over the past days, not an account exactly, but a beginning: his family's ascendancy origin in Ireland, his childhood in his grandmother's house following his soldier-father's early death, the world war he had gone to fight in. Then his marriage, his travels, his books. An outline had begun to emerge.

Hannie had told him almost nothing and he hadn't asked. He had waited. Now she sat, folded arms resting on the table, telling him her story or the bones of it.

She had told it many times and many ways and it surprised her a little, how she was telling Ned now. She told him less than the whole but far more than she'd meant to, and she told it nearer the truth.

Perhaps it was her age, she thought. At fifty-two she had little appetite left for pretence, could not be bothered any more with best behaviour. Perhaps it was her desperation or the way he took it. He sat there quietly, looking at her as she talked, accepting what she told him without comment or apparent judgement. It eased her and it loosened her tongue. It made her think there might be more between them than she'd expected, that this plan of hers might be marginally less deranged than it seemed.

She didn't hide her origins, her past marriages or her need now for a new one. She didn't hide her financial situation. She spoke briefly of Joss, her son, whom she had left in Africa. She made it clear that she wanted him near to her when she settled, that she didn't care for smartness or reputation, just that the school was steady.

She had thought of looking for a job, she said, but she had no experience, references or qualifications.

'Do you have friends?' he asked, leaning back in his chair, his legs stretched out and his feet crossed under the table.

'Influential friends? No. I have acquaintances. A few people I can fall back on in a crisis. I had a friend once but she's dead.' She didn't explain further. He nodded gravely. They both knew the sort of job she could get at her age and in these times.

'You'd better think about marrying me,' he told her. 'No great shakes. I'm sixty-nine. No money to speak of. Farm takes every penny and all my time. Quiet sort of a life, not much in the way of excitement, not very social.' He paused. His eye swept the crowded restaurant, the muddle of smells and voices, the busy faces.

'But at least you can breathe there,' he added passionately, 'at least it's a life. Not like *this*.'

Here Hannie held up her hand as though to stop him.

'We've had a week together, Ned, a pleasant week. It doesn't have to go any further, you don't have to solve my life for me. You could just get on your boat now and go back to Ireland. We could put all this down to experience, leave it at that.'

He regarded her gravely. 'Are you trying to save me the pain of rejection, Hannie?'

'I'm trying to make you think before you speak.' She lit a cigarette, leaned back, inhaled. 'I'm not in this for my ego, Ned, I'm not collecting skulls. If you ask me, I'll probably say yes.'

'I'm asking you, Hannie.'

'I'm not much of a catch,' she said quietly, looking straight at him.

He liked that, that she wasn't doing the coy wistful thing and looking at the table as another woman might.

'You wouldn't be sitting here if you were.'

He smiled suddenly, his face twisting. 'Your loss, my luck,' he added. 'Whatever it was that you lost.'

It wasn't a question. He knew there was something and he wasn't going to ask. Hannie sighed deeply. She rested her head heavily on her hand, the heel of her palm pushing up her cheekbone, and stared at him with a weary intentness.

'Can I have till tomorrow, Ned? I want to go through it one more time. I want to be sure.'

He nodded. Her words didn't leave much room for illusion. He didn't quite know how it had come to this but still he didn't want to draw back.

'Just the same,' Tom was saying, 'there must have been something. Hannie ran a tight ship and if that was the deal she had with Andrew, there must have been something big to break it.'

'Someone else?' Beth's voice came softly. Hannie stood breath-still in the hallway.

Tom snorted. 'It was an arrangement, you heard her. And Andrew liked things that way. Divorce too expensive, too disruptive, liked his women as mistresses and no fancy ideas about becoming wives.'

Beth's voice, softly again. Hannie couldn't catch the words.

'Wrong tree there, old girl. He'd have turned a blind eye, part of the deal. He'd only have asked for a bit of discretion.'

Beth, anxious now: 'Tom, I'm sure I heard a car, I'm sure she's back. It's making me nervous, talking like this.'

'Nonsense, we'd have heard her coming in. Anyway, she's living off us, isn't she – using us – what're you worrying about? Have you written to Kenya lately? Might be an idea. See what happened to make Andrew dump her. Drop Martia a line, or Dora Seaton. Don't say she's staying, just that we saw her at the wedding.'

'Tom, I couldn't, I really couldn't . . .'

'I don't see why not. I don't see why you always have to be so wet about things. She'd do it in your place without so much as stopping to catch her breath.'

'Oh Tom, she wouldn't.'

'She damn well would. And if you think otherwise you're a bigger fool than I took you for. Write tomorrow. Don't push for an answer but make it clear you'd like one.'

'I can't, you shouldn't ask, it's not right, Tom, Hannie's my friend.' Beth's mutiny ended on a low wail.

Very softly, very quietly, Hannie stepped back through the panelled hallway, back through the door through which she had come. Then she stood in the darkness, waiting. Noisily she re-made her entrance.

Hannie poured another gin and set herself to go through it all again. How easy he'd been to bring to the point, she thought. A word or two here, a sentence left hanging. Ned Renvyle had rushed into the breach.

Not so easy to work the same process on herself. Especially in the long insomniac nights when she paced about her room. Already she'd been over and over it, arguing it backwards and forwards, all the time knowing it was so much wasted effort because the truth was you couldn't ever know. Life with another human being – marriage, call it what you would – was always more than the sum of its parts, and it was always the small unknown, unnoticed things that made it unbearable or redeemed it. Beth, worrying about sex, had seized on the least of her problems. She didn't marry for sex, though fortunately most men did.

But she didn't think it was sex that had brought Ned Renvyle to the point. Clearly he could do without it, or he'd have lived a different life. And he wasn't queer, she was sure of that. So if it wasn't sex, what was it, and why her?

Companionship most likely. And to complete his picture of himself, his life. Return to his roots, a home, a wife in it. Romantic. That was his pattern.

He'd never lived with a woman, not really, but he thought he had. That brief marriage, all those years ago. Isobel, a distant cousin, become an army nurse for the war that had over-run the world. He'd met her again in India afterwards, and they'd come back on the same troop-ship in 1947, happy to be thrown together, a childhood friendship renewed. They'd been married not long afterwards in London. Six months later she was dead. It seemed she'd gone home for a visit, this Isobel, and fallen off a horse. A hunting accident. A grim look on Ned's face as he'd said it.

Idly she worked out how old he'd been, wondered what he'd been like then. Tongue-tied, she guessed, all suppressed feeling. Twenty-four, a melodramatic age. Astonished deep down inside himself that he'd survived at all.

Funny the way he talked about Ireland as home when he'd hardly ever lived there. She never spoke of Java as home, nor Africa either, she never spoke of anywhere. She would lay money he always had that look when he spoke of Isobel. Years of habit. A candle always burning before the shrine.

He had a portrait, he'd said; she could see it in her mind's eye. Some girl with dark cloudy hair, a pale, arrogant face. His class, one of his own.

He'd been lucky. What price his precious expeditions if she'd stayed on her horse?

And he'd never remarried. Had it all gone into his journeys? Perhaps. Perhaps he had a low sex-drive, perhaps he'd just done without . . .

But he liked women, you could tell that, for all his asceticism, he liked women. Well, nothing unusual in that. Men who loved hardship often loved softness between. They just liked it earned.

Prostitutes? Possibly. It went with his class. Maybe he'd bought sex the way he'd hired porters to carry his gear? Or maybe it was married white women, the wives of the men he stayed with in out-of-the-way places.

No. She shook her head to herself, the gesture underlining the mental negative. Not other men's wives, that wouldn't be done in Ned's book, not unless they threw themselves at him. No, not then either. He'd be pompous about that, would think them predatory, be ashamed for their husbands, for himself . . .

Hannie stopped herself, this wasn't the point, she was getting side-tracked into stupid speculation. Sex wasn't difficult.

He might have odd ideas, plenty of men did, but all she had to do was find them out and pander to them. And they'd have separate bedrooms. That, too, went with his class. For pleasure there were always other men.

She brought herself back to the problem. Marriage to Ned. Or not. She walked herself round the room as the thoughts walked round in her head. She stopped, lit another cigarette, poured more gin. The house was quiet beneath her.

She could marry again in Kenya, but she'd have to take a step down, perhaps quite a big step down. She moved in a small tight caste and her history was becoming too well known. Correction: Joss's history was becoming too well known.

And it wasn't only Joss and his reputation that worried her. It was Africa, the demise of the glory days of white colonial Africa. Which she'd lived on like a tick on a sheep's back, sucking the rich blood.

Well that was all changing now, even South Africa no longer a sure bastion of privilege and ease. Mandela was free, apartheid was crumbling, once the factions left off quarrelling and pushed together they'd be hard to stop. Time to pack your bags Hannie, time to move on. Survivors couldn't afford to hang around to see how things panned out.

Hence this trip. Getting started was the hard bit. She could marry Ned and as Ned's wife she'd be in. After that she could take her time, look around, see what else was on offer . . .

She walked across to the mirror and stood squarely in front of it, meeting her own eyes. Who was she kidding? She was no Jessica, tending an immaculate C.V. She grinned at herself, a painful, self-conscious grin. She was getting older, less employable, already there were too many job changes. And there was Joss.

Reality. She might as well start getting used to it because this was the way it was going to be from hereon in.

And if no alternative offered itself, if she had to stay with Ned?

A farm again. Well, she wouldn't starve, it would be a home

for Joss. And she was older now she might settle. Who knows what you can settle to if there isn't a choice? Certainly she, Hannie, did not.

And he might not be too bad. Beth said she didn't know anything about him, but Africa was full of men like Ned Renvyle, men who found the world noisy, suburban and over-crowded, with the wrong people running things. Romantics who couldn't accept the world as it was now.

But he was decent and straight and he wouldn't be cruel. And he had a hundred and thirty acres, some of it 'marginal', whatever that meant. It didn't sound much, not when you were used to Africa, but there must be enough to live on or he wouldn't be asking her. She had made herself quite clear about Joss from the start and he'd accepted it: a reasonable, fee-paying boarding school until he was eighteen.

She couldn't leave Joss where he was much longer. The school was only letting him stay on over the summer because she had written and begged them, using Andrew as her excuse, his recent death, his empty place on the board of governors, promising that she was making other arrangements.

Other arrangements. She said the words aloud, her voice full of mockery and self-disparagement. Ned was her other arrangement, the best she could do for the moment, perhaps the best she could do at all. She went for the bottle, slopped more liquid into the glass. It was nearly four in the morning, the sky had lightened, sunrise was not far off. She no longer had any assets, only a liability, it all came down to that one thing. Joss, her fear for Joss, her need to build a life that would protect him.

And how would Ned react if Joss did something again? *When* Joss did something again.

He would stand by her. That's how he was, how Andrew wasn't, despite the schools, the lineage, the family history. Ned would stand by her because that was what he'd expect of himself. That was why she had come this far with Ned. None of the other reasons mattered a damn.

She crossed to the opened window and stood with the cool air of dawn flowing round her.

Or maybe she'd let him go, take a chance on another one . . .

With the years closing in, the mirror giving her relentlessly back to herself?

Who was she kidding, she asked herself again. He was the best she could get, so she'd take him. Against the time when she would take what she could get.

She leaned her elbows on the sill and stared out at the thinning darkness. The security lights still burned, the swimming pool glowed blue by the shrubbery, pale rectangles of light lay over the shaved grass. And beyond the lawns and walls the orange glow of habitation and the low roar of traffic that had not ceased all night.

She felt her hopelessness, the fight gone out of her. In her mind the soft thick darkness of another continent, the great, soft stars that bloomed through the turning night. Who knows, she thought bitterly, she might have more in common with Ned Renvyle than she thought. She longed for Africa, its endlessness and space.

'So Beth thinks I'm too old for you,' he said. 'What does Tom think?'

'He thinks I'm taking advantage of you. He thinks you'll rue the day you met me. Or something like that.' She spoke carelessly, her eyes on the rows of lichened graves lining the path they walked.

Ned turned to her. She wore a dark blue blouse and a sand-coloured skirt and her feet were tanned in her leather sandals. She looked well, strolling about in the dappled churchyard, he was proud of her.

'Do you?' he asked seriously.

'I wouldn't be surprised.' She grinned up at him. 'Would you?'

'No,' he said thoughtfully, not grinning back. 'I think I

35

wouldn't be at all surprised. We may both rue the day. Do you want to back off?'

They'd stopped in their walk to stand by a sloping grave-stone. She laid her hand on its mossy back. She looked at him, her dark eyes gone distant and unreadable.

'No. Do you?'

He didn't speak for a minute.

'Oddly enough,' he said, 'I don't.'

He smiled then. He meant it. He thought, for all their mutual warnings, that it was straightforward. He didn't realise he would come to love her.

❧ *Chapter 5* ❧

'*T*he Mona Vullagh Mountains,' Ned said. He waved his hand at a long blue line of hills to the right. 'And those are the Comeraghs beyond.'

Hannie looked. She thought she was seeing foothills. She sat waiting for the mountains to appear.

'Irish mountains are small,' Ned said. 'Small and blue, small and brown. You'll get used to them, once your eye adjusts they'll seem quite high.'

Ned was smiling all the time now as he drove. Hannie watched these mountains that weren't mountains and said nothing. They crested a rise and below was a bay with a town built round a harbour.

'Dungarvan,' Ned said, as though they'd reached somewhere significant. They drove into the town and he parked on the quay under a battered notice offering boats for hire.

'Dungarvan's our nearest town,' he said. 'We'll get out, take a look around, you can see where it is you'll be living.'

Hannie got out. The air was sharp with the stench of fish and seaweed. She stood looking down into the harbour.

'Tidal,' Ned said. She nodded.

The harbour was deep and wide and empty of water. There were beached half-deckers under the wall and four small sailing craft lying about on the muddy sands. It was quiet, all but deserted. The tide must have turned, she could hear the trickle of the water running back into the harbour, seeping in around the beached boats. Wading birds dug in the silt, a few gulls rose and fell on the moist air, a single grey heron stood watch by a lone puddle.

Smallness, quietness, soft grey light. Whatever she had expected, it hadn't been this.

'King John's castle,' Ned was saying, waving his hand to the right where abandoned warehouses and high walls of dark stone crumbled against the greying sky. 'Important town in the fourteenth century.'

The weather was breaking up, the day going cold. He walked her through side-streets, past rain-stained, stone-built houses, often dilapidated or deserted, the slates off, the gutters full of weeds, saplings sprouting from the chimneys. Away from the harbour the town revived. The main square looked almost prosperous, the tall, elegant old houses painted up in pastel shades, the clear colours lending them a raffish, down-at-heel gaiety as they leaned in together, disdaining the street life below.

Hannie stood on the pavement surveying the shops and businesses. A bank or two, a heating supplier, a gents' shoe shop, a building society. The rest was pubs, take-aways, small plain grocers with not much in them.

Nowhere you'd want to linger, nothing you'd want to buy.

It had started well, she reminded herself. Setting off last night there'd been the expectation, the excitement and flurry of departure, standing in the darkness by the packed car she had felt her spirits soar.

It was movement, the release in movement, the scrunch of feet on the night gravel, the map and sandwiches and torch lying ready on her seat.

'Oh Hannie,' Beth had wailed, 'I feel as though you're going away for good, as though I'll never ever see you again.'

And Hannie had laughed, free at last of this house, this friendship, free of herself as she had had to be here.

It continued well. She liked the night drive, the three a.m. boat, the snatched sleep on the cramped seats of the crowded lounge, the dawn light seeping in from the sea through the uncurtained windows. They had stood together on the deck as the land drew close; Ned, eager, showing her Ireland, pointing out the Wexford landmarks.

The ship had moved slowly in, long unbroken ripples fanning out across the sheened water with its passing. Hannie had stared at a herring gull perched on the railing, its unblinking yellow eye, the red stain marking its long hooked beak. It slid off as the ferry pulled in, dropped to the water, swept high again to join with a clamouring cloud. It was a perfect morning, the air vivid with salt, the empty harbour pearly and pale in the shining stillness.

They'd stopped when they got to Waterford. They bought breakfast, then walked along the quays inspecting the trawlers and tugs and the big cattle boats with their foreign names and foreign flags loading up with hay. She'd seen worse, she thought confidently. She liked the busy port, the wide river, the tugs and buoys and pilot boats. There was a world beyond this place.

A buoyant mood. Standing here in Dungarvan, it was hard to remember the feeling. She had fallen into the old trap, she told herself, the trap of thinking that once she got through the thing in front of her then all the rest would somehow be all right.

And she had got through. She had found Ned, she had married him, she'd embarked on another life in another world.

But had she thought enough about that world?

Ned touched her arm. She woke from her reverie and followed him back to the car.

A few minutes out of Dungarvan and the town, such as it was, might never have been. They headed north away from the coast, each time leaving the road they were on for one that was narrower, more winding and more pot-holed. The hedges closed in. They were high and dense and thickened with full-grown trees. Where the hedges broke there were old walls, long crumbling stretches breached like broken teeth in a rotting mouth, great ivy-burdened trees pressing up against them from behind.

Sometimes there were neither walls nor hedges, but little low-lying fields and boggy stretches of rock and rushes. Sometimes there were farms, the houses hidden, the outbuildings blank against the roadsides. Once or twice a bit of a field held a gaggle of unfinished bungalows. Then hedges and trees again for miles, their high wild branches cutting off the sky. Hannie sat very quietly in her seat, looking, saying nothing. She felt as if she were burrowing down, away from life as she knew it, back into some overgrown and forgotten past. Ned, sitting so close beside her, noticed nothing but his own emotions at returning.

'They'll want to know your maiden name and who your mother was,' he said suddenly. 'It's so that they can work out who you are.'

She looked at him, but didn't speak.

'It isn't personal,' he said, 'don't take offence. They'll just want to find the connection.'

'What connection?'

'That their mother's second cousin had a house off your great-aunt's brother-in-law in Kildare in 1926. Or better still, a horse.' Ned laughed, pleased with himself, her bewilderment. 'Ignore it, they'll lose interest once they find you're not from here at all.'

Hannie watched his profile as he drove. She didn't know what he was talking about and she didn't care, but she noticed his anxiety and his excitement. At first she thought they were for her, were about arriving here and having her see the life he wanted her to share. Then she saw that it was something altogether simpler. He was nearly home, in the place he liked best, where he liked himself best.

She saw that she was the one being shown the bride.

A figure walking the road ahead called a sheep dog in to heel. Ned slowed and raised his hand in salute. The man saluted back.

'Best not mention the previous marriages,' Ned said to her suddenly. 'Catholic country, and all that.' She looked at him sharply but he was edging the car round a deep bend and over a little bridge.

'This is it,' he said, 'this is home.'

The house was built of rough stone, rendered with plaster, and sat in a muddle of yards and sheds. It was long and narrow, with a newer wing built on at right angles, mature trees around it and a short shrubby drive to the road. The whole impression was not so much shabby as workman-like and a bit down-at-heel. Probably mid-nineteenth century, Ned said, though he wasn't sure, he wasn't much interested in houses except for the big Georgian piles of his class and childhood. It was her domain, he said, she could explore it thoroughly herself and do what she liked within reason.

As soon as he'd done with the house Ned had taken her down to the river. It was tidal here, he explained. At low tide the pull of the sea all but emptied the river. A thick silt of pale mud called a slob lay wherever the water had been.

Step on to this slob, he said, and you went to your knees before you stopped sinking. Bring the boat in on an ebbed tide and you waded through mud like the Somme.

He had pointed to the middle of the water where it was flat and almost still, the current there curiously stationary. That was sea-water pushing back up the river, meeting the river's flow, he said, the one briefly cancelling out the other. Then the stronger sea-flow won and by high tide you'd think the river ran backwards. There was six or eight feet of a drop between tides, and except at the lowest point of the ebb the water was brackish with salt.

It seemed he couldn't get enough of showing and explaining. There was his boat, called a 'punt', on a very long mooring because of the tidal drop. Here was the 'cut' where it lay, a little man-made creek sliced at right-angles into the bank.

You had to know what you were doing at every moment on this river, he said. The ebb tide was worse than the flood, the rip of the current made fierce by the pull of the sea.

41

The near bank where they stood was rough grassland falling off into rushes, grazed by ambling sheep. At the river's edge a few saplings clung, ash and alder and willow, their roots knotting themselves frantically into the eroding soil. A path wandered between meadow and water.

She stood with her arms folded and her feet in the boggy ground. A light chill wind tugged at her skirt and hurried the sky. The weak sun shone in a vague glory, luminous behind the moving cloud. A squall of rain blew over, pocking the water, and was gone. The river went smooth and pewter-coloured and white gulls dropped out of the sky and dipped to kiss other white gulls waiting under the water. Rings of black light spread out where they touched.

She looked across the sweep of the water. The far bank was bosomy with great, still trees, their deep green just bronzed with late summer. Downriver these trees thickened into dense woodland. Upriver the trees thinned and the river bank lost itself in stretches of tall flagged reeds that moved with the wind.

You could see the house from where they stood. Its raggedy outline of roofs and buildings peered over the hummocky meadow like an old woman too anxious to see to be altogether discreet about not being seen.

The river flooded easily, Ned said. Heavy rain, big tides, the waters ran fast and furious over the banks and into the woods and the meadows. That's why the house was built up and back like that. He was proud of this strong dangerous river and its complexities, she heard it in his voice and in his words.

Hannie looked and listened but said little. She was tired now from the night journey and the stress of expectation. It was all smaller but oddly wilder than she had expected. She hadn't grasped what he'd been saying about seas and tides. How could she, what had such things to do with this place? It seemed so lost and inland – how could so short a journey bring her so far away from anywhere?

↞ *Chapter 6* ↠

*N*iamh moved down the washing line, feeling the clothes as she passed, lifting a shirt here, the leg of a pair of jeans there, pressing the fabric to her cheek to test the stage of drying. She liked to iron straight from the line, liked the burning off of the last damp, the slight glaze, the smell of the fresh, folded clothes that she carried to the hot-press. As a student she hadn't ironed, it was hardly done to be creaseless in Fine Art, but left to herself she liked ironing and she liked shaking out pressed trousers in the morning and pushing her long arms into smoothed and folded T-shirts.

Nothing dry enough yet. The afternoon was damp and still, it smelled of grass and leaves and growing things. She ran her hands down her sides, down the narrowing-in of her waist, till they rested firm on her hips.

She stood so, liking the feel of her hips under her hands, absently inspecting the swelling apples on the mossed tree behind the line. Further back, on the straggle of lawn that was more like a field, Ned had planted six young apple trees, old-fashioned varieties local to the area, the strains carefully mixed for pollination.

'Worth the trouble,' he'd said to her. 'All this homogenisation.' He'd shaken his head in disapproval of the easy-grow, heavy-cropping varieties the garden centres sold.

It was like Ned to select carefully, to plant carefully leaving the right distance between each tree, to stake and to label. He was thorough in everything to do with the farm, never just settling for what was to hand. He'd get an idea, read up on it, ring someone who knew, then he'd write off and order exactly what it was that he'd decided on.

Often as not her father was the someone-who-knew whom Ned consulted. Her father liked Ned, he was considered capable of learning and forgiven his inexperience.

Her father would most likely have heard by now about this marriage, Niamh thought. Ned's latest acquisition, and one he certainly hadn't been consulted on. She'd maybe not phone home for a bit or she'd get the benefit of his opinion.

Niamh bent to pick fallen pegs out of the springy grass. A widow with a teenage son who'd been living in Kenya, Mrs Coady had said. Not African but Dutch.

Afrikaans?

No, not Afrikaans and not Dutch from Holland, either. Some island that used to be Dutch but wasn't any more. Part of Indonesia. God knows what she was, a mix-up like that. Never been to Ireland in her life before.

They'd said Hawaii in the post office. Niamh had been in buying stamps and they were all talking about it, the old people tut-tutting and the young ones enjoying it: Ned Renvyle had a woman half his age and he hadn't married her either.

A young lad with a lick of black hair falling over his eyes and a pale, clever face said he'd seen her. He was down by Haydn's cross, he said, bringing in an old cow, and she'd come round a bend in the road with nothing on her but a grass skirt and a big long loop of flowers around her neck.

Ned Renvyle had her from a newspaper ad, he said. And there were more where she came from.

The whole post office was sniggering but the postmistress had spotted Niamh out of the corner of her eye. She threw out a hard warning look, someone had jabbed the black-haired lad with an elbow and they'd all gone silent. Later when Niamh was coming out of Foley's with the paper she'd seen the same boy and he'd started rolling his hips as if he'd a hula hoop on them. Niamh had grinned and he'd grinned back and then she'd remembered herself and looked away.

An old love, Niamh guessed. He'd probably known her for years, loved her for years, the husband's death Ned's opportunity. In her mind Niamh saw a letter in a wooden drawer in a woman's desk, a foreign stamp on the envelope and petals pressed into its fading pages.

Funny the way these clichéd images came up strong like that every time, she thought. Funny the way they kept their potency despite the tired and corny symbols. If you painted them you'd be laughed out, and yet they had something – a fragrance – all those women hoping and dreaming down all those years.

Maybe if you made it like a tiny installation you would get away with it. Drawers from an old desk, letters falling out of them, flowers and sealing wax and broad-nibbed handwriting. Everything real and old, the colours enhanced, a bit over the top.

But not by itself, by itself you'd never throw off the cliché.

A whole show of clichés, that's what you'd need, she thought. Women's dreams of love set in the narrow context of the lives they'd lived.

She could see the roof of the house and a slice of the gable-end wall from where she stood now, a column of smoke from each of the chimneys rising straight up into the still air.

The new wife, lighting fires to air the place. Mrs Coady would be offended, she'd lit them all the day before, and anyway the place wasn't damp.

She was offended herself, she decided. This little romance-fantasy she'd been dreaming up was only a way of pretending to herself that she wasn't.

If only he hadn't gone and done this.

And if he had to do it, if only he'd married someone his own age. She made herself stop. She supposed you could be as lonely at seventy as at any other age.

It was no good, she was too angry. He was old, he had had his life, why did he have to be grabbing for more?

Niamh tucked back a loop of the dark straight hair that was working loose from the knot at the back of her head. Should she go over now, she wondered, or should she leave them alone a bit longer? The uncertainty was making her anxious, destroying her pleasure in the washing line and the tree. She didn't want anything to change now, just as she'd settled in, just as she'd fallen in love with her little house and its raggedy garden, just as she was doing what she wanted to do. These last weeks had been as close to perfection as she could have imagined.

She would go over this evening, she decided. She would take the fresh loaf but not the wild flowers, the bunch she'd picked before breakfast, now drooping in a jam jar on the table.

To hell with it, she'd go now and get it over with. She straightened up out of her indecision, lifted her arms and stretched, her back arched, her round breasts in the blue T-shirt pushing forward like the figurehead of a ship.

'She's only just got here,' Ned was protesting into the phone. 'No, I'm not hiding her, of course I'll bring her over, but not yet.' He was looking at Hannie. Hannie was shaking her head.

'No, she's not sick and she hasn't got three legs.' He was laughing into the phone. 'Perhaps in a day or two.' He looked at Hannie again but he was still getting a negative. 'When she's got used to the place, found her feet a little . . . No, you don't need to ring again, I'll ring back as soon as she's ready.' He put the receiver down.

'It hasn't stopped since we got home,' he told Niamh. 'It's like Christmas, everyone ringing up, asking us over.'

He sounded embarrassed and pleased at the same time. Niamh glanced at Hannie. She was smoking and drinking tea, a full ashtray on the table beside her.

'They want to get a look at the new wife,' she said, addressing Niamh for the first time. Her voice was light, her eyes mocking.

'It's only natural,' Ned said, a little defensively.

'Of course, it is,' she agreed. 'But it's for their benefit, not mine. They can wait till I'm ready.'

'I doubt they'll do that,' Ned said. 'If we don't go there, they'll come over here, you'll see. Might as well do as they want, go and drink their whiskey, it's the same difference.'

Niamh's loaf lay on the table beside Hannie's elbow. Its greaseproof wrapper was unopened. She wished she'd left it sitting on her own table, the flowers drooping beside it.

'It's a lovely house, isn't it?' She heard herself and cringed. It was a plain spare house with an ugly roof and not much grace to it. She sounded stupid and over-eager to please.

Hannie reached across for the teapot. 'It needs re-painting.'

Ned looked surprised. 'Does it? I put a new roof on last year. Everything stripped right down, new beams, cement tiles, it's completely sound. Plaster's a bit stained, I suppose, but it'll do a few years yet.'

'Inside,' Hannie said.

'People go on about slate, can't understand why. Cement's tougher and cheaper.'

Niamh opened her mouth to protest and closed it again. Ned was a funny mixture. In ways he was almost cool, and then he'd come out with stuff that would have shamed even her father.

'This kitchen's dark,' Hannie said deliberately. 'Another window would make a difference, don't you think? In the end wall, perhaps?' She was looking at Niamh, challenging her to agree. Niamh couldn't believe she was being hooked in so fast.

'It will all seem dark,' she said stupidly. Now they both looked at her. 'Ireland, I mean. After Africa. Mrs Coady said you came from Africa.'

'I was born in Java,' Hannie said. 'But it's many years since I lived there.'

Niamh stared. She couldn't think what this woman was doing in Ned's kitchen, nor could she think of anything else to say to her. A few minutes more and she'd go. Leave them to argue about the house or his friends or whatever else they were into.

She'd draw those flowers, she thought. Try and get that half-alive, half-dead look wildflowers had when you picked them and put them in water. The I-can't-thrive-look. And maybe she'd look up Java in the old school atlas that she'd brought from home.

'You didn't mention a cottage with a tenant.'

'It was empty.' Ned was surprised to feel that he was justifying himself. 'It needed a tenant. Fires lit, windows opened, that sort of thing. No damp course, you see.' He put down the paper and smiled patiently at Hannie. 'Ireland's not like Africa.'

'Niamh,' Hannie said as though trying the word on her tongue. 'Eve with an N. Who is she – this almost-Eve, and what's she doing here?'

'N-I-A-M-H.' Ned spelled it out. 'It's an Irish name, nothing to do with Eve, or not that I know of. Her father farms near here, he's by way of being a friend. And he's been a great help to me, so when he asked if I knew of anywhere to let . . .'

'You thought of the cottage and it suited everyone?'

'Exactly. Three birds with the one stone, so to speak. A favour for John, a tenant for me and a place for the girl till she finds her feet.'

'It's a strange place for a good-looking girl to come to find her feet,' Hannie said. Her voice was neutral. 'Or is Ireland unlike Africa in that way, too?'

Ned smiled. 'No, not in that way, but she wants to be an artist and she needs a quiet place to live and paint. John's against it, but he doesn't want to play the heavy-handed father. He thinks if she has a go she'll find for herself that it's no way to live.'

'Enough rope to hang herself,' Hannie said. 'And you don't agree with him?'

'No, I suppose I don't. It's outside their ken, painting, she's stepping out of their world and he's afraid for her. He says she's an odd sort of girl, too soft for the farm, the sort who'll be on at you and on at you to save a calf then when it can't be saved she'll give you no peace till it's killed. Can't bear the waiting in watching it die. Well, the girl's by way of being John's calf, the youngest, the gentlest. They wanted a steady sort of life for her but when she wanted to go to the art school in Dublin they didn't stand against her. They thought she could train and then teach in a country school near home till she married . . .' Ned trailed off, shrugging his shoulders.

'And she has other plans?'

'Exactly. John says he'll pay for a year while she has a go. When the year's up she can do teacher training. He says she's a good girl at heart and too responsible to be idling. All she needs is a little time and she'll see things his way.'

'And you want to help her to be a painter?'

Ned nodded. 'I'm looking out for commissions for her. People's houses, children, that sort of idea. Things that will help her to pay her way while she learns her trade. I want her at least to have the chance to try. She's a good tenant,' he finished defensively. 'She's turned that cottage inside out, everything's been stripped and aired and washed to an inch of its life. She's a worker all right.'

'That is not quite the same as a painter.'

'Perhaps not. Time will tell.' Suddenly he didn't want to discuss it any more. He picked up the paper. He liked Niamh, was charmed by her lovely, old-fashioned face and her quiet, serious ways. But more than that, he liked young people who dreamed of making their own lives in their own fashion. Suddenly he felt a little foolish and he wasn't quite sure why. He tried not to mind but his pleasure in Niamh's presence was diminished.

❦ *Chapter 7* ❧

*T*he incoming tide was almost full, the river ran wide and dark, its surface swollen with little eddies and currents that creased and dimpled the water. The great trees on the far bank leaned forward and dipped their green boughs in the river. They made with the living waters a closed circle of surrender and completeness. At night there were no lights here, no sounds but the river's flow, the night birds, the scufflings and death cries of small animals. The valley had an atmosphere that was dense and secret, knowing nothing but itself.

Human absence. But an absence altogether unlike that of Africa where men and beasts moved light as thought across the land. This absence was more like presence, it conspired with the centuries of human occupation, denying their passing. Everyone who had ever lived in this valley was still here, still moved in its light, still lived in its emanations of water and land. Standing here was like stepping back to meet them, Hannie thought, stepping back into a past that was also present and future. The place was thronged and dense with lives lived.

A little evening wind had got up. The river shone and shifted, flakes of white light seemed to float on the moving water. Standing beside it, Hannie remembered another place and another river, a greener, sunnier river where it merged into the sea.

It was the place, she decided, the lostness of it. The sense that fatally she must be taken in or rejected and no compromise offered, that the life here would close over her or push her out.

The fifth time a bride, she remembered the first time. Suddenly, and with no warning, in a country more remote from that Indonesian trading station than even the flatlands of Holland, she was beset by her memories.

Piet Boonjes stood before her. Piet Boonjes, solid, Dutch, an island trader; the age those years ago that she was now. Piet, his small blue eyes, his fatty freckled shoulders, his sagging dugs and sagging belly and legs gone skinny, handing her money to add to the store of cash she'd been skimming from his takings for the past two years.

His money, her cut. But mostly she hadn't bothered to justify it like that. She'd just stolen what she could, taking care it was never so much that he'd notice.

But he'd noticed every penny and when the time came for her to leave he'd known how much she had and given her more.

'Tell me where you want to go, Hannie.' He'd held out a bundle of dirty notes. 'I will speak to the captain and arrange your passage. Put this money with the rest, you'll have enough now for a decent start.'

She had taken the money without looking up. She couldn't, it was too far beyond her comprehension. His acceptance of her, his acceptance of life. She couldn't believe he'd just open his hands and let go of her, letting his money go with her.

He'd laughed at her, but not unkindly. 'I thought a year at most but you've stayed two, Hannie. A girl like you, less than half my age. Take it, it's not a gift, it's yours, I owe it to you. On this deal I can truly say I haven't lost.'

She'd looked up then, meeting his eyes in his round clown's face with its comic-sombre air of burden and sadness. The tufts of grey hair stuck out all around like a small boy just climbed from his bed.

'Go, since you must, but write to me from time to time. I will miss you, but only a little. I will have compensations . . .'

He had always had compensations, though she hadn't at first noticed or understood this. Half-caste children ran round the tea gardens. Benign watchers followed her course, knowing she could not last. Everyone knew, even him. Only herself thinking it some secret she hatched and tended alone.

Piet was Indonesian-born Dutch, a hard, shrewd trader, with kindness only for women and natives and small children, shunning the fellow Europeans he despised. He had taught her books and storekeeping, who to cheat and who not to cheat, how to deal. Her mother had brokered the marriage and he had acceded to it; she saw now that she had merely played her cast-part. Piet had married her without expectation, she saw that too. As he might have taken a bale of cloth against his judgement. Wanting it, knowing it would not sell.

Her passage was arranged and did not cost her. She hadn't written, though he'd sent money to a poste restante in Jo'burg those first years. She'd thought of him, but mostly only when she refused a man. In the end the letter she'd sent had asked for a divorce.

The letter back didn't come from Piet. She could marry whom she liked, it seemed, for Piet was dead.

She was astonished then; somehow it hadn't occurred to her that Piet could die. He'd been in a Japanese camp in the war and she knew he would not easily let life go.

'There's a time when it's nothing to die,' he had said. 'You're so weak and the door stands open and all around they're walking through that door. But if you come back to life after that, it's a different story. My God, you hold life so tight in your hand, you'll never loosen your grip.'

His clenched fist had beaten softly on the flesh of his thigh as he spoke and his narrowed eyes had stared furiously ahead of him at nothing. Hannie recognised what she was seeing. Her mother had been in a Japanese camp for women. Her mother, too, had survived.

She was sorry then, for herself as much as for him. She had lost the last anchor mooring her to her first life. She had lived these months without it, never even knowing it had gone.

Sometimes in the early evenings, Piet had gone with her to the river to bathe. He would stand waist-deep in the sunny green waters, watching the shadows of fishes move over the sand. The fish floated above, bright and translucent, attached as by wavering threads to these more-real, darker, deeper selves. She would stand beside him, watching the shapes on the sunlit, sandy bottom. He would point and chuckle, he never tired of it. It was his indulgence, his gentlest time.

Would it come to that for her too? Could she ever be so satisfied?

She'd been nineteen then, her whole life ahead of her. Those shut-away years with Piet had been painful with impatience, but not with fear. Now here she was with Ned in just such a closed and forgotten place. Ageing, with no money with which to escape, no place to escape to. And no hope for the future to make it easier to bear.

But also with Joss. They were seeing the school next week, she wanted that done before he arrived from Africa. Get him in on Ned's clout before they smelled a rat and asked for an interview.

Briefly she acknowledged to herself the mistake she had made in coming here. Then she set the knowledge aside. She turned from the river and walked back up to the house.

❧ *Chapter 8* ❧

*M*rs Coady threw the sheet out from herself like a sail thrown to the wind. Hannie caught it with practiced ease. They settled it on to the bed, smoothing out the starched whiteness. The slanting sun laid a window of soft light across it. The window repeated itself on the blanket they threw over it, and on to the next and the next.

The same sun pulled rich gleams out of the polished furniture. The two women bent and stretched, lifted and spread, the house quiet and empty around them.

She knows what she's doing, Mrs Coady thought, it's a pleasure to work with her. They'd been at it all day now and there was the rhythm of harmony between them.

Her son was expected, they were changing things round, preparing a room for him. They seemed to have done nothing but change things round since she arrived.

Move this, Mrs Coady, move that. If she needs a dressing table, she must have one. Whatever she wants, Mrs Coady, whatever it is that women need.

She'd shifted things here and shifted things there, his mother's dressing table from the house in Fermoy, the picture from the study that she'd taken a fancy to, the curtains with the knots of faded flowers folded away in the attic, now unfolded, washed, pressed, hung.

Mrs Coady knew the signs. She'd see her walking around the house looking, and then she'd be walking around with him, pointing here and pointing there, planning. There was to be a new bay in the drawing room and a glass-covered porch by the back door and the kitchen was to be opened out to take in the two little end rooms with a window looking on to the garden. The new garden that Joe Casey's digger was manoeuvring into being. And last week an automatic washing machine had arrived from Waterford.

Ambrose Power, builder and odd-job man, said as how he might as well move in. 'Fair play to the women,' he added hastily. 'I never saw a bachelor change a house though he lived in it sixty year. If it wasn't for the women I'd hang up me hat and stay home.'

There'd been no money before. Only for roofs. Always had a thing about good snug roofs, had Ned Renvyle. Anything else you could whistle for.

'Can't have what you can't pay for, Mrs Coady,' he'd say. Which was news to her. And there was no shifting him till this one turned up and persuaded the money out of him.

'It's not that he's mean, exactly, Mrs Coady,' she'd said, swishing the dregs of her coffee around in the mug and knocking it back.

'It's just he's got out of the habit of spending. It may even be it's a habit he never picked up in the first place.' She stopped, looked thoughtful, and then spoke again in that voice that was not foreign like the Dutch and the Germans, but not English either and certainly not Irish. You wouldn't know, listening to her, where it was she came from at all.

'Still, it's never too late to teach an old dog new tricks, now is it?' she was saying. 'And I wouldn't say he'd had much of an example, living around here?'

'No example at all,' Mrs Coady agreed. 'Unless it's a horse they'd be wanting.'

'They' meant his class, the Anglo-Irish, who lived in the great mouldering houses scattered about the valley. This one never pretended to be one of them, she never pretended to be anything. No airs and graces to her, but a distance like a wall when she'd a mind to it. She'd sit you down and she'd be talking or you'd be talking and the next thing she was somewhere else altogether and you'd be left hanging there, the ladder pulled away, the sick feel of empty space under you. You never knew where you were with her.

Any more than his friends did when they came calling in their wellington boots and their padded jackets and their old cars held together with bits of twine. It just depended how the mood took her. He didn't say anything. He was keeping his head down, ignoring the talk, pretending it wasn't happening.

But he was disappointed when she wasn't how he wanted her, you could see that. Well, he might as well get used to the feeling. She was like a wrong horse. One minute all pretty ways and gentle as you please and the next away off with herself and no holding her.

She was no one's, all right.

He looked a fool, standing there beside her, and he'd look a bigger fool before he was through with her. It was hard to watch – a decent straight sort of man as he was. He was proud of himself and proud of her still, for all she wouldn't behave for him.

They were finishing up the room now, she looking around, checking that everything was just so. It looked well. She'd had the broken sash on the window fixed and the chimney swept and she'd painted the walls and the ceiling herself. She'd sanded and re-stained the floor and waxed the boards till they shone. She wasn't afraid of dirtying her hands when she'd a mind to, you could say that for her, if you said nothing else.

It was funny she'd chosen this room though, away down the end of the corridor and looking out over the back field. And funny she wanted a school up there in the North, and no bringing him home at weekends and half-terms till he got a bit used to the way of things here. The empty room at the front of the house got the sun in the morning and longer into the day. There was to be a fire lit in here, for the boy was coming from Kenya and would have to adjust to the climate. Fine, settled weather they were having, and she always on about damp and cold. What would she say when winter came, what would she make of February?

Mrs Coady had asked for a photo but she'd said she had none. No photo, no stories, and no great rush bringing the lad home from Africa, either.

She was sorry she'd asked, she wouldn't do it again, she'd only opened her mouth out of kindness, pitying Hannie's strangeness in a strange place. Whoever heard of a woman with no picture of her own son?

☙ *Chapter 9* ☙

*H*annie watched the new life shaping up around her. She smoked more, said little. At least now she could smoke where she liked, when she liked. Sometimes it seemed the only compensation.

Ned also watched. He'd been pleased by her interest in the house till he realised she was serious in her talk of alterations. New windows here, walls knocked down there, floors torn up and replaced. Now. Not some time in the future when it suited. His pleasure quickly turned to apprehension.

At first he'd tried to warn her. It wasn't easy getting building done in Ireland, he said. Especially not fidgety bits of alterations, when the builder couldn't see what was wrong with the way it was to begin with. He'd start all right, but when a job came up on the farm he'd tack a bit of polythene over the hole in your wall and go off and attend to it. Priorities were priorities. When a better job came up he'd be gone for a month, calling now and again to say he'd be with you the next day for sure.

'I've dealt with natives all my life,' she said.

His heart sank at the statement. He wondered how many fences he would have to mend, how many hard-won understandings he would have to re-negotiate. He didn't look forward to the process. As he had learned not to look forward to introducing her to his friends and neighbours. Not that it always went wrong. Sometimes, for no reason he could see, she would decide she liked someone, or that they were worth an effort. And she'd leave them dazzled and amazed as she had him. But he never knew what to expect.

Ambrose Power seemed to like her. Joe Casey traded cigarettes with her and told her things that made her laugh. When they didn't come she didn't seem surprised. Watching her, it began to dawn on him that she didn't need to learn the ways of the country. She wasn't particularly sympathetic or patient. It was more that she was like that herself.

For Hannie the activity of the building work was enough. It kept her occupied, kept her from brooding too much on the place and on what she had done to her life and to Joss's. She refused to think about Ned, though she knew that she wasn't as he wanted her to be, she knew he was disappointed. Tough. He'd just have to get used to her the way she was. She had put so much effort into reassuring him, into appearing light-hearted when she didn't feel it. At least now they were married she could stop all that. Besides, she was doing up his house for him, he had nothing to complain about.

Joss looked taller, older; it was a shock. Somehow in her mind she must have lopped off a few inches, dropped a year or two. Babied him.

So he'd seem easier to manage, more amenable to her needs and wishes?

He hadn't seen her, or maybe he had and she just couldn't see him seeing her for the Ray-Ban wraparound look. He was wheeling his luggage trolley slowly out through Arrivals. Fair hair, grey cotton sweater, off-white trousers, and those black mirror-sunglasses, very appropriate for Cork airport. He looked cold and tense and tired underneath the tan.

Which meant he'd be angry and aggressive with her. She felt herself flooded with tenderness and dread in equal parts. Thank God she'd persuaded Ned to stay at home.

'Of course I'll drive you, you don't know the way.'

'I'll find the way, Ned, it'll be good for me to begin to get to know my way around.'

'You might break down. The Volkswagen's not reliable any more, it needs handling.'

'I'll learn that, too.'

Ned had walked across the kitchen, stared out of the window, then walked back and stood over her.

'I ought to be there with you when he arrives, Hannie,' he said. 'Make sure he knows he's welcome.'

'He hasn't seen me for two months and he's been travelling all night and half yesterday. You can make him welcome when he gets here.' She had spoken carefully and reasonably, as though addressing an over-persistent child. Finally he had accepted her refusal.

And all the way here there'd been the tenderness and the dread that Joss inspired in her these days. An aching tenderness, a compound of cherishing and love and pity. The dread was simpler.

She had tried to think clearly while she still had the chance. What was she going to tell him if he pressed her? A firm line? That this was it, the future, whether he liked it or not, and he'd better start getting used to it?

But if he was vulnerable and frightened, if he pleaded with her, saying it was his life too? If he wanted her to reassure him, to promise not to make them stay here if he hated it? What would she say then?

Would she crack and comfort him and say it was the best that she could manage? That it was only to be going on with, that it might not be for ever?

She'd anticipated it backwards and forwards, taut as a bow-string with the strain.

'Hallo, Mother.' He took his glasses off, pecked her on the cheek, looked at her out of his light-blue eyes, put them on again. 'What have you done with the geriatric?'

The fine weather persisted – days of hazy gold sunlight and warm sweet air. The river moved against the great still trees and the fields swam in the dreamy light. To the north the blue mounds of the Comeraghs lay drowsy and heaped.

Everyone smiled like idiots and sighed and said over and

over how lovely it was. Hannie thought they'd taken leave of their senses. Joss shivered in his cotton clothes, refusing the woollens that she'd bought for him. He walked the farm and the river banks without comment and spent long hours in his room. The mirror-sunglasses he never left off.

Joss hardly spoke in Ned's company. He was well-mannered and replied readily enough when directly questioned, but somehow the end of his answer was also the end of the conversation.

Ned let him be and did not press him. If Joss wanted to take his time and get to know him slowly, that was understandable. He approved of old-fashioned manners; he was almost relieved the boy wasn't a chatterer. He supposed Joss and his mother talked when they were alone together, and in time they would learn to accept him, too. Meanwhile the boy was only settling in and everything was strange to him. Ned set himself to patience.

He did very well, or he thought he did, interfering only when it came to the wearing of sunglasses at the table. He requested discreetly through Hannie that meals be eaten without them. She looked at him steadily, saying nothing. He felt her will against him. The next day Joss sat down to lunch, removed the glasses and laid them on the table to his right. Hannie looked at her plate. When the meal was over and the chairs pushed back, Joss picked up the dark glasses wordlessly and replaced them on the bridge of his nose.

After that Joss always removed them for meals with a careful ostentation. Ned stubbornly refused to think his request unreasonable, but he found himself disconcerted by the expressionlessness of his stepson's revealed blue eyes. He began to wish the glasses back in place.

❧ *Chapter 10* ❧

'*T*hey're protected,' Naimh said, looking up from her stance on her hunkers at Joss. 'You can't just kill it and get it stuffed, it's illegal.'

'So?' Joss sneered out the word.

Niamh flushed. If you said illegal someone always let on you were chicken. And if you said cruel, they let on you were soft.

Bad move either way with a weirdo like Joss: words like that only encouraged him.

The small owl in Joss's tight hands roused itself suddenly and struggled frantically in his grasp. It lunged at him with its beak but he held on, his knuckles showing white through his tanned skin, the blood springing up where the beak had struck home. It subsided. Joss didn't loosen his hold for a moment. Despite herself Niamh was impressed.

'We'll have less of that,' Joss said to the owl, his voice low and reassuring. 'We don't want to be damaging ourselves, do we? Nor spoiling our pretty feathers?'

He stroked at it awkwardly with his forefinger, still keeping the vice-tight grip.

'There's a whole long future ahead to be thinking of. Posterity, presentation. All that shite. Think of a nice glass case on the wall in Joss's bedroom, eh? It's not going to look very good now, is it, owl? All this flaffing about, breaking things.'

'Danno won't touch it if you kill it,' Niamh said flatly. 'He won't stuff an owl that hasn't died naturally.'

'But maybe it *will* die naturally, Niamh,' Joss replied. 'Maybe it'll starve to death on account of its poor broken wing.' He laughed softly, still stroking the bird with his finger, then looked up into Niamh's tight face.

'Of course it won't starve to death, stupid. What would be the point of that? A mangy poxy little owl that looks like it just flew out of Belsen? Squinting at you out of its glass case? Towit, towoo, a merry owl. I-am-the-ghost-of-a-Joss-starved-owl.'

Joss made his eyebrows go round and raised and his small mouth pouted forward with his owl-sounds. He looked so funny, Niamh laughed.

'Towoo, towoo, towoo, Niamh! What a merry way to scare yourself shitless in the small hours, eh . . . ?' Joss laughed, Niamh couldn't stop, their young fresh voices blithe and easy in the sunshine.

Hannie, flattened against the byre wall, ears stretched for every nuance of the conversation, sighed with relief and let her head fall back to rest on the warm stone. He wanted to talk to Niamh, that was it. That was what all the circling and inspecting had been about, the signs that she knew of old, the small details of obsession that she had to be constantly on the watch for. He had wanted to attract Niamh's attention.

And now it was done, and they were there together, Joss sitting on an old plank set across two drums, the bird in his hands, his back against the byre wall, Niamh squatting on her hunkers beside him.

Ned was wrong in supposing that Joss talked much to Hannie. Joss talked to no one, had talked to no one for years as far as his mother could see. But this not-talking didn't mean detachment or indifference. For stretches – sometimes long stretches – Joss was with her, as silent and close as her own shadow. Then suddenly he'd be off, his needs driving him, his attention totally elsewhere. The process was invisible, psychic not physical, but of an intensity that made her feel almost deranged. What she did know – instinctively, unmistakably – was the precise moment of his psychic arrival somewhere else.

Not half an hour earlier she had known it. She had stood in the yard in the empty sunshine and as surely as she knew the colour of his hair she had known that it had happened, that Joss had stopped circling and had settled.

She didn't know where, she never knew where. He might have fallen down a well, he might have drowned himself in the river, he might have killed someone. She had stood there, quite motionless, a flat empty feeling of despair settling back inside her, a rat settling into its familiar nest. Then her ear had caught voices and she'd followed those voices around the side of the byre.

'Take it to Danno,' Niamh was saying now. 'He'll put a splint on its wing, he knows about owls, he'll save it if he can.'

And then he'll release it back into the wild, she thought, keeping the thought to herself. Joss was weird all right, he might have other plans, but then again he might not. He knew about birds, you could tell that from the way he held the owl, the way he was liking looking at it, the same as she was. This talk of his might all be an act.

'Who is this Danno that Niamh speaks of?' asked Hannie.

'Danno? Taxidermist. Poacher. Lives in a sort of shed by the river. Does a bit of this and a bit of that. Odd fish, Danno. Why?'

'Joss found an owl with a broken wing. Niamh says he must take it to Danno, that Danno will fix it.'

'I expect he will. And if he doesn't fix it he can always stuff it. Badly. Danno stuffs everything badly, but he doesn't seem to notice. No more do his clients, they keep taking him things, James Beresford's pleased as punch with a pike Danno did for him, doesn't seem to notice how grotesque it looks.'

'Pike are supposed to look grotesque, are they not?'

'Frightening-grotesque, not lumpy-grotesque. How do you know about pike, Hannie? Don't have them in Kenya, do they?'

'Andrew had one on the wall. A family heirloom from some Scottish river.'

They were sitting outside on a bench by the wall, drinking coffee in the hazy Sunday morning sunlight. It was quiet and still, a day off from Ambrose Power and his sledges and drills. Joe Casey's digger had finished its work and beyond the little garden where they sat the new lawn lay raked and waiting to be sown. Joss was off visiting Niamh, or she hoped that was where he was.

'Didn't know Joss was interested in birds,' Ned said. It was half a question. Hannie stretched up her hand to pull at a late rose on the wall.

'He is. Birds, and also insects.' She turned the rose this way and that, inspecting the shaggy pink flower, the round black indentations on its smooth green leaves. 'This rose needs spraying.'

'It does, they all do, I just haven't got round to it. So you know about roses. Andrew had those too?'

'The English must have their roses, even in Africa. I looked after Andrew's roses, or rather the gardener did, and I instructed him. Would you like me to look after your roses, Ned?'

'Yes, please,' said Ned. 'The spray's in the shed, and I'm sorry there isn't a gardener to be instructed.' He paused a moment. 'I believe I am a little jealous of Andrew, Hannie,' he said, surprising himself with the remark.

She smiled vaguely, letting go of the rose. It swung, a diminishing pendulum, on the still air.

After that Joss was around Niamh like a shadow.

Or a cat, Mrs Coady thought, as she watched him prowl and stalk and sidle close. Very like a cat. So sleek and still. Not a hair out of place. The small mouth, the neat small tongue to lick cream.

A thief too, she wouldn't mind betting. Not the son you would think she would breed. But you never knew what would come out, you couldn't choose, and you always loved the bad ones best, for they'd no one else.

Niamh didn't seem to mind him. But Niamh liked cats. At least till they brought something in half alive and half dead and sat themselves down to torment it.

She slung the mat she was carrying over the line and beat at it with the back of the broom. Satisfying clouds of dust flew out of it. She wondered about the father.

❧ *Chapter 11* ❧

*H*annie took Joss to Cork to buy clothes and kit for school. Not all of it, but the bulk of it. There were specifics she'd have to get in the school shop when they took him North.

She'd asked Ned for money and he'd taken out his cheque-book and written a cheque out to cash. She could change it in Cork, he said, he didn't keep cash in the house.

She knew that already. And that he had no time for credit cards and didn't like banks, though he paid all his bills by cheque.

She could buy what she liked when she liked, he had told her. If she wanted anything she had only to ask and anyway all the local shops kept books under the counter, he would settle her bills when they were presented. There was to be no joint account.

She went first to the bank in Cork to cash the cheque and then to the school outfitters that Ned said everyone used. Methodically, she worked her way down through the list that the school had sent.

It seemed an enormous amount to amass, everything dark and heavy and thick. Joss was docile, almost co-operative, only occasionally attempting sabotage and never refusing out-right. She was so surprised and relieved that she told him to choose something for himself when they'd finished. He gave her a long look and said there was nothing in the shop he'd wear unless he had to.

When she came to pay she found that Ned's cashed cheque wasn't enough to cover their purchases. She had no other money, no credit cards or chequebook to fall back on. The last of her own money had gone on Joss's fare from Kenya.

She picked up the list and began to edit. Joss drifted off to another part of the shop, leaving her to sort out the situation. She knew from the turn of his head that he was despising Ned for under-providing and despising her for landing them both with him.

Abruptly she stopped trying to work out what to keep and what to put back and instead she wrote out Ned's name and address and asked that their purchases and the bill be sent on. The assistant who was serving her disappeared to consult with a senior. Out of the corner of her eye she watched the two heads scanning the paper, the older one nodding assent. Ned's name was good for something, after all. When the young man came back she asked him to recommend a good restaurant.

They ate lunch off a starched white cloth with a good bottle from the list and waiters in attendance. Joss helped himself to the wine and she said nothing. He watched as she paid the large bill with cash from Ned's cheque. She felt defiant, placing the notes on the salver, she wanted to spend Ned's careful money wastefully, to dissipate it in ways he would certainly not approve. And she cared nothing for such surroundings, was indifferent to the manicured food, the snobbish, over-priced wine list. Joss liked it, but she wasn't doing it for Joss.

Why *was* she doing it? she asked herself. Why did she suddenly mind Ned's minding his wallet? He hadn't minded it when it mattered. When it came to paying the school fees, he hadn't hesitated. Why had her gratitude so quickly turned to vindictiveness?

Because now it was all settled.

Ned had arranged things and gone with her to the school and made it all possible. The school had taken Joss because of Ned: Ned's name and Ned's presence, they'd hardly bothered with her at all. She had sat in her good suit drinking tea and keeping her thoughts to herself while the headmaster and the housemaster and the matron all ignored her and basked instead in Ned and in Ned's modest, admirable reputation.

They hadn't even queried the choice of a school so far from where they resided. Ned had served the Empire, it was natural that he should want his wife's son educated in its territory. Besides, he was a Protestant. There were Protestant schools in the South of course. Some would consider them dubious.

She had been so anxious on the drive up, so grateful for his willingness to help her and for his unspoken decision to accept what she asked for and leave her motives unquestioned. It was all she had thought of. She felt that if Joss was settled she might even be grateful to Ned, for ever. Or grateful enough to get by on for at least a bit longer.

Well, that had been then, she thought sourly. It seemed that her gratitude had worn thin before Joss was even despatched.

Ned tried not to blame Hannie for her loyalty to Joss and he tried not to imagine pacts between them. He tried not to notice that the boy's politeness was often a form of rudeness and he told himself it was perfectly natural that Joss should resent a new authority, at least initially. He had known Joss would be a problem.

Nevertheless, he was disappointed. Gradually he became aware of the cause of his disappointment. Joss did not inspire affection, nor did he seem to wish to have affection extended to him.

Ned found himself blushing at this realisation. What had he wanted? A son to love and be loved by? He got up and went out to the near meadow. The old mare he occasionally hacked around on came to the gate whinnying softly and blew into his hand. He liked the comfort of her. He grew calmer and tried to think more clearly. He didn't like this alliance of mother and son and he didn't like being shut out by them. And he didn't like this blank-faced boy in the mirror glasses, yet he wanted to like him and be liked by him. Most of all, he realised, he didn't like what he was learning about himself.

He knuckled the mare's bony face and she rubbed for more. Hannie had married him for a home for the boy, he knew that, she'd as good as said it, and he had accepted it. But already it seemed he'd begun to forget it.

Things were bound to be difficult at the beginning, he told himself; her loyalty was divided, that was where her coldness came from. The boy would be gone in a few days, he and Hannie would get used to each other, the school would settle Joss down.

It was a good school, straightforward and disciplined, with a sound reputation. He was relieved she hadn't wanted Joss nearer and home every other weekend, the way it seemed to be done now. He'd been surprised at the time but she seemed sure of what she was doing, and maybe it didn't seem far to her, being used to Africa. Then again maybe she was thinking of him and of their marriage, breaking him in gently, aware that Joss was difficult. Ned was pleased at this thought. He rubbed Connie's face again, dismissed her with a final pat. Yes, Joss would settle at school, make friends, get used to the climate. He'd be easier when he came home for the Christmas holidays.

Hannie, too, would be easier. He must be patient, he must give her time.

Hannie was aware that Joss was making things more difficult for her with Ned. With the boy standing watching and challenging, it was hard not to question her judgement in making this arrangement for their lives. She knew that this line of thought wasn't useful to her and she didn't want to be wasting her time in futile rebellion and resentment. She wanted to accept Ned as he was and thus be free of him: the chameleon's trick that had served her well in the past.

But when she was with Joss it was as though his wraparound glasses were clamped to her own nose. She criticised Ned with her actions and with her eyes. She allied herself with Joss against him.

It was partly because the stakes were so high for Joss. A new life, a new school, different influences. This was a chance for him and there might not ever again be such another. Her instinct told her to stay close to the boy, to support him sympathetically and emotionally and not let him be isolated through any intimacy of hers with Ned.

But it was also an emotional reaction against Ned and against the place she now found herself in. She hadn't anticipated so closed a life, nor that Ned's expectations would weigh so heavily upon her. At night she dreamed of blocked holes and locked rooms, of sealed and shuttered windows. She escaped from dream into consciousness and lay awake in her trap. She felt this life bearing down on her like a pillow pressed over her face and her panic and suffocation unbalanced her. Joss also unbalanced her. Try as she might she could not get through his refusal of her. She could not read him or reach him and his anger and avoidance of her enraged her and worried her sick by turns.

He escaped her to Niamh who accepted him without comment, like a cat that had wandered in and might perch on her sill or wind itself round her feet for a day or a week before disappearing.

He was there now. Hannie rose from her work of sorting and labelling and packing and crossed to the window. For a long time she stood scanning the deserted yard and the empty sheds as though they held some clue to Joss's heart that she might read if she looked hard enough.

Then she returned to the piled underwear, the marker pen and the labels. She was glad Joss was going in the morning, though she dreaded the pain and apprehension she knew she'd feel on his behalf once he'd left and her anger had subsided. Nonetheless she might be less emotionally swamped. She knew she would have to create some sort of a working relationship with Ned soon or the life here would rapidly become unbearable to them both. With Joss gone she might regain sufficient equilibrium to try.

Or to decide not to.

She knew Joss wouldn't write her letters or phone her. For a moment she wished she'd chosen a school that was nearer, that she could visit and be visited from. She refused the thought. The further away the school, the easier the damage-limitation. That was the hard-learned fruit of experience. She mustn't start now on fantasies that Joss was other than he was.

At least he'd had Niamh to hang round while he was here, Hannie thought. At the same time she hated Niamh for the intimacy that Joss had bestowed on her. An unsought intimacy, probably also unwanted, she acknowledged bitterly to herself.

Niamh had a passion for moths and butterflies. Joss, too, liked insects, though ants and beetles were more in his line. It was a bond between them, this shared interest that wouldn't be most people's taste. Niamh had books that Joss consulted, they discussed species together, she could tell him what was rare, what common as mud.

But Niamh's interest was essentially more aesthetic than lepidopterous and she especially liked moths and butterflies in death. It was the way death inhabited them that fascinated her, the way it lived in them, invisible but for its stillness, yet intensely respectful of its own power. The small corpses she collected seemed to her to collude with some aspect of death's sense of itself: a sense altogether different from that which she'd seen displayed in its grosser occupation of human beings and farm animals. There was a propriety in its dealings with these insects. It was as though they'd been given notice and had served as their own undertakers. They had laid themselves out, wings spread, feet neatly crossed, bodies sleek in their furred coats now doubling up as shrouds. Then, having prepared themselves, the master had been invited in.

Niamh collected up their spent bodies wherever she found them. She perched them on windowsills and shelves as she passed, she laid them carefully on the flat surfaces of stones. Sometimes she retraced her steps, gathering in her harvest. Sometimes she just left them where they lay. Ned had noticed her preoccupation and begun to collect for her. A dusty saucer, full of his gleanings, sat on a scullery shelf.

Joss also joined in the game but instead of adding to Niamh's stores he raided them, creating tiny dramas that were parodies of the living forms. Meticulously Niamh's corpses were re-distributed and resurrected. Furred brown moths clung by their stiff dead legs on to climbing roses, butterflies crawled the bright faces of late marigolds, small silvery moths hooked the porch geraniums. Niamh liked this, the way it made you look afresh at both corpse and flower, the way Joss sometimes changed things into art. But she wasn't so sure about all his insect activities. And she didn't share his fascination with fungi at all.

There were growths everywhere: it was the warm early September weather, the light night rains and heavy morning dews. He asked her endless questions but she didn't know the answers. She knew only the big horse mushrooms dotted about the fields. She liked picking these, easing them carefully out of the ground, breaking them open to check them for grubs. Not so Joss. These edible growths were too plain and serviceable for him, he only kicked and hacked at them, scattering soft shards of flesh across the bright grass. It was the stranger growths that he liked: their rich discolouredness, their spongy fluted branches, whiter than death.

Best of all he liked the big dense fungal clumps that grew in the rough grass on the edge of the pot-holed drive. These were not single forms but multiple manifestations, accretions of chestnut-coloured platelets, layer on spiralling layer.

'Like cities,' Niamh said, kneeling in the damp grass, peering into brown streets and alleyways. 'Or those old walled towns in Italian paintings. You know the ones. Improbable. Like snail-shells. The houses all glued to those lumps of rock sticking out of the planes.'

Joss didn't know, but he liked these impermanent cities. He lay on his belly for hours inserting ants and grasshoppers into their maze of alleys, prodding them into activity with long blades of meadow grass.

Niamh observed with a detached interest. She was getting

used to Joss, making assumptions about him. His weirdness might just be loneliness, she decided. He might be an artist looking for a form.

Hannie also observed, but she did not disturb Niamh's assumptions. Niamh was a grown human being, old enough to be making mistakes and learning from them. Old enough to be acting her age.

Hannie slipped her hand into the last name-tagged sock, grasped its fellow and pulled the first one over it to make a pair. She tossed the bunched socks into the open suitcase. Then she rose and went downstairs, trailing her hand down the polished banister, feeling the lonely emptiness of the late-afternoon house. She wanted to go and fetch Joss out of Niamh's, to harry him over this packing, to force him into sharing these last hours with her, but she made herself hold back.

What was the point? There'd be no confidences, nothing he'd say to her now in intimacy, but wouldn't say tomorrow with Ned there. He was punishing her, she was fairly sure of that, but whether for Ned or for school or both she didn't know. And he seemed all right about tomorrow's journey. He'd be into crossing the border, he'd said, and seeing this famous North with its bombs and guns.

'Less boring than here, Mother. At least there'll be something going on.'

But he didn't know how far it was, he didn't know how he'd feel when he saw them turn the car and drive away.

Neither did she, she told herself. He might like it. On past form it wasn't beginnings that were the problem, it was what happened after he'd begun.

She crossed the hall and on an impulse went into the drawing room and looked out over the front. They were there, both of them, standing on the edge of the drive, Joss doing something, Niamh watching. Hannie moved closer to the window, careful not to be seen.

It was a ceremony. Joss had gathered together a pile of large round stones and was meticulously bombing his cities, his face impassive as the brown walls fell.

Hannie stood a few moments longer. Then she turned and went to the kitchen to prepare the evening meal. Fried chicken, his favourite dish. He'd be angry with her for doing it, angry if she didn't.

'Condemned man eats hearty last meal, eh, Mother?'

That's what he'd say when he'd finished.

❧ *Chapter 12* ❧

O n the day following Joss's departure the weather broke and it rained for three days. Hannie watched the water running down the clouded windows and gathering in puddles on the leaky sills. Draughts blew through the ill-fitting frames, bad-tempered winds plucked at the guttering, the tall Scots pines at the back of the house moaned and complained. Rain swept the valley in wavering curtains and the river lost itself in a hissing blur of grey.

Hannie walked from room to room, smoking too much and hating this dank sodden world she had come to. The kitchen was full of dust from the walls that Ambrose Power and his mate Liam were knocking down, the floor was mud from the wet that their boots had tramped in. For once she was narky and short with them.

The Change, their looks said, women are divils at the Change. They were disappointed in her, that was clear. Where had she gone and who was this harridan left behind in her place?

It was ever so, she thought. Women raged and men mis-understood. Then they felt injured and hard-done-by. She put on wellingtons and a waterproof and went outside to tramp about in the drizzling rain.

She walked up the drive, away from the house, and came on the rain-blackened ruins of Joss's bombed cities. They were crushed and pulped now and smelled of excrement and decay. She stood over them, thinking of Joss in the rain in that grey Northern town on the wide grey lake. Despair settled upon her, the rain ran down her face and dripped off her hands.

Despair changed to rage and she kicked at the cities, scattering the ruins till all that was left was a blackened pulp in the long wet grass. She felt no satisfaction. The ugly feeling that had driven her was still in her. It was no use, nothing was any use, she could not protect him, nor keep him safe from himself. Strange growths came up out of the dark earth, they blossomed and decayed and you could not change that, no matter how you kicked and raged and trampled.

Finally the rain stopped. It was a different landscape: colourless, sodden, beaten down. Overnight a whole world had vanished. Hannie stood by the paddock fence and stared at the mud and the dying vegetation. Nothing was as it had been. The tall ghost-stands of willow herb were battered and flattened now, the fluffy seedheads that last week shone in the light like silk threads were all matted and draggled and done. The rain had stopped, but the sun had not returned. It was cold, the day was dark.

Hannie stood on, staring blankly at the rain's aftermath. She was awaiting a huge sun, floating up over the rim of the land, throbbing the life back into this cold spent world.

It would not come, she realised. That sun lived in Africa, there was no such sun here, nor ever would be.

A grey Cortina drove up, battered and muddy. Hannie watched as a woman got out, opened the boot, and stood looking down into it with an air of quiet satisfaction.

Alison Beresford. A small grey woman in her late fifties, deep-bosomed and slender, wearing trousers and clean wellingtons and a plain, light-green headscarf. Hannie recognised her at once. One of Ned's oldest friends, she lived with a husband called Vere in a crumbling grey house just a few miles away. Hannie watched her now as she straightened up and scanned the house front with quiet, determined eyes.

The boot of the Cortina bulged with muddy polythene bags that had leaves and bits of cut stem sticking out of them. Alison was rummaging about in there, opening bags and closing them, obedient to some order of things hidden in her mind. Hannie stood silently beside her.

'Oh yes,' Alison was saying as she found the bag she was looking for and heaved it out of the boot, 'since we were children. Or rather, since I was a child – he must have been in his teens. They'd just come to live with Mrs Valender at Oldcourt. His grandmother,' she added, with the air of one making clear things clearer.

'Of course he seemed terribly grown up and glamorous. And tragic. His father had just died, you see, Oldcourt was his mother's home. About fifteen, I suppose he must have been. And I must have been about five.' She hauled at another bag.

'Geraniums, cobalt blue. Masses of foliage, very fast spreaders. So useful in the right place, but you do have to be careful. Bullies, really, they'll take over the bed if you let them. Heavenly blue flowers, but only for about two weeks in June. Some people hate them, say they're not worth their keep.'

On some of the bags Alison had scrawled clues as to content with a black felt-tip pen. She would look at the words, then open the bag anyway, and stare hard at the tangles of root and mud and leaf.

'He went to the war of course, but afterwards, after Isobel died, we thought he might come home ... But he didn't. He began on his journeys instead. This one's a little white saxifrage, so dainty, good on a wall or under a tree.' She handed Hannie a bag and waited for her to open it and look inside.

'There's a small pink geranium in there with it. Quite dull, but makes neat little clumps and flowers for ages and ages.' She dived back into the boot.

'He always came backwards and forwards, all through the years. Then when Mrs Valender died, Oldcourt was sold and his mother moved into Delaney's – which was only a step away, so it made no difference really, we saw as much of him as ever. Then she died too, but he still came when he could. He would go to West Cork for his cousins, but he'd always come here for a few days at the end and he always stayed with us.'

Alison dumped the last of the bags with their fellows by the Cortina's back wheel. She straightened up, tightening the scarf under her chin in a gesture at once absent and automatic.

'There,' she said with quiet satisfaction, 'that should keep you busy. And don't be disappointed if the bearded irises don't flower straight away. They will when they get round to it – they simply hate being moved.'

'Alison came,' Hannie said, setting the casserole down on the table. 'She wants us to go there on Friday. "Family-supper-in-the-kitchen", whatever that means. I said we were busy.'

Ned frowned. He stabbed a potato, then reached for the butter. 'Remind me,' he said, not looking up. 'I've forgotten.'

Hannie said nothing. He looked at her.

'We're not busy,' she said, 'I just said we were. She wants me to help with church cleaning and flowers.'

Ned lifted the lid off the casserole. 'And will you?' he said neutrally, spooning lamb and mushrooms on to her plate.

'No,' Hannie said, moving the lid out of the way, still not looking at him. 'She'd been doing her border, splitting up her perennials. She brought us a bootful of off-cuts for our new beds. A bit of everything – even things she doesn't much like, or thinks probably won't grow in our soil. She says it's so much nicer, having plants from someone else's garden. You think of where they came from and they give you extra pleasure.'

'You don't like her,' Ned said.

Hannie looked at him, a long straight look. She picked up her knife and fork and began to eat.

'She's a nice woman.' Ned said, 'It was kind of her to bring us plants, and she's absolutely right about associations.' Hannie kept eating. 'Besides, it would have cost a fortune, buying perennials from a garden centre.'

Ned reached for the salt in the silence. 'You have to give

people a chance, Hannie,' he said reasonably. 'You'll never make friends if you won't try.'

'Why would I want to make friends?' she asked. 'I have Joss, I have you, I am busy all day, why would I want friends?'

Ned sighed. 'It will be easier if you make friends,' he said carefully. 'Easier to settle.'

She put down her knife and fork and rose from the table. She picked up the phone.

'What're you doing?'

She didn't answer him. 'Alison?' she said into the phone. 'Alison, this is Hannie Renvyle. Change of plan. We can come on Friday after all . . . About eight? That will be fine. Yes. I, too, am delighted.'

She sat down and resumed eating.

'I asked her if she'd help with the church flowers,' Alison said.

'And would she?' Vere was sitting at the long table, riffling through the new edition of the *Farmer's Journal*.

'She said she didn't qualify. She said she was an animist.'

'A what?'

'An animist. She comes from Java. She said in Java animists are the norm.'

He looked up, almost interested despite the fresh attractions in the journal.

'A Protestant animist or a Catholic animist?' He smiled, pleased with his little joke.

'A Lutheran animist.' Alison put the boiled kettle and two mugs on the table and sat down.

'She won't get out of it that easily. Tell her Lutheran equals Protestant and as such she's expected to do her bit.' He had lost interest, had already returned to the journal.

'She said her father was a Lutheran. The animism was on her mother's side.' Alison was pouring hot water on to the instant coffee in each of their mugs. 'What do you suppose she meant by that?'

Vere sat up, looking startled. 'Was she serious?'

'Totally.'

'I wouldn't know,' Vere said slowly, reaching for his coffee and abandoning the journal altogether. 'But if I was guessing, old girl, I'd say she meant a touch of the tar brush.' He looked at his wife speculatively. 'I wouldn't put it past old Ned, either. Would you?'

That night Ned came to her room. Afterwards, instead of going back to his own as was his habit, he stayed and slept beside her. Hannie dreamed, this time not of locked rooms and blocked corridors, but of Piet.

She woke in the darkness, Piet there in front of her eyes, Ned snoring gently beside her. The dream was a strong thick taste in her mouth. She lay finding her way back out of it, not wanting to return there when she slept again.

The dream was short. She was standing beside the river here, very early in the morning. It was like grey glass, and a mist crept up from the water in little trails and puffs. In the intense quiet a bird rose, its wings beating the still surface, breaking the smooth grey glass. She saw Piet standing, his feet astride, his hands clasped loosely together behind his back, his belly sagging. He lifted his head and glanced sideways at her. She wanted to ask what he was doing here, so far from home, but she couldn't speak. She saw that he was laughing at her. He rocked his weight from foot to foot, his belly jiggled. He would not tell her why he laughed, she had to guess. She could not. She looked down at her hands. They were greenish-grey and covered in small shiny scales like the skin of a fish. Then she knew she was waiting for something but she didn't know what. She knew that Piet knew, and she looked up from her hands to ask him, but he'd gone.

∾ *Chapter 13* ∾

*A*utumn was fully upon them. The river shone, a moving sheet of light. More and more she abandoned the house, Ambrose and the alterations. She would be outside and halfway down the avenue almost before she knew she'd gone. Above her the poplars, golden-green and thinning, streamed in the high blueness. A pheasant walked over the green meadow. The burnished oak trees stood against the thin, intense sky.

She learned to walk everywhere with her head tipped far back for the sky that was up there like grace, shining with light and swept empty and clean by the wind. She thought she could stand anything as long as there was this grace, this light. Only the wet grey days were too hard.

There were layers to the wind. Low down it was still and breathing, but throw your head back and you saw another world. Winds romped the sky, possessing the tall poplar trees, riding them, throwing them about like ships thrown about on the sea.

She would come home buoyant. She had been to the harbour: she might not yet sail on the ships, but she knew where those ships lay. It was like seeing the seagulls on the river. It promised that there was somewhere else.

Some days. On other days this illusion of escape eluded her. All illusions eluded her. What was the use of somewhere else if you were never in it? She would flee from the house and the yard and the half-planted garden and walk about for hours. Then she would trudge back across the fields, feeling the thinning grass, the dying light, the dense suck of the trampled mud where the cattle had clustered.

Every day the year's change came faster. The air thinned and the trees thinned and the colours sobered. The skies closed down. She felt bereft, shut in. She ranged further, pushed beyond the meadows and into the stands of ancient woodland that clung, here and there, to the river. She liked these at first: their secretness and their neglect. But each day the light died a little sooner and somehow she began to fear them. The snapping of twigs, the frantic dusk alarms of the roosting birds, the patter of leaf-fall, the wet black smell of decay. They seemed full of small shiverings and dyings.

Thirty calves bawled and cried in the sheds by the house, refusing the meal that was brought to them. Ned spent hours in there, calming and coaxing, trying to wheedle them into feeding. It was no good, they wanted none of him: they were desperate for milk and their mothers.

'Try the treacly stuff, they love that . . . in the yellow bags . . . You know the one, the stuff that's got loads of molasses in it.' Niamh hung around, throwing out vague suggestions, getting on his nerves.

Ned didn't know, but everyone else did, so every time he drove out through the gates he came back with a different sack that someone or other had recommended.

'Leave them alone,' Hannie said. 'They'll stop bawling when they're tired enough. They'll eat when they're hungry enough. Just let them be.'

Ned said he knew that, but they'd lose condition fast when they were upset like this and anyway they were his calves and he didn't want them to suffer. Hannie heard the annoyance in his voice, so she folded her arms and shut her mouth and went back inside, banging the kitchen door to behind her.

Ambrose was sitting at the table with Liam, having their morning tea-break.

'They do be missing their mothers,' he said into his mug.

'Missing their food, more like. Bloody calves, bloody fuss, shouting their bloody heads off. Empty bellies is what's wrong with them, they'll forget their mothers the minute their bellies are full again.'

'Ah no,' Ambrose said gently, 'it wouldn't be just milk, it's their mothers, too. 'Tis hard for them all, and some show it more than others.' He was still staring into his mug, avoiding looking at Hannie.

'Sure I mind a calf the brother had,' Liam said. 'Weaned and grown and away from the cow for a year or more. And then didn't he put him into the same field as the mother and wasn't he trying to suck her right away? A big, lump of a bullock, as if he was only a calf again.'

'Exactly,' Hannie said furiously. 'Bothering her long after he's grown up and well able to fend for himself.'

Ambrose kicked Liam under the table, finished up his tea and rose to return to the job. Liam, looking surprised, did the same.

'Twould be noisy inside as well as out today, Ambrose told her. All the old stuck-down lino was to be chipped away, then the floor levelled up and the new skim of concrete poured.

'No point in laying new tiles on a bockety floor,' he said. 'We'll be all day getting that old stuff up. Sure we might as well get all the noise done with in the one go.'

Hannie put on her boots and abandoned ship. The yard was loud with the bawling of calves as she walked away. The house reverberated with hammers hitting on chisels.

On the edge of the woods she chose a path that was new to her. It ran through stands of old hardwoods, dense with tangled undergrowth and unthinned saplings, opening here and there on to patches of neglected planting. She followed this path till it petered out. Off to the left behind a tangle of laurel and rhododendron, she found another one. It was narrower and windier than the first, more an animal track than a path, but she followed it stubbornly, ducking under branches, crashing through brambles, skidding on timber hidden in falls of moss and leaf. The path ended abruptly in a thin screen of leaves. She burst through and stumbled into a once-cleared clearing, cluttered now with mossy piles of abandoned logs.

Near the centre of this clearing rose a big old spruce, dead but still erect, the upper part of its trunk snapped abruptly off at twice her height. She walked around it, expecting the dark marks of a lightning-strike but finding none. Instead she saw fungal growths like red-brown misshapen kidneys, near to the ground but climbing the trunk in tiers.

There was something shocking about them, indecent, she felt she should turn her eyes away. Like coming on a bad car accident unawares, she thought. People with bits of themselves on the outside instead of the inside, their private internal organs casually on display.

Growths everywhere. Perhaps it was the damp? She reached out her hand and made herself touch the flesh.

She had expected softness, a slimy dissolving, but the fungus was dry with the hollow hardness of old wood. She pressed harder into it with her fingers, but still it did not indent. Something at once frightened and violent rose up in her and she had to damage it, to break it or mark it, it didn't matter which. She tried to snap off a piece but it was like twisting thick old leather. She wrenched, but nothing happened and the violent feeling grew more frantic with each failed attempt. She wrenched again. It gave abruptly and she staggered back, a piece of the leathery growth clutched in her hand.

She regained her balance without at once realising that she still held it. When she did she started, then hurled her malignant trophy furiously away. It arced from her and smashed into the thinning brambles.

There was a short burst of silence, then a sudden wild crashing. A black dog rushed from somewhere behind her and threw himself at the undergrowth in pursuit. Two more Labradors appeared and danced and circled around her and the empty place was suddenly filled with noise. A man stepped from between the trees, calling the dogs. The first dog emerged from underneath the brambles, the half moon clutched in his mouth, his tail thrashing in triumphant pride. He circled the man again and again, neck arched like a horse's to show off his trophy. He was fully grown, she saw, but still very giddy and young.

The man bent to the dog and removed the fungus. He turned it over and back, inspecting it, his face without expression. Hannie knew at once that he'd been watching her. Watching from a place of concealment and not intending to be revealed. It was like Africa, this place, eyes hidden everywhere. Only the missile and the young dog's exuberance had flushed him out.

'Root fomes,' he said quietly, weighing the thing in his hand. 'Always a killer. You think it's only external, but it rots right through to the heart.' He shifted his eyes along the broken trunk, noting the other growths.

'That's why the tree died, d'you see? You didn't break it off, you couldn't have. The tree's so deeply rotted the wood crumbled when you pulled.' He reached down and rubbed at the tree where the wound from the ripped-away fungus showed. The wood powdered off under his touch.

Surreptitiously, Hannie watched him. He was tallish and lean and not ill-made, but curiously without presence. His features were regular, his hair dark and just touched with grey, his eyes grey and veiled behind heavy glasses. He wore wellingtons and an old, torn waxproof and trousers made out of some brown stuff, long discoloured and stained. He was camouflaged, she realised. Everything about him was some-how damped-down, concealed, restrained. Only his thick dark eyebrows were energetic, even when he was saying nothing.

'The owl died,' he said. 'I thought she'd make it but she didn't. Boy settling all right, is he?'

For a moment Hannie thought she had misheard him, then light dawned. This was Danno, the man who stuffed birds.

'I haven't heard,' she said bluntly, surprising herself with the flash of bitterness in her own voice.

He heard it too, she could feel his recoil. He didn't like emotion or contact with people, she realised. She could feel him wanting to get away but by effort of will making himself stay. He was like one of those large shy brown deer she sometimes glimpsed here at dusk: blundering and ungainly when startled, their first instinct always flight.

That he knew who she was did not surprise her. At first she had thought herself invisible here for no one stared or even seemed to register her presence, but she had soon learned the reality. Everyone knew her, it was as though her photo had been pasted up in the post office and passed through the houses and farms.

'The owl was doing well, or well enough, tell him. Something happened, I don't know what. She lost heart and I couldn't turn her round.'

'Like the tree.'

He looked puzzled.

'Heart rot,' she said, gesturing towards the growth he still held in his hand. 'You said it rotted right through to the heart.' She stopped. She had a sudden strange impression that they were talking about Joss. She shook her head to dispel the illusion.

'Heterobasidion annosum,' he agreed. 'There's a fair bit of it in these woods. They're old and neglected, they need thinning and replanting, but no one gives a damn –' He broke off and involved himself with rounding up the dogs. His eyes, she noticed, had not once rested on her directly.

Ready to make his escape now, she thought. The instinct for flight again. Like a lizard. A flick, and it was gone into its crack. No, not like a lizard, there was something overtly sexual about a lizard, there was a curious, damaged sexuality about this man.

She would hang on to him, she decided, make him show her the way back. She felt easy with him suddenly and faintly contemptuous but also hostile.

~ *Chapter 14* ~

'**W**ho *will lend a dipper of water to save a fish in a carriage rut*? He quoted that to me. Then he paid my passage and let me go. He was a strange man, I didn't understand him, I still don't. He said he had dropped me into the rut, so it was only right he should lift me out.'

Niamh was warming the teapot and gazing at Hannie with her big, shiny dark eyes as she sent the water swishing around in its base.

'Black tea or jasmine?'

'Black.'

She was very self-possessed, Hannie thought, with her neat clean kitchen and her laid table and her choice of teas. Hannie took out her cigarettes and began to smoke.

'I dreamed my hands were covered in scales like a fish,' Hannie said. 'The dream wouldn't leave me alone, it kept coming back to me. I thought and thought but still I didn't connect it with that saying. Then I came walking here through the mud and the ruts and Piet's little fish dropped into my mind. He liked Confucian philosophers – their little stories and homilies. He often quoted them, he didn't mind their neatness or their smugness. He liked that, he said, it helped ward off life's pain.'

She was here for tea at the girl's repeated invitation. Young woman, she should say – that was how the girl referred to herself. Hannie ignored the proffered chair and mooched around the kitchen, talking and looking at things. Briefly, she wondered at this insistence on being a woman. Her own generation called themselves girls relentlessly till they died.

Niamh filled the teapot and settled the cosy down over it. She somehow couldn't quite grasp that this woman was Joss's mother, but she liked having her here, liked the funny jumps and disconnections in the way she talked. She felt a bit awkward with her but not shy in the way that she did with Joss or Ned, she was too interested. She didn't ask questions or interrupt in case Hannie noticed she was talking about her life and stopped. Niamh wanted to hear all about Piet and their marriage. She wanted to hear all of Hannie's crowded, exotic past.

'I hated these Confucians and their homilies. He used to say them to me all the time because he knew how much I hated them. I knew by looking at him when another one was coming. His mouth would go pouted and shiny as though he was sucking a boiled sweet. Then he'd laugh at me because I looked so sour. *Better a boiled sweet than a lemon*, he'd say . . .

'There was one I liked, though. I haven't thought of it for years. About a man on a white horse in a whirl of red dust. A young man, handsome and distinguished, and all the people coming out to watch. Lord Tung – that was his name – Lord Tung. He rode about the place looking for adventures and fine women. Piet knew he only had me till Lord Tung came riding by. I think perhaps he said it so often because he wanted me to know that he knew. And I never realised. I was too stupid and too young . . .' Hannie's voice trailed off into silence.

Niamh waited, hoping for more, but nothing came. She called Hannie to the tea table. She talked as she poured tea, buttered bread and sliced the apple tart. She spoke of her pleasure in the cottage, and her appreciation. She spoke of her work, the back room she was sorting out, the paintings she would make from the drawings done in the fine weather. The rain ran down the window panes, the fire danced. It was like a painting on a plate, Hannie thought. So smooth and shiny and clean. She ate nothing. She smoked and drank tea.

Niamh was very attractive, Hannie decided. She had fine eyes, a wide mouth and smooth dark hair pulled into a knot at the nape of her neck. She was tall, her figure was slender but full, and she had slim, strong wrists and large graceful hands. There was something of the Madonna about her, an effect curiously accentuated by the jeans and sweaters she wore. Did she know this, Hannie wondered, did she deliberately cultivate the Madonna effect?

Probably not, she decided. Mostly because it wouldn't occur to her that she needed to. Niamh expected the kindness and indulgence with which she was treated, it had clearly never crossed her mind that the world might have been a harder place had she been plain and spotted, or buck-toothed with a cast in her eye. She was artless because she could afford to be.

Niamh's assumption that she was loved for herself alone offended Hannie, who had grown up without any currency other than that provided for her by her youth and her looks. She knew, very exactly, the value of this currency.

Niamh used this currency, but she used it unconsciously and her behaviour produced in Hannie the same reaction that people who have had to scrape for every penny feel when they watch the next generation using unearned money thoughtlessly. To spend such currency idly was bad enough, but it was careless to the point of criminality to use it without ever being aware of what it was: a finite quality that won affection and privilege but would, with time, expire.

Watching Niamh now, Hannie came closer to understanding precisely how much indulgence she had been granted on that score in the past herself. It was a painful realisation, for with it came the knowledge that the currency in which she had traded was all but spent.

So perhaps it was simply envy she was feeling? Well, so be it, she didn't care. She was happy to dislike Niamh, she enjoyed her own ill-will.

'Do you like jasmine tea?' Niamh was asking. She picked

up the box on the table. 'I don't much myself, but this is the real thing. One of my sisters went to Hong Kong and brought it home for me – thought you'd like this, Niamh, she said, it's a bit peculiar. That's my family. If it's peculiar, give it to Niamh. I like what it says on the box, though – there, look, on the side –' She pointed at the words and read them out. 'Aromatic infusion. Homely refresher. Ideal gift.' She laughed, her voice blithe.

> His blouse was the pale yellow of gosling down;
> his face and figure were fine as a painting.
> Always he rode a snow-footed horse,
> whirling whirling up the red dust . . .

Tramping back through the rain, Hannie recalled a snatch of Piet's verse. Remembering it, she fell upon another painful little revelation. She was still waiting for Lord Tung.

'Because they are wasteful and stupid,' Piet would say of his fellow Europeans if you asked him why he shunned them. 'Because their greed is endless and they do not have the sense to be content with a full rice bowl.'

Well, it seemed that neither did she.

She had a full rice bowl now, why else had she married Ned? Yet she wasn't content, she never had been. It was always the same. At first the marriage – the full rice bowl – was a big deal, but before very long the same deal looked smaller and when it did she found herself a lover.

You're a fool, Hannie, she told herself now. You can't just go on doing the same things over and over all your life. The same things now, when you're fifty, as when you were twenty, or thirty, or forty. Look around you, where is this lover, this dashing Lord Tung of yours?

I'll tell you where.

At home by the fire, smoking his pipe and scratching his belly and counting his snot-nosed grandchildren.

She pushed open the back door, kicked off her wellingtons and flung them at a corner. But she could not kick off her thoughts so easily, no matter how she tried. They itched at her like flea bites.

She'd begun on the house because it was what he wanted, however he might resent the expense and complain of inconvenience. He'd said as much. He wanted a garden, flowers on the table, the place made into a home. A living life in the house that existed whether he entered it or not.

For her it was part of the deal, her way of earning the shelter provided. It meant she was not compromised.

But she saw now that deep in herself there was another reason. She was doing the house for the man who would come here and see her work and know this was what she could do. She was advertising, displaying her wares. So that the future might be different.

But no one was going to come, she saw that too. Her life here was a closed loop and would not change: Ned's friends, their modest, badly cooked dinners, their modest, penny-pinching lives. The same people, the same conversations: farm subsidies, the price of feed, what breed for the perfect cross, what had happened to what once-great house, the way things were now, the better way they'd once been.

And there was to be no salvation from outside, no wild card dealt into her hand, no young Lord Tung to take her up on to his horse and whirl her off. Lord Tung was grown elderly and married. She'd have to find her own alternative to Ned. Or walk away from him on her own two feet.

She stopped doing the house. She sent Ambrose off and told Ned she'd changed her mind about the shower and the new bay in the dining room. It was enough to be going on with, she said, she might think again in the spring. She wasn't short-changing him. She would still cook for him and clean and help him on the farm when needed. She'd run his house and go to bed with him and entertain his friends. But the things that were still unfinished, she left unfinished.

Ned made no comment. He couldn't help but see how she'd

improved the place, and he liked to open the door and see that a woman lived there. But winter was coming on, he was glad to have the house private again, Ambrose gone, and no more expectation that he find the money to pay for what she wanted. He accepted that he should provide, but it was money he was convinced he did not have. Except for the farm.

❧ *Chapter 15* ❧

You could get to Danno's by one of two ways. There was a path through the woods that followed the line of the river, or an old, narrow road, its thinly tarred surface broken by roots and rain and years. Hannie came by the path on her first visit.

Danno's house was built on a narrow strip of ground that dropped very steeply down to the edge of the river. It was small and old and single-storeyed, white-washed a long time ago and roofed in slate. The site was dank and awkward and everywhere there were steps and little runs and platforms, inexplicable except to the initiated. Cages and wire enclosures, some empty and some holding injured raptors, clung like molluscs to its walls. It was dark and damp, with a cluster of lean-to sheds huddling off to the left and the woods pressing in close, shutting out the light. Beyond it the river flowed, high and fast with the autumn rains, sinuous and muscled like a salmon.

Hannie banged on the door and then waited with her back to it. She had no explanation for her visit, had brought no excuse in the form of an injured bird or the ubiquitous pot of jam. She'd been walking over this way and thought she might call. Just curiosity. She thought she might take a look and then never come back again.

Nothing. She knocked again. A voice called something from inside but no one came. She knocked a third time. The door opened abruptly and Danno appeared, a scalpel in his right hand. He took in her presence without once looking at her directly.

'There's a knob on the door and it turns. Have you no hands?'

After that first visit Hannie came often. She would open the door and let herself in and sit in his dusty, chaotic room that smelled of outdoors and feathers, smoking and talking as he worked.

He never once called her Mrs Renvyle, it was Hannie right from the start. He never asked her questions or offered her anything to eat or drink, he never welcomed her, nor invited her back, but she came anyway, relieved of some burden by his privacy and his indifference.

Autumn and winter were his busiest times, he told her, the times for indoor projects and making the money to last him through the year. People brought him game birds to be stuffed, sometimes a frozen wild bird or the corpse of a pet, sometimes a big boastful fish from the river. He tied flies to sell to the fishermen, he carved the tops of the ash plants he'd cut and dried in the summer, he soaked the bundled sallies from last autumn and wove them into baskets.

He was busy. She could sit if she liked but he probably wouldn't talk to her and she wasn't to look at the hawk directly. If she wanted tea she could make it herself.

She sat. The room was untidy and plain and roughly finished. The walls had been painted a dark-cream colour a long time ago but were discoloured now and marked with big shambling patches of damp and dirt. Leather leashes and nameless tools hung from nails on the walls, photos of owls and hawks were pinned roughly about the place, there were grubby reference books on a long high shelf and assorted piles of things lay in heaps on the floor and the seats. A door gave off each end of the room and a single window, much larger and more recent than anything else in the house, ran most of the length of the back wall. This window was full of the river, of its moving mass of water. The river dominated the room and was its meaning.

At the left hand end of the room there was a sink with a kettle and a wooden draining board. On the dirty tiled floor three dogs sprawled. At the right hand end was his long wooden work table and an old blue office chair, battered and torn but still revolving. Beside it, between desk and window, was an open-fronted box about two and a half feet high with a length of old blanket pinned across the window behind it. In the box an injured female sparrow hawk was recovering. Leather jesses loosely bound her feet but she could move around within the box and fly up on top of it to perch if she'd a mind to it. The blanket, Danno said, was to stop her flying straight at the window and knocking herself cold.

Hannie never saw beyond this room and the small one to the left of it. She presumed the one to the right was where he slept, but the door was always shut and she never saw him come out of it or go in. He might have slept in a cupboard for all she knew – on a bit of old mattress or a nest of rags, it would have been like him. There was a lavatory built on at the back, but no sign of a bathroom.

The small room at the left hand end of the house was a sort of store where he kept unworked ash plants and big bundles of sallies and any sort of work-in-progress. On long shelves running all around the room, were the birds and animals that were being stuffed, some all but finished, some with splints on legs and necks, some with clips and bits of wires sticking out of them. On the very highest shelves were the finished items awaiting collection. Also the ones that had never been collected. He told her this lightly, with a flick of his head at a pair of chub that swam in a painted box. She couldn't tell if he was angry at this omission. He was always secret and impenetrable. Like the river, its wide opaque surface, its unknown depths.

She didn't care, she didn't need to like him or know who he was; she sat talking about her life before she came here, aware that he couldn't see the pictures constantly forming and dissolving before her inner eye, but relieved nonetheless to be describing them. He worked silently on a bird or an ash plant as she talked, and when she got up to leave he barely nodded. She didn't know if he had listened but it didn't matter, his silence was not unaccepting. It helped her to emerge from the sense of non-existence she so often had here, and it meant she could begin on the process of joining things up.

❧ *Chapter 16* ❧

*M*rs Coady was washing the new tiled floor in the kitchen. It looked well now, she thought, a big long room with the light coming in from both sides and the new window facing south for the afternoons. The curtains were new and the walls were a warm egg-yolk yellow. 'Like the sun, Mrs Coady,' she'd said. She'd made the curtains and painted the room herself.

That was before. She'd no interest in the house any more, she'd no interest in anything much any more, she just walked around the place and wrote letters to the boy and sometimes she visited Danno or Niamh.

It was hard for her, he was a fine man but he wouldn't be everyone's cup of tea, and her so much younger. She never said anything or complained but sometimes she spoke of the light going and the shortness of the day. 'I just can't get used to it,' she said, 'it feels like death.'

She was always cold, she wore anything that came to hand, often his clothes, she didn't have enough warm ones of her own. Mrs Beresford had hinted a bit but he didn't catch on, in the end she just said out straight it was time his wife had some new clothes. He'd looked surprised, and then the next thing they'd gone off to Cork and she'd come home with sweaters and a pair of trousers in a heavy cord. She should have had winter underwear, nothing like an extra layer to keep out this damp cold, but there was no sign of any around, no vests or leggings on the line. She wouldn't complain, and sometimes he didn't see the nose on his own face.

* * *

A letter came, a queen's head on the stamp and a Northern postmark. Ned handed it to her, he watched her careful blank face and saw how her fingers trembled as she took out the single sheet and read.

'All well?'

'So it would seem.' She lifted her coffee cup and drank. 'But he needs more sports kit, he's sent a list, he's on a team.'

'Which team?'

'He doesn't say, just that he needs it by next week.' She put down her cup and began buttering a piece of toast. 'If I send him the money he'll buy what he needs himself from the school stockists in the town.'

Ned understood. She wanted a cheque. He went and got his chequebook and wrote one for the sum required. That was all she really wanted from him, he thought, not knowing why he minded so much; it had, after all, been the deal.

When he left the house she got out the writing pad. She wrote urgently, though there was no urgency, she knew that Joss would already have opened a charge account at the school suppliers, would already have acquired whatever he wanted and sold on what she'd bought only weeks before. When she had finished she sealed the envelope and addressed and stamped it. She had to stop herself going straight out to the post. It was pointless: the only post of the day left at four.

That evening she told Ned she thought she might try her hand at poultry. Ducks for the table and a few hens for eggs. He approved, it was traditional for the farm wife to rear poultry, it fell into his scheme of things.

'And we can give away what we don't eat.'

Hannie nodded. She didn't intend that so much as an egg be given away or eaten without first being paid for, but she didn't say so.

When she thought of what she might earn she was discouraged. It seemed so little she was nearly ready to give up before she started but she had no choice. She needed no ready money so he gave her none. Even if this poultry scheme earned her nothing, at least it would give her access to Ned's chequebook and bank account as a matter of right. And she saw the time ahead when she might need money badly. Money she didn't have to explain or account for.

❧ *Chapter 17* ❧

'*A* poofter? Danno Tuomey? Not bloody likely. More like old Brandy, I'd say: N.B.I. Not Bloody Interested. Happens sometimes – not a lot, but more than you might think.' James Bering stood in the crush of people by the parade ring at Clonmel races and bellowed his opinions down at Hannie. She gazed up at him, her gloved hand sharing his race card, her shoulder pressed comfortably against his chest.

It was as Ned had said; they all knew Danno, the taxidermist-fella-who-stuffed-things. They went to him with dead animals for their walls and mantelpieces. Sometimes they wanted to know what he thought of a dog.

Not a bad-looking woman, James was thinking. Tanned still, but been living out there for years, could take time to wear off. Or Vere's tar brush theory might be true . . . Could do with a visit to the hairdressers, something decent to wear . . .

James's brother Vere stood on the other side of him, not speaking, absorbed in the horses as they appeared. Ned was across the ring with the rest of their party.

James had been explaining the going to her, translating the marks he had made on his race card about the runners and their past form. He had been enjoying himself – in full flight and oblivious of the carrying power of his voice in the quiet, soft-spoken crowd.

No one looked at him directly and you would not have known that the neutral faces around him listened at all. But from time to time a pencil hovered and a card or a folded newspaper was marked. Racing crowds were the same anywhere, Hannie thought. Suckers for a tip. Scouring the place for Someone-in-the-Know. Ready to ditch their most cherished fancies and bet all on a thrown word.

Hannie knew about racing – every colonial society had a racecourse so she knew how to look at a horse in the parade ring and how to read form. She let James know she knew – at least enough to whet his interest in explaining the local situation to her. She was flirting with him in a low-key, idle sort of way. She knew he did not like her. For the moment it amused her mildly to wheedle her way round his dislike. And it pleased her to annoy his wife Marjorie, who didn't much care for him but knew her rights.

'Don't know why it happens,' James was banging on from above her, still on the subject of Danno's lack of sexual orientation. 'There'll be theories, of course. Traumas and rot like that. All nonsense. Had Brandy since day one and never a flicker out of him. No mystery to it – born that way.' Brandy was an ancient liver-and-white spaniel who dozed all day by the range in Marjorie's kitchen, living proof of Danno's situation.

She nodded now and laughed because she wanted to, which was an unfamiliar way of feeling these days. She saw Ned's eyes on her from across the ring. He was watching the circling runners with Alison, just as she was doing with James. Hannie grinned at Ned and waved. She watched his beaky contained face break open with sudden pleasure. She was surprised – embarrassed almost. She turned her eyes back to James.

James's gaze was on the ring and the led horses swinging their way moodily round the rails. 'Danno Tuomey, a poofter . . .' he was saying, shaking his head and chuckling softly. 'That's a good one.'

A big bay was led in, the number 12 emblazoned in red on his grey stable blanket.

'I like him,' Hannie said, referring to Danno, aware that James didn't. He looked at her with sudden strong approval.

'Good woman, yourself,' he said warmly. 'Red Kestrel. O'Shaughnessy trained. All heart. Fast, but carries a lot of weight.' He lowered his voice. 'Only his third time out. Another Arkle in the making, so I've heard. Keep it quiet. I'm off to see what the bookies are saying . . .'

James pushed his hat firmly down on his head and plunged off through the crowd. Vere, who had been standing quietly on the other side of James, expanded slightly to fill up his space. Despite being twins, the two men were not physically much alike. Mentally they were even further apart, though this was not so immediately obvious, as Vere's voice was seldom heard above the noise James made wherever he went. Now Vere smiled vaguely at Hannie and returned his gaze to number 12, who was making a mutinous progress around the ring.

'All heart and no discipline,' he said, quietly. 'That's why they brought him out late. And hates this sort of going. So you like Danno Tuomey, do you? And why is that?'

Hannie shrugged. 'He's easy to talk to. I tell him about my life in Kenya and he doesn't change the subject. Then I remember I existed before I came here.' She smiled up at him, the slight foreignness in her voice and diction accented. 'That can be a pleasant reminder.'

Vere smiled back. Peculiar woman, he thought, where on earth had old Ned found her?

'Are we really so parochial?' he asked.

'On the journey here,' she said, 'Ned told me you would all ask my maiden name. Then when you didn't know it you would ask me my mother's maiden name. When you found you didn't know that either, you wouldn't ask me any more questions at all.'

'What else did he say?' asked Vere, suddenly interested.

Hannie looked at him, unsmiling. Then, with a slight wilful toss of her head, spoke with deliberate indiscretion.

'He said, "Best not to tell them about the marriages. Catholic country, and all that."'

Vere roared with laughter. From across the ring, his sister-in-law glared at him ferociously but he didn't notice.

* * *

The last race was over, the crowd was dispersing, the darkness coming up out of the ground like smoke. A traveller woman thrust oranges at Alison. Giving them away, she said, dragging her emptying black pram across the rutted ground. Alison shook her head but James bought a Mars Bar apiece off her, though no one much wanted them. Red Kestrel had fallen at the last fence, but had got close enough for James to feel he'd had a race. He was resigned but not discouraged.

They tramped across the muddy parking field, looking for where they'd left the cars. Ned handed round a hip flask. Hannie had lost her high spirits, they'd slunk off like the daylight. Her wet feet burned with cold and her hands were numb through her leather gloves. This was not racing, this rite held in mud and bounded by darkness. She tramped along, her head bowed and her shoulders hunched against the cold.

Glancing across, Ned noticed her with sudden clarity, as he might have noticed a stranger. He saw that she was utterly discouraged and slowed his pace. Then he remembered her flirting with James and with Vere, ignoring him, ignoring their wives. She hadn't wanted him when she was full of herself, he decided, so why should he help her now? A stubborn self-righteousness possessed him. He stuck his chin out and pushed on over the freezing mud.

They thawed out in Marjorie's kitchen with a couple of bottles of red wine, a reheated casserole and some dubiously labelled whiskey. Hannie got as drunk as she could manage. Now, she sat huddled in the corner of the car, not moving or speaking, just glad to be through with it all and going home.

Home? Was that what it was? Not home as others would mean it, but something all the same. A refuge. She closed her eyes and rested her head against the frozen window of the elderly Volkswagen. Her car. Or at least the car she drove unless Ned wanted it. Ned used the Land-Rover, but only for short distances. It drank petrol.

Ned was looking straight ahead, his eyes intent on the unravelling ribbon of twisting road which ran beside a once-great estate. The headlights discovered it out of the darkness: the bare, over-arching trees, the crumbling demesne wall, the clusters of houses where pockets of land had been sold off. Beech and ash and lime. Old trees, sufficient and unstriving in the deepening night. Over and over the lights gathered them and let them go.

Hannie sank further into her own dazed state. The heater blasted out hot thick air, its warmth poured over her. Her kicked-off shoes, stiff and dry now from Marjorie's Aga, lay in the caked mud on the floor and her thawed-out feet throbbed and itched with vicious persistence. She'd have worn wellingtons if she had known. She wasn't asleep, but somehow she was separated from herself, time and place dissolved into this unending tunnel of lit darkness. It was a sort of reverie of aloneness: a curious, stale aloneness, informed by night, discomfort, and hot, beating air.

She came to herself with a jerk. The car had stopped and Ned was getting out to open their gates, his movements careful so as not to awaken her. She went on pretending to sleep. He drove the car through, then got out quietly again to close the gates. She sat up. He appeared beside her, smiled at her, touched her hand.

Driving home through the night Ned had glanced across at her huddled form and thought her asleep. He had turned his gaze back to the unwinding road but with that small shift of attention something had changed in him. This was not just some fellow traveller behaving unreasonably, he realised, not some tracker or bearer deliberately making things difficult. This was Hannie, and she was his wife.

He had felt her there then vividly, the unlikeliness of it: her life curled up in the corner, her slack limbs, her body softened by sleep and age. If only they could pull together they could make some sort of a life for her and she could be happy or at least content. He had been flooded with a heightened, almost impersonal tenderness. His self-righteousness had dropped away.

He stood on the step now, fiddling the key in the door. The lock was stiff or the key needed filing down, it was always awkward. He was thinking he must see to it and at the same time he was trying in his mind to find some way of telling her his thoughts from the car. It had all seemed so obvious and simple when he was driving, but now he didn't know how to begin to speak.

He got the door open, groped for the light switch and felt her pushing past him. He called her name softly but she was already on the stairs and she didn't answer. He mustn't put it off and just let things drift, he decided. He'd get the whiskey and some glasses and take them to her room and they would talk.

But Hannie didn't go to her own room; she went to Joss's room and she locked the door. She pulled off her clothes, drew back the covers and got straight into bed. The sheets were icy and damp. There was a soft knock and she heard Ned's voice calling her name, but she didn't answer. She switched off the light. A few minutes later she heard his footsteps withdraw. She gathered the bedclothes tight round her neck and made herself small in the cave in the freezing bed.

It was no good, she would never sleep, it was too cold, she was too over-wrought. She switched on the light again, got out of bed and pulled on her discarded jumper. Then she rooted in Joss's drawers for clothes and socks, glimpsing herself in the speckled mirror of the dressing table as she searched. She stopped rooting and stared at her dim reflection. She pulled her hair back from her face and held it like that with both her hands. Even in the poor light she could not avoid the truth of herself. Hair greying and losing its curl, throat sagging, skin gone spongy and white. Nothing bankable there any more, nothing that might help her. She pulled on a pair of Joss's tracksuit bottoms, got back into bed and lay there with her eyes tight shut, too low for sleep.

There was an incident from the afternoon that she could not get out of her mind. A thickening, tallish man of about her own age had bumped against her in the crowded bar, jolting her arm and causing her whiskey to slop itself down his shirt. He had apologised promptly then disappeared, re-appearing a few minutes later to put a double into her hand.

That done, he had stood back and stared at her. An open, arrogant gaze, a blatant assessment he did not bother to hide.

'Richard Thornton,' he said, introducing himself. 'You must be the new wife.' He nodded his head towards the back of Ned's. 'Welcome to sunny Ireland.'

He was dressed in a thick sweater, worn jeans, leather boots and a torn, fringed suede coat. He had grey curling hair and a confident self-satisfaction. She knew at once she was being patronised and insulted. She knew he had come back with the drink to size up her sexual potential, knew that already she had been dismissed as too ramshackle, too close to his own age, too old.

'Glad to see old Ned's got himself shacked up at last. Do him the world of good, a woman about the place. Hope you won't die of boredom, though. Not everyone's cup of tea.' He grinned a big easy grin and jerked his head to where James and Alison stood with Ned. They looked glum and diminished in the warmth and life of the crowded bar-tent. They looked in-bred and shabby and austere. None of the energy of power remained, only the habit. They looked what they were – the end of their line.

Hannie heard the note of easy contempt in Thornton's voice. They were old buffers. So was she, for the company she kept. Hannie hated him – his curls, his self-satisfaction, his fringed coat. She would rather have Ned, she thought furiously. At least he was honest and not cruel. She turned her back on Richard Thornton and walked away.

Now, in the cold bed, it was not so easy.

The music business, Vere had said. He had made a pile, could live where he liked, do what he liked. He had the old

Cantelon house but he wasn't here much. America. A womaniser. Young women, half his age, one after the other. Seemed to have no trouble getting hold of them. He'd had a lot of work done on the house – everything as new. God knows what it had cost. The last word, or so they said. Locals very impressed.

Vere, clearly, was not. But he was wistful about the young women; the wistfulness of a life not fully lived. Then he had shrugged his thin shoulders slightly, letting it fall away. She saw that he settled for less without much struggle. Most likely had always done so. She felt his defeat.

Now, in the freezing night bedroom, she felt her own. She had met Lord Tung – not nodding by the fireside as she had fancied, but abroad still and roving. And he had seen her from up there on his fine white horse and had coldly passed her by.

Dust and ashes were in her mouth and she could not spit them out. In the arrogant eyes of Richard Thornton she had grasped what her life ahead must be. The future – whatever future she might have – lay where it had always lain, in marriage. But not, as she had imagined, in some marriage as yet unmade. It lay in the marriage she had now, with Ned.

Change of plan, she thought, grinning bitterly into the darkness.

She must knuckle down. She must stay married to him until he died and left her what he had. Then things would be different. She would be able to live for the rest of her life without being married to anyone at all.

~ *Chapter 18* ~

*T*here was another letter from Joss. Hannie read it, Ned watched. She finished the letter, replaced it in the envelope and held it in her hand as she talked.

'He wants to stay with a friend for half-term.'

'He must be settling in then, making friends.'

'Yes. A place called Omagh. He says it's not far from the school.'

'About fifty miles.' Ned pushed back his chair, aware that he wasn't being shown the letter. 'It's a bit soon, don't you think? And we don't know this boy.'

'Girl,' Hannie said flatly.

Ned looked startled. He still hadn't really grasped the facts of co-ed boarding. There was a short, tight silence. 'He can come home now and go to Omagh in the summer,' he said finally. 'He can't just go traipsing off to strangers –'

'Why not? They've invited him.'

'It's too soon.'

'So you just said.' Hannie'd got to her feet and started vigorously clearing the table.

'He lives here now, Hannie. He can't just go gadding about the place, he has to come home.'

'Why?' she challenged. 'There's nothing for him to do here, no one his own age to talk to, why must he come? Because you say so?'

'Because *you* want to see him,' Ned said quietly.

There was another silence. When Hannie spoke again she didn't look at him. A knife danced on a plate as she lifted it on to the tray.

'Yes, but I also want him to be happy. He'd only be here and he'd have to go again. There are several of them going to Omagh. If it makes him happy to be with other young people then I want that for him too.'

'It will do him good to be here, Hannie,' Ned said reasonably. 'He's not a child now, he can't just do what he wants, he'll have to learn –'

'He *will* learn. Life will teach him, it always does. And he's tired of travelling, tired of traipsing around.'

'He'd have to travel to get to Omagh, too.' Ned's voice was suddenly sharp with irritation. 'He's only been in Ireland a couple of months, Hannie, it will disorientate him going to Omagh at this stage. He should come home, get to know the place, settle in.'

'Listen to Ned Renvyle the famous explorer. I must settle, Joss must settle – all you ever think about is settling! Why must we settle? Because it suits you? Because you want it that way?' She banged a cup furiously down on the table. 'He can go to Omagh for two days, then come here for the rest of the time. And don't worry, you won't have to pay for extra petrol, he can get a bus direct from Omagh.'

'There may not be one.'

'There *will* be one.'

'– cutter ants,' Joss was saying. 'Big dark ants with jaws like scissors. They eat vegetation. You'll see a line of them trailing through the grass and you just think ants. Then a minute later you look again ... There's a line all right, but not an ant in sight, they've mown that grass right down to the roots, cleared a highway. Amazing!'

'Like locusts?' Niamh asked vaguely, not moving her eyes off the large dead moth that lay on its back on the windowsill.

'No, stupid, like veggie ants. What do you call this moth?'

'I don't know, I never saw one before.' She pored over the moth. 'It's huge, isn't it? And look at its horn-things.'

'Huge?' Joss sounded derisive.

'Huge for here,' Niamh said.

'Nothing here's huge. Everything's small and brown. Insects, birds, flowers. Small and brown . . .'

The smooth black eyes that stretched round Joss's face pointed in her direction. He's like a moth himself in those glasses, Niamh thought. The blank, expressionless eyes.

'The flowers aren't brown.'

'Might as well be,' Joss said. 'You should go to Africa, see some real insects. Everything's bigger, stronger, more interesting.'

'I like it here,' Niamh said steadily.

'Lucky you,' Joss sneered.

Hannie's hand moved of its own volition to wave, but she realised in time and lowered it. Joss didn't like waves, kisses, fuss, didn't even like her standing waiting for the bus to leave. She turned to go.

To hell with him, she thought suddenly, she needed it even if he didn't. She turned back and stood at a decent distance, stubbornly watching the back of his poised blond head behind the glass. Joss looked round once, saw her and turned resolutely away. He was wearing his dark glasses so she couldn't see what his face said. He didn't look round when the bus moved off.

It hadn't been an easy visit, she thought wryly. It had started badly, and then got worse. She hadn't been very clever about it either. She'd dug a big hole over the Omagh trip, and then jumped into it in plain view of Ned. She had wanted to believe Joss, that was the problem, wanted the picture he offered her, everything healthy and normal, everyone young and blithe. At the same time she'd known perfectly well it was just a ploy. Joss wouldn't go to a happy teenage house-party in some country town called Omagh. He'd go to a city, find himself company, stay away till things fell to bits. Then he'd come home.

And it wouldn't be the first time, either.

But Ned shouldn't have interfered, it was his instant assumption of authority that had angered her so. Joss was hers, for good or ill, the only thing she had that was wholly hers. No one was going to order him around but her.

So despite her defiant words she'd written at once to Joss saying he had to come home and he mustn't accept any invitations. Then she'd phoned the school and said she'd pick up the boy herself at the start of the half-term break.

So he wasn't to be sent to Belfast after all, they asked innocently?

No, he wasn't to be sent to Belfast. She'd collect him and bring him home. And she'd phone again if there was any change of plan.

She told Ned the Omagh girl's mother had rung and cancelled. She'd broken her arm, she said, and just wasn't up to all those kids. Ned made no comment. Joss was getting bolder, Hannie thought. She'd have to watch or he'd outwit her.

She had collected him herself from the school but he wouldn't speak to her at all on the journey. At home he'd produced only monosyllables and he'd spent all his time with Niamh. She'd been beside herself. When he was at Niamh's she'd ached to have him with her, but when he was with her and all she got were blank yeses and nos she fumed with helpless rage. Ned had said nothing. It was just as well, there was nothing he could have said that wouldn't have made it all worse.

She'd planned to drive Joss back, but the clutch had gone on the Volkswagen and Ned said he needed the Land-Rover, he hadn't said why.

She wished they could have driven. On the long monotonous journey he might have tired of his silence and opened his heart.

Pigs might fly. Suddenly, all her anger evaporated and she saw him in her mind, not difficult and devious as she'd been thinking him, but a vulnerable, awkward boy, sitting alone in a crowded bus, a tinny trickle of music spilling from his headphones, the empty miles opening out before him. She would drive him the next time, no matter what, she told herself. And she'd fetch him as well.

A child ran across the empty tarmac. By the bus shelter his mother waited, her hand outstretched. The child took the hand and together they moved away. An old man in a shabby dark suit and a cloth cap also moved away.

The bus had gone, the other witnesses to its going had gone, there was nothing left for her to do but leave as well. Instead she crossed the street and pushed open a door and went into a bar. It was dark and quiet with only a couple of men on stools at the counter and another reading the paper at a table by the fire. They glanced up discreetly, looked away again. She crossed to the counter and stood waiting for the barman to appear. She looked around her. From the mirror behind the bar stared a white-faced woman with untidy hair. She stared back, not realising at first that she was looking at herself. Then the barman came out of a door at the end, polishing a glass as he walked towards her. Suddenly she remembered she'd given all her cash to Joss.

Even a month ago, finding herself in a bar without cash wouldn't have bothered her. She'd have ordered a drink, waited to have it set up, opened her bag – no purse. What a surprise.

And some man would have offered to pay.

Not now. Suddenly she didn't blame Lord Tung or Richard Thornton, or whatever it was he called himself. She wouldn't have bothered with herself either.

⨳ *Chapter 19* ⨳

*S*he was losing her looks, Mrs Coady thought, but she didn't seem to care. The warm-brown colour had faded from her skin, it was going yellowy-looking and stained, and you'd notice the grey coming through in her hair where before it was bleached by the sun.

'The sky's fallen down, Mrs Coady,' she'd say, standing at the back door, staring out at the low damp day and the cling of moist air in the yard. Then you'd see her around the house, her hand moving to switch on lights she'd already switched on, wanting more brightness, unable to thrive in this squinting daylight.

'I miss the colours, Mrs Coady,' she'd say, her face all strained and pinched up with the cold. She was sorry for her then; there were many that found the short days hard, and them not used to the warm sun and the bright air the way she was.

Tom was on at her to pack in the job and stay home. They didn't need the money, he said, and he was tired of her coming in so dispirited and out of sorts. She was tired of it herself, and she wasn't working for the money, though she let on that she was, that she liked having money that was hers alone to spend or waste as she wanted.

She didn't tell him the truth, that she still couldn't face the house every day because it reminded and reminded of Joanna.

She'd get over it, the same as she'd got over the sleeplessness, but she had to take her time, to find her own way out of the dark maze. It was two years before she'd slept the night through after Joanna died, but she'd got there in the end.

Tom thought she didn't talk about Joanna because she was protecting him; that she didn't want to be reminding him on account of him thinking the accident mightn't have happened if he'd thought ahead.

But it wasn't that, she wasn't protecting him, an accident was an accident, a mistake, no one's fault or intention, that was what the word meant. It was just that she needed to be private, even from him – especially from him – she needed to manage it in her own way. And you had to go on living.

People had said she was wonderful, she was so brave, but she knew that behind her back they had said she was hard and it wasn't natural and they'd have liked her better if she'd taken on like Tom. Well, the world hadn't stopped, though for a while there she'd thought it had, and it wasn't as if Joanna was their only child.

Still, she was the youngest, the afterthought, there'd been a special sweetness. It was five years now, the world had all but forgotten Joanna, but she hadn't, there wasn't a day when she didn't see Joanna in her mind and think of her.

Hannie'd cut back her hours, there wasn't enough work for the two of them. Which was true enough, there wouldn't have been any need for help at all if she'd spent less time traipsing about the place and rolled up her sleeves. And she was able for it, she had proved that from the start, she was a worker all right when she'd a mind to it.

Hannie hadn't told Ned about the hours, Mrs Coady was certain of it, she'd seen him leave out the money for wages on the table, the old amount, and Hannie had said nothing. Then, when he'd gone out, hadn't she subtracted the extra and taken it and hidden it away in a drawer?

She was saving it for Joss most likely, for the times when she would need it and she didn't want him knowing about it.

Hannie was withdrawn and morose. It didn't worry Ned overly, he thought it was worry over Joss or the pain of adjustment and the season pressing in on her, the sombreness of it.

Sometimes he hatched schemes and plans but he never really tried to realise them because he didn't know what she wanted or how to change things, and in the end it was easier to stay quiet and watch and wait and endure. He endured as he would have endured the hardships on one of his journeys: stubbornly and without surprise or complaint. Knowing that either it would pass, or it would not.

It should have been easier, once she'd realised her fate, Hannie thought, but it wasn't. Decisions were one thing, living with them was another.

The problem was that of a life which has been lived in action and movement and then finds itself abruptly arrested. Hannie felt like a victim of shipwreck or marooning. She had survived, but the price was this existence with Ned in a hidden valley from which there seemed no escape. Profoundly she didn't want this break in her life, this empty space that was like a mirror showing her back to herself. She was not reflective or used to reflection. She had no wish to confront herself or to understand herself or her life as far as she'd lived it.

More particularly she didn't want to be understood by Ned. She didn't even want to be seen. And she felt him constantly watching her and waiting, drawing conclusions, trying to fit those conclusions together. She felt her privacy violated by this meticulous, attentive observation.

Farm life threw you together, she knew that from her short-lived farm-marriage with Stan. But Stan had only wanted her sexually; apart from his frequent welcomed invasions of her body, Stan had been totally taken up with himself. Ned was different and that difference was more than a different landscape and different time of life. Ned not only wanted to understand her, he wanted intimacy and he wanted to incorporate her into his life. She hadn't expected this, and she hadn't expected to feel so pressurised and observed.

When she couldn't stand it or herself any longer she went

to Danno's and talked about Piet or Africa. Danno didn't take any notice of her. He just got on with carving the knob of an ash plant into a fox's head or putting the rand on a log basket or whatever it was that he happened to be doing when she landed in.

Besides he was growing used to her, her fiery energy which burst out in anger and complaint and then suddenly left her and leaked away into nothing. He didn't try to reassure her or placate her. He didn't know what it was she was trying to figure out or think through and he didn't care. He just let her come in and walk around his room, talking and talking until it was enough for the time being and she could leave him and return to her life.

She talked about Piet a lot but she never once spoke of Ned. 'My first husband,' she called Piet, making it clear she'd had several. He liked to hear her talk of him, his trading station, his time in the Japanese camp, his little homilies and sayings. Sometimes he'd wondered that Piet should be so vividly there in the front of her mind after all these years, but he didn't ask.

'A fish in a carriage rut.' That was what she said she felt like. It was an apt enough image, he thought, but he doubted Ned Renvyle would ever do as her Piet had done. He'd think she'd get used to the carriage rut, would grow to like it, wouldn't even realise she needed water not air. But she'd only herself to blame for it. She'd jumped into this rut of her own accord and she didn't seem to be about to find a way of jumping out of it.

❧ *Chapter 20* ❧

Cold winds blew from the North and winter came early. The river was burnished where the sun reached – a dull, matt gleaming, like hoarded silver paper smoothed with a child's wet finger. The trees were emptying. Ned loved the ash best – its slender nakedness. A stripe of soft light followed each limb, each twig, where the weak sun shone. Here and there, in the copses of cherry, tattered red leaves hung on. There was a poignancy about them, a defeated courage – the pennants of lost armies trailing home, the winter pressing. The oaks under the lea of the hill still clutched their old brown leaves. The rest were swept bare, the leaves gone.

Colour leached from sky, woods, fields. Only the ivy kept its strong dark green, it glittered in the pale light, burdening up the hearts of the trees in great hanging masses that swung in the cold winds like gallows fruit. The ash were mauve-grey on the hill, the spindles had lost their leaves, their last berries stood in pinpoints of cerise against the grey. By the river the tall buff skeletons of charlocke and thistle rattled in the bleak wind. On the paths, black sludges of fallen leaves.

Even the sounds thinned and grew monotonous: the hungry bleating of sheep, the wing-whir of pheasants in the mornings, the dry rattle of magpies all through the short, dark days.

Late one afternoon, the light dying, Ned decided to talk to Danno about shooting the vermin on his land. He had done it himself at the start, had liked walking the land with a gun in the early morning, but the farm took more of his time now and Danno wasn't above poaching across his bounds. Might as well legitimise the situation, make an arrangement, Ned thought. Danno could go on shooting the odd bird in return for a haul of dead crows and the occasional fox.

Danno was agreeable, the business was done and he should have gone but he hung on, trying the sentences this way and that in his head and liking none of them. Danno sat at his work table fiddling with a half-stuffed pheasant and saying nothing. No matter what way Ned tried he couldn't slide over the fact that he wanted to ask his wife's friend what could be done to make her happier.

'You could get her a dog,' Danno said, when he'd got the gist of what Ned was saying. He heard himself, and a twisty little smile worked his mouth. 'Not a house dog or a pup,' he went on. 'A grown trained dog she has to work and exercise. One she can be proud of.' He looped a fine wire under the wing-feathers and chose his words with care. 'She shoots, she can handle a gun, can't she? I've heard her speak of game-shooting in Africa? Well, she can go along with you when you shoot. As a gun or as a picker-up, it doesn't matter. So long as she's there in her own right, not just stuck in a corner with the wives.' Danno paused; he was glad Hannie couldn't hear him.

'She might not take to it,' Ned said, his hands deep in his pockets. The pause in the room lengthened. 'There's no telling with her,' he added, staring intently out of the window at the deepening gloom beyond.

'She rides, you know. Sits a horse as well as any woman. Marjorie Beresford offered her the use of those two mares of hers any time she wanted, said she could use a bit of help exercising them since her back went. As good as begged her.' Ned waited, but Danno did not comment.

'No interest,' he went on. 'I told her if she doesn't want to go to Marjorie's there's always old Connie. I might as well be suggesting she go to mass. How do I know it would be different with a dog?'

'You don't,' Danno said. He didn't say anything else but kept his eyes and his hands on the pheasant he was wiring.

He was angry and embarrassed at this conversation. Ned should have known better than to ask him – did know better – but chose to ignore what he knew. Ned should have kept it to himself that his relations with his wife were not all they should be.

He knew, of course, and Ned knew that he knew. But Ned shouldn't have brought it out and set it there in the middle of the room for them both to look at, it was a gross intrusion. It hadn't been Danno's idea that Hannie come calling on him.

'It's a shot in the dark, but it might be worth a try,' Ned said. He had cheered up, his voice had regained its confidence. It was the opposite for Danno. His hands shook as he worked and he knew he'd have to re-wire the legs when Ned had gone. Who did these people think they were, he thought furiously? Those days were long over and done.

And if Ned believed a dog would solve Hannie's problems he must be either desperate or stupid.

Ned turned it over in his mind as he drove back home. Odd fish, Danno, difficult childhood, there were stories. Mrs Coady said he was an outside child. Some said he was a spoiled priest as well.

Somehow he gave the impression that he didn't much like Hannie. That she'd taken to visiting, though he didn't want to be visited.

It was typical of her, Ned thought. She wouldn't like the people who wanted to be her friends and she took up with someone who didn't. Maybe he shouldn't have gone there, shouldn't have asked. Danno certainly hadn't made it any easier.

Chapter 21

'Wonderful woman, Alison. Been the making of old Vere, don't know how he would have managed without her. How any of us would have managed, come to that.' James stood at the fire, one arm resting on the high mantelshelf. He stared moodily into his half-drunk whiskey, swirled it around in the glass. Then he sighed, tipped back his head and threw in the remains. 'I'll have a word,' he said, as though that sorted the problem. 'Get Alison on board . . . Give Hannie someone to talk to . . . Shouldn't be running around with oddballs like Tuomey and girls half her age . . .'

Ned said nothing. He avoided looking at James. He knew the avoidance was cowardly, but there was nothing he could say, certainly not that Hannie didn't seem to like Alison. He wished sincerely that he'd talked to Hannie himself when he'd meant to, and left his worries unshared. James was about as sensitive as a concrete bollard, but even James would have kept his mouth shut and his thoughts to himself if Ned hadn't started in on it. Wives were wives, in James's book, and you pretended it was all roses and sunshine even when you could feel the flood water lapping around your ankles. Unless the husband raised the thing, and declared the subject open.

James was pleased with his solution. He sincerely admired his sister-in-law and was confident of her tact and abilities, which had been exercised on her husband's family over the years and as the need arose. She was neither bossy nor managing and could be relied upon to gently insinuate herself into your affections and equally gently to nudge you in the right direction when you needed it. She was intelligent and self-deprecating and still reasonably presentable in late middle age. As a young woman she had been a beauty. She was, in James's view, the perfect wife.

The only thing that was quite beyond his understanding was why she had saddled herself with Vere and, in time, with his extended family. She must have 'fallen for him' he would say to himself, or Marjorie, when he had cause, once more, to examine the puzzle. 'Falling for people' was something women did. Marjorie said nothing. She was grateful for Alison's influence on James and her as yet undefeated ability to call him back from the bottle. She did not much care for Alison and she thought her dull company, but she knew a good thing when it came and sat down under her nose.

James strolled over to the drinks tray and helped himself to another whiskey. You could wait all night before old Ned would think to offer you one. Fellow was a natural ascetic. Tents and camp beds and deserts and all that. Made an ass of himself over this Hannie woman. A baggage, if ever there was one. A strap, as the country people would say. Must have got carried away with himself. Plenty of time to regret it now.

Ned watched James quietly and followed all his assumptions. He was neither surprised nor offended by them, but Hannie certainly would be. He was aware that talking to James – even to the limited extent that he had – had been both unwise and disloyal. But it was done now and couldn't be undone. He just hoped that Hannie wouldn't appear before he got rid of James.

They had been at the mart together, had run into Niamh's father, and somehow the result had been this misplaced confidence. With James at his elbow, Ned had steered his way out of the building and down through the pens for a last look at the calves he'd just let go. The cattle were anxious and unsettled and a steady reek of shit and fear was acrid in his nostrils. The mart was busy and he could hear the echoey boom of the auctioneer's voice on the Tannoy. The wintry sun had all but gone; its last rays lifted the wet concrete yard and the metal rails of the pens to a cold glory, and aureoled men and beasts with radiant light.

The air smelled frosty and keen above the cattle-reek. Ribbons of peat smoke from the chimneys of all the little houses round the mart ran straight up into its clear stillness. The sky to the west was lemon, the night was ready to fall. Something in Ned quickened. He felt the timelessness of this life, the ancient repetition of ceremony and act and season. He had spent so many years searching for myth in other lands and among other peoples, yet it was here all the time and could be lived from the inside.

John Comerford was standing over by the mart wall watching him with the quiet steady gaze of a man who has been doing it for some time and knows that his attention will be rewarded. When Ned saw him he nodded quietly and smiled. Ned made his way over to him.

'That's a fair price you're after getting,' Comerford said.

'I've done worse,' Ned said, his spirits rising at this approval.

The mart was always an ordeal for Ned. He knew that his inexperience showed, that he didn't yet know the nuances of pricing, of when to sell and when to hold back from selling, and he was afraid that he was mocked behind his back. He told himself that he didn't care what these farmers thought of him, but he was lying, he cared a great deal, and all his prickly pride was invested in the regard of one or two men.

'You were selling yourself?' he asked, though he'd seen Comerford's calves under the hammer just after his own. Asking was courtesy, it was part of the ritual dance of the conversation.

'I was,' John Comerford said. 'And I'm not sorry either.' He looked up and then down at his feet. 'There's a change or two in your life, or so I'm hearing?'

Ned agreed that there was. 'Will you thank Mrs Comerford for the jug? Hannie was very pleased with it, she said she'd be writing.' He must remember to tell her to do so.

James appeared. He nodded at Comerford but he didn't join in. It was clear he was ready to leave and was waiting to extract Ned. James was a dogged companion, if you were with him you were with him, there was no getting rid of him.

'Kathleen would have me ask if Niamh is being a trouble to you?' John Comerford asked. 'She was home there last week and she talked a lot about Mrs Renvyle. Kathleen says you're to tell her straight if she's under your feet.'

Ned assured him that Niamh was not being a trouble. On the contrary, he said, she was company for Hannie, who was lonely in this new country with her son away at school. It was good for her to have a young face around her, good for them all.

Comerford nodded and seemed satisfied. They shook hands and he thanked Ned again for his care of Niamh, and Ned said again that it was a pleasure and a small return.

James's old green station wagon was parked off a side-street, the passenger door secured with a knotted length of rope. Ned had to get in on James's side and shift himself across under the steering wheel. The awkward movement caught at his hip and a sharp stab jarred through his body, making him suck in his breath with the pain. James heard the sound. He passed over the hip flask he'd been nursing in his gloved hands.

'Arthritis,' he said cheerfully. 'Goes with the climate – happens to us all. They'll saw you up when it gets bad enough – doctors all butchers at heart, no interest in a pill if there's a chance they can get to cut holes in you, fire out the bones, stuff you with plastic instead. Seems to work, though. Have to live with it till then, that's the problem. There's a healer fella over at Coolnabawn you could try. Lays you out on a table and pulls you about. Some Johnny out of nowhere, married the mistress after old Henry Nairn passed on. Englishman, or so he says. Definitely not an officer. Funny ideas about food. Not half bad with animals, though – Marjorie uses him on her ponies, believe that's how he wormed his way into the grieving widow's graces. Or there's a Seventh

Son of a Seventh Son over Clonmel way. Bit too close to voodoo for my taste, but the country people swear by him. Peasants. Rag trees and water out of a holy well and a bit of clay from a saint's grave under your pillow when you sleep. Superstition.'

James rattled on in a steady flow as he twiddled the choke and crashed the gears and negotiated his way awkwardly on to the road. Ned sat back and listened and nodded. It would probably have been all the same to James if he hadn't, but he was fond of James, despite Hannie's contempt for his company. Hannie couldn't seem to grow fond of those she disliked or was disappointed in. She couldn't put away her expectations and let them grow on her like that old coat of his she took down off the peg and wore about the farm.

'What was all that about Comerford's daughter?' James asked suddenly, changing tack. 'Heard you'd let her a cottage. Marjorie said she painted houses. What's the sense of that, I said – a slip of a girl setting herself up to paint houses? – she'd never be able for it. Marjorie said I'd got the wrong end of the stick, as usual. Said the girl paints pictures, not rooms. Pictures of houses. I said well she'd better not go painting Ned's house till Hannie stops messing it around, better find her something else to paint. Houses the only thing she can do? What about animals? I've a dog she could turn her hand to, that black setter I have off O'Reilly. Wouldn't object to her having a go at Jacko if she'd a mind to it. Strange-looking creature. A Gordon setter, O'Reilly called him, but I'd say there's retriever in there and more besides. Looks like the wrath of God and hunts like an angel. Never had a dog like him, the softest mouth I ever saw. He'll lift a hen pheasant out of the nest and bring her home and lay her in my hand. "Dead, Jacko," I say, and he unhinges his jaws a fraction and out rolls the bird. Dead, my arse. Not a mark on her. Gets up and flies away once she's over the shock.'

Ned had listened more than once to the wonders of Jacko. He allowed himself to distract James.

'She may do animals, I don't know, you could ask her. She'll say no if she doesn't want to – not shy about that sort of thing. It might depend on how much you were thinking of paying her.'

James looked shocked. Ned could see that payment had never crossed his mind. James had volunteered Jacko as a favour, he was trying to be helpful.

Ned pressed on. 'It's by way of an experiment, all this. She wants to see if she can earn a living at it.'

James gathered himself. 'And what's she living off in the mean time?' he asked. 'What's she living off while she's experimenting? Comerford, I dare say. And Comerford's fobbed her off on you till she comes to her senses. Daughters! Worse than sons. Come on at you all eyes and tears. Yes Daddy and no Daddy and butter wouldn't melt in my mouth, Daddy. Before you know it you have them so spoiled they think it's your duty to keep them for life.'

James spoke with feeling. He had two daughters of his own and their maintenance in the style which both they and their mother considered appropriate had long been a sore point. Handing them over to husbands had temporarily eased the situation, but hadn't solved it.

'So if she wants to keep on at this painting game,' Ned was saying, 'she has to start making it pay. I'll mention Jacko to her if you like, sound her out?'

But James was not to be pinned down so easily.

'Bloody stupid name,' he said grumpily. 'Don't know what's come over people. Bloody stupid fashion for Impossible Bloody Irish Names. Surprised at the man. Nothing Irish about Comerford. Good Norman name, papist or no. Next thing you know she'll be changing her surname, putting the whole damn lot into some sort of unpronounceable caterwaul, won't even know who she is, who her people are. Hannie like her, does she?'

It was Ned's turn to be discomfited.

'Not much,' he admitted.

'Humph,' James responded. 'Thought Comerford said the girl couldn't stop talking about her?'

'Hannie's at a bit of a loose end, just now,' Ned said quietly. 'Niamh made friends with her boy when he was here. Hannie's taken to calling in with her from time to time. Bored, I'd say. And I'd rather she was there than spending her time with Danno Tuomey. At least the girl's educated, comes from a decent family.'

'Heard about Danno,' James said, for once not taking his eyes off the road as he talked. 'Wondered how much there was in it?'

And that was how Ned had got himself into this mess, with James tramping round the study, helping himself to whiskey, immune to all attempts to get rid of him, and Hannie due to walk in at any moment.

Life was simpler before, Ned thought. He thought it without regret or recrimination. It was simply a statement of fact.

❧ *Chapter 22* ❧

*A*lison had been got 'on board' and was quietly doing her best. 'Hovering around like a bad smell,' as Hannie, exasperated, had put it. 'Persecuting me with invitations.'

Hannie had said no to beagling in Tipperary, to an afternoon's pruning course in Kilkenny, to the selling of Armistice-day poppies to people-who-might-be-thought-to-be-sympathetic. She had refused invitations to inspect graveyards and once-great houses and poke around in ruined gardens. But she had agreed to a tree walk and to shopping in Cork. Of the two she had marginally preferred the tree walk.

'You can always tell ash,' Alison said. 'Those lovely smooth limbs, beige-grey, and the arms spread and just raised in that gesture like wonder. Ash is the masculine tree and hazel the feminine since ancient times. You'll see them together at holy wells, the ash and the hazel, the masculine and the feminine. Odd really, ash is so graceful. Perhaps it's because hurleys are made from its wood . . .'

Hannie was leaning against a crumbling wall, smoking a cigarette and staring at the blowing sky behind the empty branches of the small grey tree. From time to time Alison would pass her a twig or a bit of bark and she would glance at it absently, then drop it into the mud and resume her staring. She didn't know what hurleys were, or holy wells, and she didn't care. She was used to the foliage and blossom of Africa, its spontaneous extravagance, she couldn't see what Alison saw, what stirred in her voice and lit her face.

'Beech,' Alison said, moving on. 'Isn't it lovely? So graceful and wide and all those lacy twigs like fine hair standing out from a head. We don't have so many here, but they're very common in England. They blow down in the gales. Big wide shallow roots, the winds rock the trees and they just keel over.'

Alison was absorbed in her subject. She would reach up to catch hold of a branch, pulling it down to show twig structure and shape and buds already forming for the spring. She would rub the moss off bark to show its pattern, and suggest ways of remembering names by associations which mostly depended on an intimate knowledge of nineteenth-century English literature and meant nothing to Hannie. Hannie mooched along behind her kicking at sludges of dead leaves, hearing Ned's voice in her mind.

She's a nice woman, she means well, couldn't you just go for a walk with her?

Well she had, and this was the result. She was disappointed in Ned over Alison. She had thought him more honourable, had thought that at least he wouldn't have discussed her, would have left her to work out her own fate. She cursed herself now for letting him persuade her into this.

Alison stood at the sink, scrubbing and disinfecting flower pots to put away for the spring. They needed doing and she always cleaned something when she was worried or upset, it meant you could think things over without getting too overwhelmed by them and even if your conclusions were completely depressing at least you'd done something useful while you were reaching them.

Vere appeared in the doorway in his stockinged feet, rubbing his hands and blowing on them to get some warmth into them. He took off his damp coat and arranged it on the rail in front of the Aga.

'Good walk?' he asked. 'Interested in trees, was she?'

'Not much,' Alison admitted without looking round. 'But it got her out of the house.'

'Hmph. Wasting your time, old girl. Ned married her. Let him look after her.'

Alison scrubbed hard. 'The Jeyes fluid's finished. I must put it on the list.'

'Getting on, are they? No, well I expect he's regretting it now.'

'I don't think so. She's an unusual woman. And think how Ned's spent his life. He's always been fascinated by nomads.'

'Nomads? You're an incurable romantic, Ali. The woman's not a nomad, she's a tramp.'

Hannie woke the next day and stood back from herself. Something had nudged at her introversion and suddenly she was critical of the habit of drift she'd slipped into. She felt she'd done nothing for weeks but exist in a torpor of walking and staring. She must act, she decided, if only to defend herself from Ned and Alison. Joss was blessedly quiet but the silence couldn't last for ever, already it felt ominous. She'd have to get started on something sooner or later, be it hens or theft or prostitution. She went to the library in Dungarvan for a book.

She asked at the desk and the librarian waved her to a shelf marked DIY. Obediently she went through its contents. There were books on geese and on bees, there was nothing on hens. She went through the shelf again then crossed to the desk, annoyed, for she'd set her mind to action.

'It is odd, is it not, this omission?' she asked, her voice at its most foreign. 'And in a country library?'

'Dungarvan isn't country,' the librarian said haughtily. She stood looking at Hannie, daring her to contradict. Hannie glared back. There was a moment's impasse, then the librarian relented.

'Sure, why would we keep books on hens?' she asked. 'Doesn't everyone know how to rear them?'

Hannie picked up the book on bees and opened it. 'I don't,'

she said, looking at a diagram of a beehive and not at the librarian. 'That's why I wanted a book.'

In the end she got out the volumes on bees and geese on Ned's ticket, reasoning that their presence in the library must mean a wider ignorance than there was over hens, and a wider ignorance might signify a hungrier market. And she took out a book on herbs as well; it was sitting on the counter looking at her, Ned wanted to diversify, he'd been talking about lavender and scented herbs, she might as well show willing.

Ned came home with a pup, a little Springer bitch straight out of the litter. He put it into Hannie's arms and said it was hers. Hannie looked at it and smelled Alison. She put the pup down on the floor and it peed with fright. She prodded the pup with her foot. The little creature caught hold of her shoe and chewed at the leather. She lifted her foot and the pup fell over on to its back.

A baby will settle her. That's what was always said of a new wife. This would be Alison's version: a pup for a woman past child-bearing. She picked up the empty washing basket, put on her boots, and went out in the dusk to the line. She hauled at the wet clothes that had hung all day in the damp air. Well, Ned had bought it, he could look after it, she would not.

Later she watched as the pup played into his hands and would not eat.

'What shall I do?' he asked her, trying to involve her.

'Whatever you like,' she said sourly. But she went to the fridge and took out an egg and some milk and broke bread into the beaten-up mixture. She gave it to him.

Ned came back into the kitchen, holding out the empty bowl. The pup had eaten it all. He was pleased and relieved. Already he cared for the puppy. She was pleased, too, despite herself. For a short moment they were both pleased at once and they smiled at the little warm creature, puffed up with milk and bread, and forgot themselves.

Hannie bent down and put out her hand. The puppy came

to her and placed her neck on Hannie's wrist and her head on her opened palm. She gazed up at her out of round black eyes with only a sliver of white at their lower rim. Hannie allowed this, knowing that in letting the pup love her she would be letting herself love in return. She let herself. She was holding out against so much in this new life, for once she did not resist the softening.

A knock came to the door. Niamh came shyly in to look at the pup and dropped to her knees. 'Oh, the darling,' she crooned. 'Oh, the doaty little puppy.' She was on the floor, the puppy squirming and wriggling in her arms, biting at her fingers and her nose and the loose strands of her hair. Ned stood, smiling and watching. Hannie watched too. For a moment the kitchen was full of firelight and warmth and young things.

'What are you going to call her?' Niamh asked. She sat back on her heels with the puppy in her arms, looking at Ned. Ned looked at Hannie.

Hannie turned away, the softness going from her face which grew calm and neutral and watchful again. 'Alison,' she said decisively.

Danno smiled a small bitter smile to himself when he heard. A trained dog, he had said, not a pup. He didn't himself care for the innumerable small shoots that were littered around the country, but Ned liked his day out with a gun.

Perhaps Ned didn't want to bring his wife along just yet, Danno thought. It was a risk all right. She might or might not behave herself.

But the pup couldn't even begin to be trained for another few months, it would be a year at least before she was ready enough to be useful.

A year's grace to break Hannie in.

Danno shrugged his thin shoulders and went out to feed his Labradors. Hannie would just have to stay in her rut and learn how to like muddy water, he thought. It was her own fault. The people of Abel should not walk with the people of Cain.

Ned called the puppy Pippa. She was around the house in the day, chewing things and piddling and making sorties into the yard, but it was Ned who fed her and dosed her and played with her, she was his, now. He had tried to back off, to be cold and restrained, but when he saw how studied was Hannie's indifference to her, he gave it up and was unashamed in his affection. Someone had to love the little dog and teach her. If Hannie would not, then he must.

Besides, he liked having Pippa around, he looked forward to coming in to her when darkness had closed down the day. He would stand in the doorway between the scullery and the kitchen drying his hands on a raggedy towel, watching her thumping her tail and wriggling in anticipation. He liked washing his hands and drying them, taking his boots off, placing them together in their place beneath the hooks where his coat hung. He liked all these slow, thorough actions, the glow of the lighted kitchen in front of him, the smell of mud and bran and old flower pots in the scullery behind.

He would feed her, then he would play with her. He had given Pippa an old glove and nightly she fought battles with it.

'Look, Hannie, the glove's pretending to be dead, it's set an ambush, it's going to trap her!' The glove would be lying silently on the floor with Pippa crouched in front of it ready to pounce.

'The glove's going for her, look, the glove's attacking...' With a sudden wild leap Pip would be on the glove and thrashing it furiously backwards and forwards as though it was indeed alive and attacking.

'It's winning, the terrible glove's winning! No, it isn't, Pip's fighting back! She's got it by the throat, she's trouncing it – Little David's beating up Goliath...'

Nightly Hannie was irritated by this joint performance and

resented her role as audience. He looked so satisfied, so happy in his home and in his homelife. She felt outside of it all. She felt like a chattel.

'He might as well have bought a dog instead of a wife in the first place, Mrs Coady,' she said not long after Pippa's arrival.

Mrs Coady had raised her eyebrows at the word *bought*. She wondered if Hannie had said it to Ned. More than likely. For a survivor, she lacked sense.

Hannie hadn't, but what she didn't say spoke almost as loudly as what she did. Sometimes Ned was as exasperated with Hannie as she was with Alison. Why had she married him if she was going to refuse to participate in his life, he thought bitterly? She had misled him in their brief courtship. She'd been so different then, easy and open, an unconventional and independent companion. He hadn't misled her, hadn't pretended beforehand that he would be other than he was. Why was she always so difficult? He would go over it in his mind, rehearsing his arguments, nursing his anger.

His exasperation was exacerbated by guilt over Alison. He liked Alison and he respected her and he felt that he had trespassed on her, not least because he couldn't bring himself to tell Hannie that the pup hadn't been her suggestion but Danno's.

Sometimes though, his feelings swung the other way and he would be contrite. He should be supporting her, he told himself, not trying to convert her into something appropriate. If he had wanted appropriateness he would have chosen differently. He must help her to get used to things, explain his life and what he wanted from her. Tentatively, he tried to speak of his disappointment over her attitude to his friends.

'They're your friends, Ned, not mine, and I don't have to like them because you do. I'm not saying I won't see them. I'll invite them when you want them, cook for them, talk to them, entertain them. I'll even go to their houses with you and eat their badly cooked food and listen over and over to hilarious stories about people I've never met and never want to.' She looked at him out of those deep brown eyes that went so strangely with her light hair. '*Make an effort* you said, so I'm making an effort, but I still don't like them. Why would I? They've been looking through the same window at the same few fields for hundreds and hundreds of years, they've forgotten long ago there might be other windows, other views and other ways of being. And they don't like me either, we have nothing in common, they know what they like, and it isn't me.'

'They do like you, Hannie, Alison –'

'Alison is doing all this for you, not me. Alison is, as you said, a very nice woman, but one whom I don't happen to be interested by, Ned, and I don't want to go riding with her or walking or shopping or looking at gardens or other people's houses. Nor do I want to have tête-à-têtes with her about trees.'

'Then what will you do, Hannie?' he asked.

'Don't worry about me, I'll find something to do.'

But that wasn't enough for him. He should leave her alone, he knew he should leave her alone, but he couldn't. He wanted to talk to her, to show her what he loved and what he thought. All his life he had held back from intimacy, now he wanted to speak and have her understand what he said. And he was convinced still that she could, despite the signs, despite his friends' unspoken compassion. It was for this, he realised, that he'd married her and not someone else.

And Hannie felt smothered by him and by what he required of her. She felt burdened down by his constant efforts to close the distance.

∾ *Chapter 23* ∾

*H*annie got out of bed as soon as she woke and pulled on a sweater. It was freezing cold in the room and her breath came in visible clouds. Like smoking, she thought, shaking a cigarette out of the packet and reaching for the lighter. She padded about in the heavy socks that she wore now in bed every night for her chilblains. The window was opaque, the glass patterned with flowers of grey ice. She reached out her finger to touch and the glass seemed to jump out and burn her. Ice on the inside as well as the outside. She dragged the rickety sash as wide as it would go, then knelt on the floor and stuck her head and shoulders out into the morning.

The sky was a length of stretched silk. Lemon silk, translucent and shot through with pink. The grass was grey-white with frost and the trees were furred on every branch and twig with a coating of tiny frost-hairs. A white mist lay over the river.

Hannie threw her half-smoked cigarette out of the window and breathed in the clear empty coldness. She liked the promise in the air and the brief extravagance of colour in the sky. As she watched the sun broke through and the avenue poplars shone like white flames where the light caught their frosted branches. A momentary glory. Almost before her eyes the ice thawed and the white splendour dulled. Still, she felt better, defeat leached from her.

'Geese,' Ned said over breakfast.

Hannie looked at him. She'd forgotten all about the library books. As far as she knew they still lay unopened on the window-shelf beside the sink.

'You could start in the spring,' he went on. 'Less complicated than bees and at least there's a sure market for Christmas.

'I looked at the books,' he explained. 'My cousins keep geese, know all about them, we'll go and see them. Good time of year for it, just before slaughter, they'll tell you all you need to know.'

It seemed he had cousins who kept geese over Kenmare way. Their mother was his mother's youngest sister, he said, and he owed them a visit.

'The old girl's eighty-six, she can't live for ever. You'll like Ellen, she does all the hands-on work, Lettie runs the show.' He poured himself another cup of coffee from the cafetière Hannie had bought in Cork on her shopping trip with Alison. 'We could go for the day,' he went on, 'I'll find the time, you might as well learn all you can before you start.'

Hannie agreed. She had no desire to inspect hordes of geese or to question wellingtoned female cousins on fattening, but at least it was an outing. Ned seemed pleased. To her surprise, he got up at once to ring his cousins. She remembered it was Sunday. Cheap rate on Sunday, she toyed with the idea of phoning Joss, but resisted the temptation. Joss hated being phoned for a chat, he'd just stand there saying nothing till she got the message and fell into silence.

'The old girl's got pleurisy,' Ned said, coming back, 'she's been in hospital.' He sat down shaking his head. 'Extraordinary thing, Ellen was on the point of phoning, she had the number in her hand when I rang her.'

Aunt Cecily had been sick enough, Ned said, Ellen had held off phoning till the news was good because she hadn't wanted Ned to feel he had to visit. She was doing well now, Ellen said, she'd been wanting her own bed, but the doctor had ordered a week in a nursing home where she'd be warm and quiet and properly looked after.

She'd had a fit. Properly looked after? Of course she'd be properly looked after, she'd told the doctor, what else did he think she had two daughters for?

Poor Ellen. She was the youngest and most bullied of Ned's cousins and he was very fond of her.

Anyway, the old girl had caved in in the end, must have been weaker than she thought, and they'd found a place in Kenmare that would take her.

'House and geese no longer on the agenda, I'm afraid, Hannie,' Ned said. 'I'll go anyway of course, see Aunt Cecily, meet up with the girls in Kenmare for some lunch – but there's no need for you to flog all that way,' he continued. 'No one will be offended.'

But Hannie said she would come, geese or no geese. Ned seemed pleased. If he felt any apprehension he concealed it.

'You look very nice, very smart, Hannie, but we're not lunching at the Court, we're only meeting there, we'll find somewhere in the town that's less expensive.' Ned looked at his watch. 'You've got time to change.'

Hannie said she would come as she was. She was sick of sweaters and trousers.

'It's a four-hour drive,' he told her, 'you'll be cold on the journey.'

'I'll bring a coat.'

The roads were frosty but dry and they made good time, arriving early. Hannie was pleased, she wanted to sit in the hotel with a drink, looking and being looked at. She smoothed the fine dark skirt of the expensive Italian wool suit she had bought four years ago for a winter business trip to Germany with Andrew. She had worn it on their first visit to Joss's school but after that it had sat in the wardrobe and would have gone on sitting there for ever if Ned had had his way. She didn't care if he thought it unsuitable, it was the best thing she owned and she wanted to look quite unlike a woman who might be considering keeping geese.

The hotel building was grey and stately and there were other cars scattered about the dark-green grounds and parked under the ancient yew trees. They got out, Ned locked the car and they walked slowly across the drive to the stone steps. Hannie glanced down at her feet, liking them in their beautiful suede shoes on the dark sweep of the drive. She straightened, the sway crept back into her walk. Looking at them gave her confidence and helped her remember who she'd been before.

The wooden outer doors of the building lay open and there were soft daytime lights glowing behind the glass inner doors. The glass was old and fine and when you moved your head it had ripples in it like running water. Ned reached forward and turned the handle. He pushed but the door wouldn't give. He pushed again.

'There's a notice,' Hannie said, pointing to the paper taped to the glass.

'Closed until April,' she read, and looked around, dismayed. Ned was still fumbling in his pockets for his glasses. 'But it can't be closed,' she said, unable to accept it. 'The lights are on, there are other cars . . .'

'I expect people like to meet here,' Ned said. 'Meet here, walk round the grounds . . .'

'Why?'

'Why not?'

She felt like a child whose treat has been taken away. She stiffened herself. She would not be disappointed, she would not. And over so small a thing.

'Peculiar country,' she said calmly. 'People want to meet in December at a hotel that's closed?' She shrugged and sat down in her beautiful suit on the damp stone steps. She reached in her bag for a packet of cigarettes, took one out and lit it slowly, ignoring Ned's look. Ladies don't smoke in public outside good hotels, even closed ones, the look said. Too bad. She wasn't a lady.

'People here are content with nothing,' she said lightly.

A rackety station wagon burst through the open gates and charged to a halt. Moth-eaten dogs and women in tweeds and cardigans erupted out if it. Ned looked relieved. He hugged his cousins, rumpled the dogs, patted the car and called it by name.

'Glad to see Rosemary's still on the road.'

Hannie was introduced. The dogs were called back, introduced, shut into the car. They would walk to the nursing home, Lettie said. A dreadful place, frilly and pink, but it wasn't far. Then they would find some lunch.

They set off in a little straggle, Ned in front, talking to Lettie and Hannie with Ellen bringing up the rear. Hannie didn't bother to talk. Ellen looked as if she would have liked to have done the same, but her training wouldn't allow it.

'Ned said you want to know about geese?' she opened shyly.

It was very cold already, and would freeze again as night fell. Lights were coming on in the scattered dwellings; here and there yellow rectangles pushed forward through the gloom. Ned opened the window an inch, smelling the fields and the frosty air, watching the folded land fade into the four o'clock dusk. From time to time there were hamlets strung like beads down the side of the road, but mostly it was just fields and farms and boreens running off into twilight. Sometimes a creamery. Sometimes small towns, empty and quiet, the wide streets crossed with coloured lights that swung in the windy dusk. Once they waited while two old men and a girl-child drove a few cows home for milking. Once they stopped for travellers' horses: big dark shaggy shapes grazing loose by the road in the dying light.

Ned felt his love for this shrouded country, these small lost roads, this people he had known from childhood. Nothing in his life had moved him like this, not even the deserts, and he wondered that he'd journeyed so far to see what had always been here. He resolved not to leave again, he was home at last and he wanted nothing else.

He glanced across at Hannie. She sat slumped into herself, staring out of the window, seeing fields and mud and beasts and hedges pass before her eyes. For a moment he saw it as she saw it and for the first time he didn't blame her or condemn her because she couldn't be satisfied as he was. He would think of some way to make her happy, he decided. He felt very tender towards her, very patient and protective.

Then he stopped thinking and abandoned himself to this joy that was filling him. He could see the twin lights of a car away down the road in the valley. He could see darkness thicken and hold the land.

❧ *Chapter 24* ❧

'*M*aster them?' Danno said. 'Put that out of your head, there's no mastering them.' As he talked he was slitting open the blackbird Tommy Moran had found dead on the road and brought to him the night before. The sparrow hawk in the open-fronted box watched him sideways out of her yellow eye.

'Some men try it,' he went on. 'Whole books have been written about one man's struggle with one raptor. They're always the same. Man tries to master hawk. Fails. Tries again. Fails again. Gives up. Masters himself and leaves the hawk be.'

The sparrow hawk moved suddenly, sidling rapidly along her perch in the direction of the blackbird. There was a clicking noise from her claws and a dry scrabbling sound as she shook out her feathers.

'It's a fine line. To work a raptor you have to get its respect but you mustn't break it or even come close to breaking it or you'll drive it mad. They can't bend, you see, can't learn to come to hand like a dog and live submitted. But you have to drive it hard just the same, and no mercy, mercy is weakness, and weakness will always be taken advantage of, that's its nature. And you must get it at the right age and in the right physical and psychological state and not damaged by hunger. Then maybe you have some chance.'

'So why do you do it?'

'I don't. I patch them and feed them up a bit and cage them while they're healing. Then I let them go. To live or to die. Which is all they understand anyway.'

He stopped talking and concentrated on working the blackbird's carcass free from its feathered skin. Hannie was quiet today, he thought. Mostly she paced about, smoking and talking, disturbing the hawk. He would tell her to sit still, or if she had to move around not to wave her hands or look at the bird, but she took no notice. She did what she wanted to do, charged noisily around till she tired of it, then sat herself down, deflating like a balloon that is losing its air.

Danno snipped a last tendon and pulled out the carcass. He placed it in front of the hawk, making little noises of encouragement and endearment. The sparrow hawk stared at it coldly and didn't move. Then with incredible swiftness she shot out her foot, pinned the skinned blackbird, and began systematically pulling off the flesh in long bloody strips with her beak.

Danno lifted the bundle of blackbird feathers and skin lying on the table, opened it out and sprinkled its fleshy side with plaster of Paris. He blew off the excess carefully. He looked up at Hannie, a swift sudden look, one eye opened and one closed, one eyebrow raised in a vivid inverted 'V', the other flattened over the closed eye. He looked down again.

'Hannie,' he said, 'why did you marry Piet?'

Hannie stared.

'You were young. You must have been beautiful. Why did you marry him? Were you in love with him?'

Hannie started to laugh. She'd told Vere she liked talking to Danno because he didn't change the subject when she talked about the past and it was true, but that wasn't to say that he listened to what she said. Danno didn't listen, or if he did he never responded or commented or asked a question, there was never anything to indicate that he'd heard. Until now. She stopped laughing.

'Because my mother told me to,' she said quietly. Danno had the blackbird skin spread out, feather-side down, and he was working one of its wings on to the inside. At the same time he was scraping at fragments of left-behind flesh and feeding them straight to the hawk. He nodded without looking up.

'She thought it would give me a future,' Hannie continued, 'and that I wouldn't have one otherwise. She said there weren't so many people who'd marry me and Piet wanted me, he didn't care what people thought.' She paused. 'For me, Piet was a stepping stone,' she said, shrugging her shoulders as though she were getting rid of something. 'I had to get away from her and I didn't much mind how.'

'Why weren't there many people who'd marry you?'

'Because of her. We weren't respectable.' Hannie reached for her cigarette packet. She extracted one and lit it carefully, leaning into the flame and inhaling deeply. 'And because of me, I was making it worse. I didn't care what I did, you see, she was afraid of how I'd end up.'

'What had she done that made you not respectable?'

'Sailed too close to the wind. In Java, in the war,' she added, as though that explained everything. Danno glanced up.

'The Japanese came,' she said. 'All the men who were Dutch were taken away to a camp. Then it was the women's turn and my mother also was put in a camp, but one for women and children only. She wanted to live, she was very determined, and it wasn't respectable to be so determined, to fight so hard to survive. It was a colony, you see, everyone must pull together, live together, starve together, die together. She didn't want to die. She was beautiful and the guards were men. When the war ended people told stories and the stories followed her around.'

Hannie's accent had thickened. Danno wondered if it was involuntary, if she heard the change herself. 'Were you in the camp too, Hannie?'

'No,' she said, 'or I wouldn't be here now, I was only a baby, I was with the Amah for those years. *When the Japanese came*, people say, as though everyone just woke up one day and it had happened, but it wasn't like that. First there were rumours and panics and people tried to get away. My parents tried. They got a passage on a cargo ship, crammed in with thousands of others, but I was too little to survive such a journey so they gave me to the Amah till the war had ended. Then the ship was turned back so they went to the camps anyway and my father died there. Afterwards, my mother came and got me from the Amah. I was lucky, the camps were very hard, I wouldn't have survived them. Or I'd have been like that hawk you said couldn't be worked. Damaged by hunger. And fear. As she was ...'

'Why didn't she go somewhere else afterwards?'

'Where could she go?' Hannie shrugged. 'She was born there, it was her home, and anyway the stories would have followed her. But it was confused, there was nowhere she belonged even before the stories. You see, her father was Dutch but her mother was Indonesian, and her mother wasn't married to her father. When my father died there was no one to speak for her with the Europeans any more, no one to protect her. And her mother was dead so there was no place for her with the Indonesians either. It was hard.'

Danno was trying to ease out the blackbird's eye with the point of the scissors but it wouldn't come and he had to loosen it from the inside through the beak. When he lifted it out it looked enormous, the black centre surrounded by a firm dark blue rim about three times the area normally visible. He put it in his palm and stretched out his hand to show Hannie.

'You see that lad there,' he said, pointing to a tiny white membrane that ran through the eye. 'That's the optic nerve. Everything the bird sees is carried through that thread.' Hannie looked where he pointed. The sparrow hawk shifted angrily. She didn't like his switch of attention, or perhaps it was the removal of her titbit that upset her. She flew out from the box, trailing her leather jesses, and perched malevolently on top of it, glaring and settling her powerful wings.

'The eye of a bird takes up a third of the head-area.' Danno spoke in the same quiet voice that he used to soothe the hawk. 'More so, if it's a raptor. Is this a secret, Hannie?'

Hannie looked up from the eyeball in surprise. 'No. Why? Who are you thinking of telling?'

'I'm not, but I've read things about Kenya. I just wondered.'

'Oh, Kenya.' She shrugged. 'They could think what they liked, people do anyway, don't they? And it gave them something to talk about. If there'd been nothing they'd have made up worse.'

'And Ned? Does Ned know all this?'

'Of course, why?'

Danno lifted the forefinger of his left hand and pushed his glasses firmly back up on to the bridge of his nose. He swung round and placed the eyeball on the edge of his table where the sparrow hawk could reach it.

'He just went up in my estimation.'

The blackbird lay, an eyeless huddle of feathers and beak on his work table. He'd done enough for now. Feed the dogs, feed the birds, feed himself. He wondered if Hannie talked to Ned about these visits of hers. He knew the way they spoke of him. Peculiar Danno in his peculiar little world.

He hadn't tried to understand Hannie or placate her, he'd just let her come in and talk until it was enough for the time being and she could return to her own life. He'd never meant to like her or talk back to her.

But he was growing more used to her, even the hawk was growing used to her, she flew up on to the top of the box less, sulked less, was generally less of a prima donna. Outclassed in her own act, he thought sourly.

He stopped himself. Thinking badly of Hannie was a habit he'd encouraged himself to get into. It protected his defences and kept her at a distance. He hadn't wanted her to visit, but for a while now he hadn't not wanted her either, he realised. Yesterday he'd even caught himself watching for her to come.

He got up from his chair, went outside and collected the old soup-pan he used for feeding the dogs. It wasn't just Ned who'd gone up in his estimation.

❧ *Chapter 25* ❧

*I*t was the dogs Danno couldn't forgive, Mrs Coady told her. Wouldn't forgive – there was no sense nursing grudges when things were over and done, and Mr Renvyle hadn't acted out of anger or spite, he'd thought it was the right thing he'd been doing.

'What dogs, Mrs Coady?' Hannie asked.

'Didn't Danno tell you?' Mrs Coady asked her back.

'No,' she said, 'not a word.'

So Mrs Coady told her about it – about the two black Labradors that he'd had off Danno when he'd come to live there, young dogs, but trained up and ready, lovely creatures and first-rate hunters, his pride and joy as well as Danno's.

He hadn't had them long, five or six months, no more, and it had been spring, the lambing just starting and the hunting not long over and he'd been very busy about the place and inexperienced, and maybe the dogs had got a bit less in the way of exercise than they'd needed.

Then Micky Cullen over at Maher's Cross had had a lot of his lambs killed by dogs, and three or four ewes as well. He'd been out there straight after, standing in the field, slaughtered beasts all around him, when he'd seen two black Labradors making off down the hill through the furze . . .

He'd had to act fast, they were off down the hill, so he'd lifted the gun and aimed straight and shot them both dead in their tracks.

'Did he know they were Ned's dogs?'

'Not at the time,' Mrs Coady answered, 'not at the time, but that story wouldn't be one to be long staying home, folk soon started putting two and two together and making four.'

And the way it is in these parts, Mrs Coady told her, there were many would have found themselves two Labradors out of some place a good stretch away, and had them sitting ready in the yard as though they'd known nowhere else. Then when the Guards came looking for someone to pay for Micky Cullen's sheep they'd have pointed at the dogs for answer.

But that wouldn't ever have been Mr Renvyle's way. Mr Renvyle had picked up his chequebook and driven to Cullen's as soon as he'd heard, he'd walked into the yard and said straight out that he was sorry, and Mick Cullen had been right to shoot the dogs, and how much did he owe for the sheep?

So that was that. Mick Cullen had been happy, and everyone bar a few begrudgers thought a lot of Mr Renvyle for the way he'd acted. Mr Renvyle didn't know it, but he was made up after that, people accepted him, he'd never looked back.

Only Danno hadn't been happy. Danno had landed round that night and he'd banged on the door till he had Mr Renvyle up out of his bed. Mick Cullen had shot the wrong dogs, Danno told him, he'd trained those dogs himself, they wouldn't touch sheep, and Mr Renvyle was a fool and worse than a fool not to know it.

Mr Renvyle had given him short shrift, he'd said any dog could turn rogue and there was no point in swearing the moon was blue when a child of two could tell you it was yellow.

But still Danno hadn't been satisfied, he'd said those dogs were clean bar their own wounds, he'd had it off the Cullen boy when he'd been around there asking questions. Mr Renvyle wasn't a fit owner if he didn't know his own dogs and wouldn't stand over them, Mr Renvyle couldn't be trusted with dogs, he was damned if he'd ever have another one he'd bred.

'Was he right?' Hannie asked.

If he was, there was no proving it, but a bare two weeks later there'd been another kill not a mile from Cullens and three other dogs had been shot – knacker's dogs – and after that there'd been no more kills.

Mr Renvyle hadn't held it against Danno, he'd said Danno had trained those dogs, it was understandable that he'd felt the way he had, but it was his heart not his head had been speaking.

And besides, Mr Renvyle had said, what had his dogs been doing loose in Cullen's field in the middle of lambing? At the very least he should have had them properly secured in his yard.

Mr Renvyle had dealt with it like that, then afterwards he'd put it from his mind.

'But Danno hadn't?'

Maybe he had, maybe he hadn't, Mrs Coady told her, but she hadn't seen Danno coming round with another dog when he'd one that was trained up and ready, nor a pup either for that matter. Where had Pip come from, Delaney's, wasn't it? Wherever it was, it wasn't from Danno . . .

'There wouldn't be much love lost between them,' she finished. 'Danno's a proud one and Mr Renvyle would be the same, though I don't think Mr Renvyle knows what Danno thinks of him, I think he hardly remembers what happened, and maybe he's never really acknowledged to himself that he's given offence.'

❧ *Chapter 26* ❧

'*E*llen phoned,' Ned said, coming into the kitchen. 'Aunt Cecily's taken a turn for the worse and she's back in hospital. Making life merry hell for all, Ellen says. Seems she wants to go back to the nursing home. Poor Ellen.'

'They let her do as she liked in the nursing home. The hospital's probably stricter.' Hannie was manoeuvring a rolled neck of lamb out of the oven as she spoke. The kitchen was full of the rich smells of garlic and rosemary and roasting meat. 'Bottles under the blankets, bottles under the sheets, nobody saying a word. She reeked of whiskey. They wouldn't let her do that in hospital.'

'Strictly speaking, she shouldn't be drinking at all.'

'They should put her on a drip. Neat whiskey. Kill her off.' Now she was basting the lamb, spooning hot fat over the skin to crisp it. She might not be very charitable, Ned thought, but she was a first-rate cook. He ate better now than he ever had with Mrs Coady. Paid for it too, the bills were consistently higher.

'Horrible, greedy, old woman.' Hannie returned the meat to the oven and slammed its door. 'More life in the tip of one finger than in both those daughters stuck together.' She lifted a lid, jabbed with a fork, appeared satisfied. 'Kept all the life for herself, I expect, none left over for the girls.' She picked up the pan and drained a stream of orange-coloured water into the sink. 'Stupid, spineless, useless women, I don't blame her.'

'I'm very fond of my cousins, Hannie,' Ned said mildly.

'You're fond of Ellen. She puts her hand on your arm and

looks up at you with her watery eyes and at once you want to protect her.' Hannie lobbed some butter on to the carrots and tipped them into a serving dish. 'You're not fond of Lettie. Lettie is bossy as well as stupid and spineless, no one in their senses could be fond of Lettie.'

'Ellen was very excited. Patrick's come home from Canada.'

'Patrick? The son?' Hannie had a spoon poised at her mouth. She tasted, then put the spoon down. 'I expect he's useless, too. Who wouldn't be with a mother like that? Either useless or selfish or both.' She began stirring flour into the meat-juices for gravy. 'Ran away to Canada, did he?'

'He's an engineer,' Ned said. 'He went to Canada to work. Now he's home for a couple of months to see his family. He's there for the rest of the week, then he's coming to us.'

'Oh? For how long?'

'As long as he likes. Probably until Christmas.'

'There isn't a room ready,' she said flatly.

'He can have Joss's room while you see to one. He isn't fussy.'

'Joss is. He won't like this Patrick using his room.'

'He needn't know.'

She went on stirring at the gravy, her back and her silence so ostentatious that Ned noticed. Irritation rose in him.

'He's my cousin, Hannie,' he said. 'We haven't spent time together for years.'

No response.

'You'll like him, I'm sure you'll like him.'

'I'd have liked to be asked.'

Ned sighed. She expected him to apologise. He was damned if he would, it was his home, his cousin had a right to come to his home, he didn't have to ask permission.

'I didn't think you'd mind,' he said at last, his voice stubbornly reasonable.

Hannie poured the gravy into a jug. She took the plates from the warming drawer.

'Niamh's boyfriend is coming next week,' she said brightly.

'And Joss will be home the week after, we'll be quite a crowd.'

'I didn't know Niamh had a boyfriend.'

'She doesn't, he's a three-night stand, but she wants to turn him into something more so she's invited him.'

'He'll be staying in the cottage?'

'Of course.' Hannie plonked the plates down on the table. 'I expect she would have asked you but she probably didn't think you'd mind.'

Ned did mind. If it hadn't been for the fuss Hannie was making about Patrick he wouldn't have hesitated. He'd have gone straight out, knocked on Niamh's door and told her he had a responsibility to her father and he couldn't allow it. What exactly 'it' was, he didn't get round to formulating.

Now he sat fretting and fuming, his dinner spoiled. The girl was a grown woman, he told himself, she didn't need his protection even though he wanted to protect her, not just for her father's sake, but for her own. She was so lovely and so trusting, it was a much harder world than she knew.

He couldn't say anything now, if he did Hannie would ask him nastily what century he thought he was living in, make him feel small.

But if he was really honest it wasn't just Hannie's fuss about Patrick that kept him quiet. It was those words Hannie'd used – *a three-night stand* – she'd said it like a quotation. Yet he couldn't imagine sweet, grave-faced Niamh saying anything so crude.

He wasn't really a boyfriend yet, Niamh had told Hannie, he wasn't much more than a three-night stand, but she liked him a lot, and she was pretty sure he liked her too.

They'd had a fling in the summer in Dublin, then he'd gone back up to the North without even leaving an address. Her friends said she shouldn't go setting her heart on him.

But she knew she hadn't seen the last of him, she knew he'd be in touch again, and all she had to do was wait.

And he had. And she'd seen him again in Dublin that last time when she'd gone up to buy pastels.

Her friends still warned her, they said he was too good-looking, women went for him all the time, he had it too easy, he couldn't be trusted.

But she couldn't stop thinking about him and she knew it was the same for him.

Hannie had sat listening. She had heard the naked sex in all Niamh said. She'd begun to remember things she had carefully forgotten, emotions and sensations deliberately left behind.

It seemed all women must be fools for men before they got old and grew wise.

But in the drug of the physical there was potent, if temporary, compensation. She'd felt suddenly savage that such compensation should be wasted on Niamh.

Hannie ran the brush carefully along the line of the skirting, making a clean edge of white against the Wedgwood blue of the wall. She was on her knees on spread newspapers, shuffling her way around the edges of the room, turning the big front-bedroom into a suitable retreat for Ned's Canadian cousin. A gas heater bubbled quietly in the middle of the floor.

The cold weather continued. Hannie liked it, she felt more alive, her sluggish blood ran faster. She liked its ancientness, the threat in the air, skies fierce and then soft, mornings smoky and secret with frost. It was quite new to her. Winter's blanket, its thorned weave and rank folds, its clean bitter stars, so unlike the great flowering stars of Africa.

Ned had been tight-lipped over her insistence on the integrity of Joss's room, but her efforts with a paintbrush seemed to be in favour. He was used to the caravanserai, sleeping forms on the floor, a common roof, all thoughts of privacy and ownership redundant. Easy for Ned, who knew who he was, had had this all his life. Not so easy for Joss, moving from school to school, from one of her husband's houses to another.

She picked a brush-hair from the skirting with her forefinger and wiped the sticky gloss down Ned's discarded trousers. She was covered in paint-splatters: mixed blue and white on her clothes and her face, white in her hair from the ceiling. Ned had noticed, he'd touched it approvingly as he got up from the breakfast table that morning, then suggested a visit to the hairdresser when she was finished. She'd got up and started clearing, saying nothing. He'd gone to the study, come back with his wallet, taken out a ten-pound note and laid it on the table.

Later, when he'd come in for coffee, the note was still there, its edge tucked under the milk jug. Didn't she want to get her hair done, he'd asked her, and she'd smiled and shaken her head and said ladies' hairdressers in Ireland must be very cheap. He'd looked surprised, then picked up the ten and put two twenties down instead and asked would that cover it? She had nodded and smiled again and lifted the notes and put them into her pocket.

Now she filled in the last six inches of skirting and got up and stood looking around her. The room looked well with its matt blue walls and white trim, it would look even better when the cleaned carpet was put back and she'd hung the curtains she had washed and pressed and altered. Just the window frame and the door to be done and she'd be through with the painting. She crossed to the window, lit a cigarette and stood smoking and thinking vague thoughts of Joss, of the unknown Patrick, of Niamh's unself-conscious anticipation of sexual pleasure. She could hear Mrs Coady downstairs hoovering the study and Ned in the upper field with the tractor. The house was sombre around her.

Standing there she had one of those sudden reversals of mood that these days often seemed to accompany one of her successful little manipulations or ingratiations. Pleasure in her own cleverness would dissolve into a vague depression. Hard on the depression would come an angry self-disgust.

And she hated it, this enforced awareness. She didn't want

the mirror she kept finding herself looking into and couldn't seem to smash or push away. Suddenly she couldn't stand Ned or this house or herself a moment longer. She was overwhelmed by the need to make some violent, irreparable gesture that would shove things right to the edge and cut at the dragging compromise of daily life.

She put down her paintbrush, turned off the gas and left the room. Then she bathed, changed her clothes, took the money she'd saved for Joss from its place in the back of the wardrobe and put it with Ned's forty pounds. Downstairs, she lifted the car-keys from their hook and crossed the yard. She opened the garage doors and backed out the Volkswagen.

She woke in broad daylight in an upstairs room somewhere in Cork. The man who snored on the bed beside her was half her age and unknown to her. Other bodies, male and female, lay around on the floor, on the other bed, on the sofa. She sat up and someone put a mug of tea into her hand. It was laced with whiskey. She asked for a cigarette.

Some time later, in some pub somewhere in the city, she was searching her pockets for money and her hand met keys and closed tight around them. For half an hour she sat trying to work through the haze of alcohol to reach for a reason for being here. She found none, the last dregs of any purpose had long since fallen away. She stood up, pushed back her chair, picked up her cigarettes and headed for the door. Someone called her name, but she didn't turn round.

Hannie crossed the yard and reached the back door, so hungover and exhausted that she had to drag herself the few remaining steps. She'd lost all track of time, all care for consequences. She felt empty, anaesthetised and ancient.

She paused, her hand on the door, then pushed it open and stood at the entrance looking in. The kitchen was clean and fire-lit, everything glowed and shone, a cave of warm brightness. The puppy lay curled in her basket and the room was fragrant with the rich warm smells of meat juices and potatoes baking. A man was standing over by the fire, a man as tall as Ned with something of his angular, rangy look, despite the extra flesh he carried, the soft bulge over the belt. He cradled a glass of whiskey in his hand. Hannie half turned in an automatic movement of withdrawal. This was a place both domestic and secure. She had no business here. She should go back outside to the darkness, where she belonged.

'Ah, Hannie, there you are.' Ned's voice came to her from across the room. It was quiet and even and matter-of-fact. 'Hannie, this is my cousin Patrick, come to us a few days early. Patrick, my wife Hannie.'

Hannie stood there, her hands shaking, her hair wild, her clothes crumpled and drink-stained and slept-in. She knew what she must look like, what she must smell like. Yet the man who came forward to greet her gave no sign that anything was other than expected.

'My sister Ellen couldn't stop talking about you,' he said easily. 'She is very impressionable and you impressed her very much. She said you were very elegant and wore beautiful clothes and she didn't want to talk about geese at all, but Ned had insisted and anyway she couldn't think of anything else to say. She liked you very much and she hated being so dull for you. She said I was to be sure to tell you and to apologise for boring you so dreadfully.'

❧ *Chapter 27* ❧

*I*t was late when Ned phoned Mrs Coady, well after eleven, Tom was already in his bed.

'She hasn't come home, Mrs Coady,' he said, 'she went off in the car and she hasn't come home and I wonder if I should be worrying?'

He was calm enough, Mrs Coady thought, no fuss, no dramatics: he might have been asking where she was because he had Ambrose Power standing beside him wanting a decision about paint or tiles or underlay. But she knew what he was thinking and he knew that she knew: he was thinking she'd left him and she wasn't coming back.

It was a lot to take on, Mrs Coady said, a whole new way of life, and it might be that it was all too much suddenly, it might be she'd got into the car for a bit of a drive and gone further than she'd intended . . .

There was a small silence then he said he'd looked upstairs and there was nothing, as far as he could see, that had gone. He paused again then he asked her what it might cost to get your hair done in Dungarvan?

At first she thought she'd heard wrong, but he said it again so she asked was it only a cut she'd be wanting or was it a colour as well?

The next day he phoned again just before ten and said where was she, was she unwell, he'd come and collect her if she didn't have a car?

Mrs Coady said this was Wednesday, it wasn't her day to come, Tuesdays and Fridays were her days – two mornings a week – but she'd come anyway if he wanted her, she'd only bits and pieces of things to finish up here.

When Mrs Coady put down the phone she remembered that Hannie was saving the money she didn't have to pay her anymore now that she was working fewer days. She cursed herself for her mouth and went to get her coat.

Ned had made himself ring round the hospitals, but the exercise only confirmed what he already knew. She wasn't lying injured in a hospital bed, she'd walked out, it didn't matter that her things were upstairs and untouched, packing a suitcase wasn't ever going to be Hannie's way.

His first instinct was to tell no one. He knew what gossip was like here, how each incident was pounced on and shaken to death and the participants held up to delighted ridicule. He would face that when he had to, but he wasn't going to open the door and invite it in.

He was angry with Hannie, he felt that clearly, but what he hadn't expected at all was the feeling of loss. Having Hannie living here as his wife hadn't been as he'd imagined, it had changed his life in ways he didn't always find either positive or comfortable, yet he could find no sense of relief in himself when he thought that she'd gone. Under the anger at what she was doing to him, his strongest emotion was that of wanting her back.

Then she came back. He didn't ask her where she'd been or what she'd been doing. He wouldn't let himself interrogate her, mostly for reasons of honour but also because he was afraid of what he might hear. And Patrick was staying, Patrick was always at his elbow, Ned didn't want to draw any further attention to the difficulties he and Hannie might be having.

Over the next two days Hannie referred once to her absence but her tone was mocking and light and she made no attempt at an explanation. She seemed neither apprehensive at a possible interrogation, nor relieved when none came. He was angry, despite himself, despite his decision to say nothing. It kept coming on to the tip of his tongue, it was harder and harder to push down.

The next afternoon they were coming back from the field above the house where they'd walked with Patrick and old Bess to check on the heifers in calf. It was just after four, dusk thickened, already the trees were lost, dark shapes on the blue of the coming night. Patrick had fallen behind, he was making heavy weather of closing the gate, Ned and Hannie had walked on in silence, then noticed and stopped and stood waiting.

'People can't always be as they intend, Ned. They can't always deliver on what they've said they'll deliver, even when they truly meant to at the time.'

Hannie's words came out of the gloom. Her voice was so low that he almost thought he'd imagined it but he hadn't. Then Patrick was upon them, Bess at his heels, and there wasn't time for more. She touched her hand briefly to his arm and turned from him. Suddenly, he understood why she'd gone missing. He no longer minded that Patrick had seen more than he wanted him to see; he no longer minded her deception over Mrs Coady's hours and money. Mrs Coady was right, it was hard for her, she had lived a different life, a life opposite to the lives that he and his kind lived here: steady and cautious, with every action evolving out of some previous action and tempered by the knowledge of consequences to be lived down the unfolding years.

They tramped home, the dusk loud with the suck of their boots in the mud and the frantic evening chirring of blackbirds in the thorns.

∾ *Chapter 28* ∾

'And there she was,' Ned said, 'with her feet in a basin. And when I asked what she was doing she said it was for the chilblains, Mrs Coady said to soak them every day in warm urine.'

Ned swept his eyes round the table. He was enjoying himself, telling his story, making them laugh.

'I got straight into the car, but it was after six when I got there, the chemist was closed, so I banged on the door, made Heffernan come down and attend to me. He didn't like it of course, mumbled about his dinner and emergencies only. "Heffernan," I said, "if it was *your* wife with her feet in the stuff *you'd* be banging on the door."

'"Very good remedy, the urine," says Heffernan, "a lot in these old pishogues. Sure they're drinking the stuff now, these New Agers, or whatever it is they call themselves, you couldn't go far wrong with the odd soak."

'"Like tying rags to a rag tree. We're approaching the end of the twentieth century, Heffernan," I said, "you can surely do better than that."'

Vere was thumping the table, Patrick had his head thrown back, even Joss let out a little yelp that might have been the sound of appreciation.

'Of course Mrs Coady roared laughing when I told her. Said she'd never meant Mrs Renvyle to go trying it, she'd only said it to show her how bad people were with the chilblains in the old days, the things they would do to get rid of them. So I told her not to be telling her such things any more, Mrs Renvyle was the sort that would try anything.' Ned threw

Hannie a look full of pride and affection. Hannie saw it, smiled quietly, looked away.

'Central heating,' Patrick said. 'And proper insulation. Canadian winters are much worse than ours, but they don't just sit back and endure the way people do here, you don't have to have chilblains or rheumatism.'

'Or sit with your feet in warm piss,' Joss interjected.

'Something like that,' Patrick said, grinning at him.

Joss liked him, Hannie thought. Or perhaps he was only getting at Ned. Joss listened when Patrick spoke to him, he even threw the odd remark in his direction, the contrast was hard to miss.

'Don't like central heating myself,' Vere said flatly. 'Awful atmosphere, can't breathe in it, you get sick.'

'No draughts or damp,' Joss said softly. 'Rots the soul, makes you soft, how can the boys grow up to be men?'

Niamh giggled.

'He bought me an electric blanket,' Hannie said loudly, looking at Vere. 'I didn't even know such things existed.'

Ned got up. He crossed to the sideboard and took out a bottle of Drambuie he'd been hoarding. Bloody good dinner, he thought. He'd explained to Hannie about the Beresfords and Patrick, how they'd grown up together, close as first cousins, and she'd understood what he was saying, he hadn't had to ask would she invite them. She'd rung up James and Marjorie as well but they were in Dublin with one of the daughters, so she'd fixed another evening later in the week. Her idea having Niamh, too, company for Joss, stopped him feeling awkward and left out. She'd done them proud all right, not just with the food, but with the way she talked and arranged things and kept it all flowing; the Beresfords were no end impressed.

From another shelf Ned took tiny glasses, sparsely cut, clouded and old. He arranged them on a little polished brass tray that had come from the Yemen. He smiled to himself as he did so, he could nearly see Vere thinking that maybe she wasn't such a total mistake after all. And maybe Vere was right, maybe she wasn't, she could certainly do it when she set her mind to it, that much was clear. She'd had plenty of practice of course, social sort of a life with Andrew, parties and entertaining and the like. Good with people too, easy and natural, sometimes downright charming, the other night at his lecture in Kilkenny she'd really shone. She'd looked terrific, worn her good suit, had her hair done, he'd been proud as punch introducing his attractive new wife. Silly old fool that he was, he thought, smiling happily to himself. At his age. The lecture had gone well too, he hadn't done it for a while, been a bit anxious, surprised himself with his own eloquence in the end. Islam in Sub-Saharan Africa. Surprised Patrick too, he kept saying how good it was, on at him to develop the lecture into another book.

Ned had set one of the tiny glasses in front of each of his guests and was moving around the table filling them. The success of the evening was making him bountiful.

'Ned likes the winter,' Hannie said, pouring coffee into his cup and speaking to the table generally. 'He says he doesn't, but he does.'

'It changes the proportions,' Ned said. 'It's like the desert again, one becomes tiny in an immense landscape.' He looked at Hannie and it was clear that what he was saying was for her. 'There's an excitement, a quickening of the blood. I like that, I like the stars so high and sharp, I even like the darkness, though I wouldn't like it all year round.'

'I had a Swedish friend, once,' Hannie said. 'She said in the north of her country in winter it never got light at all.' She played with an unused fork as she spoke and it shone with the shine of the lights. 'She was like daylight herself, despite all that darkness,' Hannie went on, 'very clear, like fresh water. Her character, I mean, not just her looks. She wasn't dark like the people here, she wasn't secretive.'

'Is that how we seem to you?' Niamh asked suddenly. She had said very little all evening. Now she sat low in her chair, her eyes intent on Hannie, who suddenly saw that she was drunk.

'Poverty, rebellion and endless rain,' Patrick cut in easily. 'Mud floors and history and conspiracy. A race bred to secrecy and darkness.'

He's said these things before, Ned thought. In Canada, over the whiskey, when they ask him about Ireland.

Hannie turned to Patrick. 'Yes, but this darkness is in everyone. In you, and in Ned and in Alison and Vere as well,' she said. 'And you are the outsiders, the rebelled against.'

'Perhaps ruling is the supreme illusion,' Ned said. 'Perhaps the rulers will always take on the characteristics of the ruled.'

'Fiann O'Brian and the molecules,' Joss put in suddenly.

They all stared.

'*The Third Policeman*,' Joss explained. 'It's a book by Fiann O'Brien, about molecules.'

'About a Guard,' Niamh said, trying to help him. 'A country Guard –'

'A Guard who spends his whole life on a bicycle,' Joss said across her. 'Arse rarely absent from the saddle. Time passes and exchange of molecules takes place. The bicycle begins to take on Guard-like characteristics. The Guard in his turn becomes partly bicycle. Literally: he starts standing by the kerb outside his favourite pub propped on one leg.' Joss reached across for the Drambuie bottle and refilled his glass.

'Happens all the time,' he went on. 'See it in Africa. Half-castes. Visible exchange of molecules has taken place.' He gave a little bark of laughter. 'So Niamh is like you, you're like Niamh. You all sit round the dinner table together and everyone's happy. Till you need someone to build roads and die in trenches again. Then there are problems.' Joss flicked his blank blue gaze around the table and settled it on Niamh. 'The bicycle thinks it's the man that rides it.'

Hannie rose, holding the coffee pot. 'More coffee?' she said. 'Perhaps we should have Irish? Patrick has promised to teach me. Joss, fetch the whiskey bottle from the drawing room and bring it to the kitchen. You must learn, too.'

It was gracefully done, Ned thought, hoping she hadn't seen the look Vere'd thrown at Alison but pretty sure that she had. He wondered how much Joss knew about the colour of his great-grandmother's skin.

'He's just weird,' Patrick said, 'don't take any notice of him, Niamh, no one else does.'

'But it's true, what he said. A hundred years ago I couldn't have been in that room except as a servant.' She stood in the yard, her eyes large and thoughtful, clutching an armful of cut logs against her sweater.

'You're being silly, Niamh. Silly and insecure and melodramatic.' Patrick was impatient now. '*That room*, as you put it, is only a room in a modern farm, not a turn-of-the-century country house. Besides,' he added more kindly, 'the loss would have been ours, not yours.'

'That's not the point,' Niamh said stubbornly. 'My grandmother would've been unfit company.'

'Sure. It's the way it was then. It isn't the way it is now. Ned's not patronising you, Niamh, he's not doing you favours. He invited you to dinner because he likes you and he wanted you at his table. Don't be so touchy for God's sake, your father's three times more likely to help Ned out than the other way round. And as for the cottage, you pay your rent, don't you? You're not here on charity.'

Niamh flushed. 'Not much,' she said. 'Not as much as I should.'

'Do you *want* to pay more?'

Niamh looked startled, then she began to laugh.

'Well then,' Patrick said, 'don't suggest it, Ned might just hear you. Anyway, you're talking from gross ignorance, you never knew Ned's mother. If you had you might just think your grandmother a very fortunate woman.'

'Why, what was she like?'

'A true horror.'

'How do you know?' Niamh had cheered up, her eyes shone.

'I remember her. Besides, my mother's her sister, a living reminder, just in case there was any danger of my forgetting.'

Niamh grinned. Her thick blue sweater was matted like an old blanket and she wore mittens in grey and red hand-knitted stripes. Some aunt, over-fond of the knitting needles, Patrick thought. Or perhaps it was the mother. He wondered if she'd wear them when the boyfriend came. Probably, he decided. She had very little artifice. He was glad she was here, he thought of her as a shield or a token, protecting Ned from Hannie and her strange son.

And she was accurate enough, twenty years ago she might have been in the cottage, but she wouldn't have been in the dining room. What no one had said though, was neither would Hannie or Joss. Well, they were Ned's problem. He was naive, Ned, despite all the books and the travelling. Perhaps on account of the books and the travelling: a kind of bubble of unreality he'd deliberately created for himself. Not a bad lecture though, must build him up a bit more, talk him into starting on another book. Something to get immersed in, a sort of inoculation for when everything fell apart.

✎ Chapter 29 ✎

'Niamh has the polishing cloths,' Mrs Coady told Hannie. 'She was up for them first thing, said she didn't need them for long, just finishing touches.'

'He's hitching down from Dublin, he'll be here late afternoon or evening, depending on how the lifts go. She's told him to start early. *You know what country roads are like,*' Hannie mimicked. '*No cars and no one stops after dark.*'

Mrs Coady laughed. 'She's a bit anxious, all right. She has that place like a palace. *I want everything to be perfect for him, Mrs Coady.* She'll learn.'

'Probably the hard way.' Patrick was standing by the window with a mug of coffee. 'That house looks more like a dowry offering than a setting for an independent woman. I told her she'd defeat herself. "*Do you think so, Patrick?*" she says. "*Oh, but I'm not trying to trap him.*" So I said I didn't mean it, I was teasing.'

'You should've told her to spice things up a bit, ease off on the domestic detail, put in some squalor and sex.' Hannie finished wringing out the floor cloth and fired it neatly into the empty mop bucket. 'I don't know what young people are coming to, nobody thought about soap and water in my day. I hope at least she's had the sense to buy some bottles.'

'The funny thing is that she isn't,' Patrick said. The two women looked at him. 'Trying to trap him, I mean.'

Hannie snorted. Mrs Coady put her hands on her hips, and stared at him in disbelief.

* * *

Hannie slipped the string round the ivy stems and pulled them tight. She wound the cord a couple more times then tied it firmly. She lifted the bundled mass, heaved it on to one shoulder, then bent again for a second bundle, settled it, and began the trudge home.

The sky was racing with cloud but already the light was slipping. The surface of the river shone dully. Two swans drifted past quite silently, their white forms resting on the pewter water, their long wakes catching the shine from the dying sky. On the far bank the darkness was thickening, the land between river and sky was black and lost.

Cold God crouched in the woods and floated on the water. Hannie felt him, his great age, his stubborn indifference. She couldn't remember the sun or its heat. Only the death of the sun, the long shadows cast here at midday in the sunlit fields.

Above her head wave after wave of black birds washed across the sky, great soundings of crows going home to their roosts in the woods across the river. She closed her eyes and stood. The sky reeled with the enormous clamour of their voices. After a time the great traffic of birds ceased, the sky stilled, the darkness came seeping up out of the earth like smoke.

A stick snapped. A blackness broke from the trees and moved out on to the path towards her.

'Oh Hannie, it's you, I didn't know who it was, you were such a strange shape in the dark.' Niamh's white face loomed towards her. Hannie stopped and waited. Niamh turned to the darkness behind her. Another white face moved forwards.

'Hannie, this is Ciaran. Ciaran, this is Mrs Renvyle, otherwise known as Hannie.'

'Hannie as in Hannah?'

'No, not Hannah, Hanneka.'

'Pleased to meet you, Hannie-as-in-Hanneka,' drawled a young man's voice. 'Niamh here was showin' me around, but we couldn't see for the dark.'

The voice was throaty and light and detached. Hannie was suddenly mildly curious to see his face.

'Ciaran's not used to the country,' Niamh said. 'He's not used to the dark.'

'What time do they turn on the streetlights round here? Does everyone go walkabout in the middle of the night?'

'No streetlights, and it's not the middle of the night.'

'Whatever you say, sweetheart.' There it was again, that odd detachment. As though all this was happening to someone else. Someone stupid.

'We were going to Danno's,' Niamh's voice was eager. 'Ciaran wants to see his sparrow hawk.'

'Correction. *You* want to show me his sparrow hawk.'

'I want to show you all his hawks, and you want to see them.'

'That's how it is, is it?'

'That's how it is,' Niamh said, laughing. She was laughing a lot, little laughs of happiness and excitement. Hannie wondered how long it would be before these little laughs of hers began to irritate him.

'What are you carrying, Hannie? Is that ivy?'

'Ned wants holly and ivy, he says it's traditional,' Hannie told her. 'There's plenty of berried holly in the upper field. He'll cut that himself, I've been cutting the ivy, but it took longer than I thought.'

'Tuesday's the shortest day,' Niamh said.

'So everyone keeps telling me.'

'That's a con, so it is, you think you only have to get to it and then the next day everything'll be okay, but it's ages an' ages before it gets any lighter.'

It was odd, standing talking to someone you couldn't see, Hannie thought. He seemed to find it odd too, but Niamh sounded perfectly comfortable. 'Will we skip Danno's?' she asked him. 'Walk back with Hannie?'

They moved off. She had a good fire going, she explained to Hannie, and plenty of booze. They'd be as well going on home and sitting by it, Danno's could wait. Of course if Hannie wanted to join them, she added hastily . . .

Hannie declined.

She dumped the ivy by the step and stood working her wellingtons against the iron scraper, pushing the caked mud out from the insteps. This done, she waggled each foot in turn in the low tub of rain-water beside it. Ned was fussy about cleaned wellingtons. Everywhere Ned, Ned and his systems, everywhere she turned they were in place. He had explained each one carefully to her at the start. When she ignored them he explained them carefully again.

She lifted the bundled ivy and shoved it stem-down into the water-butt, thinking of the young man she'd seen briefly in the spilled light from Niamh's door. Tall with a muscular build, and attractive, just as Niamh had promised. Much good it would do her, except in the short run.

❧ *Chapter 30* ❧

*I*t was all different now: Patrick and Joss in the house, Ciaran with Niamh in the cottage, the house open and warm. Ned liked the generous feeling of the way his life had become, but he missed the silence. Sometimes he had to make himself remember that when he'd had the silence he hadn't always wanted it.

He stayed working outside for as long as weather and daylight allowed. Mostly he toiled alone but sometimes he prised Patrick from the comforts of the hearth and the two men worked together, making their way round Ned's scruffy acres, draining ditches, re-setting hedges, repairing gaps in fences and walls. Ned liked maintenance, the quiet, steady activity of anticipating problems or putting things right where the damage had already been done. It was useful having another pair of hands, though in some ways he'd rather have got Mick up from the village as he'd done in other years. Mick was less chatty than Patrick and cleverer when it came to dry-stone walls, but Patrick was surprisingly competent once he got started and Patrick didn't have to be paid.

Ned suggested to Hannie that he bring Joss out with them, teach him the work. Hannie agreed in theory, it would do the boy good she said, but perhaps he should start in the summer and have these few short weeks just to settle in? She was relieved when Ned dropped the subject, she didn't know herself quite what it was that she feared except that Joss might reveal too much of himself and she needed to keep him concealed from Ned for as long as she could. She was more relaxed when he was at Niamh's playing cards with

Ciaran; he liked that and it kept him happy and away from Ned.

She took basic precautions. It had been easier in Africa.

'Don't let him do that,' she would say to a houseboy without having to explain herself or worry about what they might think.

'Don't leave Pip with Joss,' she told Niamh, and then had to think of a reason. 'He's not reliable with dogs, he'll just take her for a walk and come home without her.' It was a weak excuse even to her own ears, and did nothing to chase the surprise from Niamh's eyes.

Boredom was the danger with Joss. She glanced at the calendar, mentally marshalling her resources. Christmas was almost upon them, Patrick was going back to his mother and sisters in two days' time and Niamh was off home the day after, on Christmas Eve. Ciaran had refused Niamh's familial invitations, he seemed set on going North, but was promising a quick return.

That was something, Hannie thought. Joss was impressed by Ciaran, who treated him with an easy contempt which he seemed to respond to. Christmas itself would be a distraction, and after that there was the New Year. She wondered about a party.

'Where's Niamh?' Ned asked. 'She promised to make us a wreath for the front door, I haven't seen her for days.'

Hannie laughed and said Niamh had other fish to fry just now and he should stop being such an old fogey and try to remember as far back as his youth. She was washing the breakfast dishes, lifting the plates out one by one and setting them in the drainer. She laughed again and turned to him, looking up into his eyes, and he flushed with shy happiness. His hand lifted without him asking it to and he touched her hair, which was silvery-blonde now from the hairdresser she'd gone to on the morning of his lecture. She didn't look away, her eyes held his and there was a humorous gentleness in them. Then

Patrick was at the door with Pippa trotting behind him and for a moment he stopped and then came on and they knew he'd seen them. Ned dropped his hand and made to fill the kettle. He was embarrassed, but somewhere also a little stubbornly proud.

Later that day he knocked on Niamh's door, a big bunch of berried holly dangling by a string from his hand. It was early afternoon, Niamh answered his knock, she was more or less dressed but her feet were bare and her hair was tangled and wild.

'I've been fencing with Patrick,' he said, trying not to look at her, trying not to see her face against the blue-painted door, the puff-lidded eyes that wouldn't look up, the scraped chin, the mouth all gorged and bruised.

'We were just in time,' he heard himself saying stupidly. 'Another day and the birds would have stripped it bare.'

Niamh took the bunch and thanked him quietly.

'The kettle's boiled,' she said, 'I'm making tea . . .'

An invitation was implied but she didn't sound as though she meant it and still she wouldn't raise her eyes. Ned shook his head. He didn't mention wreaths or front doors and he blushed and mumbled as he turned and walked away.

He'd been fencing all right, but she hadn't, she'd been swimming in sex till everything had blurred and merged and lost its edges. He felt irrationally shamed by his age and his innocence and he wished he'd listened to Hannie and had some tact. Then embarrassment overtook him and he began to imagine that they were standing together at the window watching him and he had to make a huge effort not to turn round and look. In his mind he saw the strutting young man he had met but hardly spoken to, and the young man was mocking him, and Niamh wasn't exactly rushing to his defence.

It was different for the young man, Ned realised. He was becoming himself, it was the making of him, at the same time as it was the un-making of her. He even looked different: as though he could see further and run faster. And she was losing herself, that was clear enough, she could hardly even remember who she was.

He thought of Hannie and he wondered if this same losing of herself had happened to her, if sex for women was at the beginning like entering a river where they submerged themselves and became featureless, before finally re-emerging on the further bank.

Abruptly he forgot Niamh. He felt he'd seen a map of a country that he'd glanced at a long time ago and then discarded in favour of other more pressingly interesting maps. He had meant to return to the first map, he knew that now, but he'd forgotten it and left it all too late. Now he wanted to find Hannie, to ask her questions and listen to her answers, to understand through her this country he'd lost sight of years ago and then glimpsed again near to his journey's end.

He looked at his watch. He was anxious to finish the fencing before it got dark, had only come back early with the tractor to fetch more posts. Patrick was working on now, if he went off to find Hannie he'd leave Patrick to run out of posts and they might not finish the job before the light died.

To hell with the posts, he decided abruptly. He picked up the two great bundles of holly they'd cut for the house and made for the back door. He had his hand on the door handle when he stopped himself.

Maybe she'd want to see him as little as Niamh had, he didn't want to feel he was intruding again, he didn't want to be shamed twice in the one hour. He looked down. The holly berries shone against the deep, spiked leaves.

> *The holly bears a berry*
> *as red as any blood.*

The words of the carol sang themselves in his head.

> *The holly bears a bark*
> *as bitter as any gall.*

He slipped the holly string from his hands, laid the bundled holly on the doorstep and went back to find Patrick.

'I must admit I did question the tastefulness of the enterprise at the start,' Patrick said, reaching across and spearing a slice of Niamh's home-made bread on the end of his knife. Patrick and Joss and Ciaran were all sitting in her kitchen, discussing Patrick's mother's parrot, recently deceased. Patrick, in a light mood, had suggested taxidermy on the phone and his sister Lettie had sent the corpse by the next post.

'Then I saw Danno's work and I knew that taste didn't enter into it, I knew the whole scheme was just part of the cosmic fun. Besides, it's What-Mother-Wants, and who am I to deny Mother? This bread's delicious, Niamh, you should go into production, you'd make a fortune.' He helped himself to another slice and smothered it in butter and jam.

'Danno's work?'

'Danno's terrible taxidermy, my dear Niamh, you've surely noticed. A crooked wing on a widgeon, a cancerous bump on the flank of a basking pollock.'

'That's not fair, Danno's quite good,' Niamh said hotly. 'It's not supposed to be exact, more of an approximation.' She stopped. They were looking at her in a way that made her feel about ten years old. 'People come to him from all over,' she finished lamely.

She got up and started to clear the dishes from the rack and put them away. Domesticity – her refuge. More like a permanent state these days. When she wasn't in bed with Ciaran she was standing in the kitchen dishing out food. With a shock she realised she was equating sex with feeding mouths and washing dishes.

She wasn't working, that was the problem, she should just go into the other room and get on with it, then she'd feel better about herself, she always did. But how could she work with her house full, how could she work without quiet? Suddenly she was glad that Ciaran didn't want to come home with her for Christmas: let him go to Belfast, she'd a good mind to tell him not to bother coming back.

And if he didn't?

She found the bottle of aspirin on the dresser and tipped some into her hand. She had a hangover, that was all. She'd feel different when the pills worked.

❧ *Chapter 31* ❧

*H*annie was very busy in the house. They'd had lunches and dinners and drinks, they'd asked friends and relations and acquaintances of Ned's from around the county, all of whom had known Patrick or Patrick's family some time in the course of their lives. These people lived stranded in their big houses, houses crumbling now but still connected up like the knotting in an invisible net, thrown down years ago, then left to tear and rot away.

They knew this, accepted it, but sometimes they spoke as though the country were becoming uninhabited, as though the lands between the dying houses were all empty and laid to waste. It was like Africa, Hannie thought, the white talk of No one-lives-here-anymore, when they meant No Whites. It was like Africa but without the fury, fury that was fear-induced, fear of an overwhelming privilege threatened and soon to be lost. Here there was only resignation and occasional bitterness, the privilege so long lost it was barely even a habit of mind.

Hannie didn't mind this entertaining, especially when she had Patrick for audience and conspirator; she even enjoyed it. She liked showing how well she could do it, liked impressing the Alisons and the Marjories, and she loved the aftermath, the mockery of eccentricity, the ridicule of drunken folly. Patrick colluded with her and encouraged her. Even Ned let himself smile as some of James's wilder expressions crept into his household's daily currency.

Hannie was flirting gently with Patrick. Ned noticed without jealousy; he was glad she was enjoying Patrick, glad that his cousin liked his wife, relieved that her visits to Danno seemed to have fallen away.

Hannie herself felt easier, less trapped and desperate, and with the ease had come a certain caution. Her words to Patrick were light and ambiguous, her husband was always included, she took care to make him feel secure and proud. She wasn't making a play for Patrick – he wasn't husband material, nor was she much attracted to him sexually – but he was pleasant, urbane company, he amused her and he broke the awkward silence around Ned and Joss.

Niamh wasn't careful, except over contraceptives; she was hardly even aware there was anything else to be careful about. She was confused though, she knew that much: confused about Ciaran, confused about her feelings for him, confused about sex and the way it was changing her.

It was as though all of her that she thought of as herself had stopped living tidily some place more or less behind her eyes and had melted like butter left out in the sun. And this warmed butter had run down into her flesh and spread over her whole body, and she was left not knowing anything, not even if she liked what was happening to her until it stopped happening and she ached for it to happen again.

'I'd draw the curtains when I undressed, if I was you,' Ciaran said. 'Yon bucko's not beyond a squint or two.' He hitched his bag over his shoulder and stuck his free hand down the back of her jeans. She felt the shock of its cold intrusion. At the same time her flesh reeled and her body shouted with recognition.

'An' who'd blame him?' Ciaran drawled salaciously. 'Sensible fella I'd say, if you asked me.'

'You'll not be away that long, sure you won't?' She tried to ignore the hand, tried to sound indifferent.

'A few days,' he told her. 'They'll go nuts, so they will, they'll be on at me to stay.'

'But you won't?'

'Couldn't if I wanted to.' He pressed his fingers hard into her buttocks, driving her crotch and pelvis forward to meet his. Her flesh dissolved, she moved forward and pressed into him, he forced his tongue deep into her mouth and worked her till her whole body cried out with need. Then he pulled away from her.

'Have to go,' he said, looking at her and wiping his mouth on the back of his wrist. Then he caught her hand and held it against the bulge in his straining jeans. 'That's just so's you'll remember,' he told her.

'Hm.' Hannie stood in Joss's room, thumbing the shiny paper of the mail-order catalogue. She looked at the young woman in the picture, at her swept-up hair and her downcast eyes and the simper on her glazed lips. '*The Lingerie Collection. The return of the camisole.*' Her voice was casual and dismissive. 'So this is what Niamh's dreams are made of. Get yourself up like a Victorian boudoir and simper about the bedroom: fuck me, oh please fuck me. How very liberated and suburban.' She tossed the catalogue scornfully on to the bed.

Joss leaned by the window, cigarette in hand, watching her. Or at least she supposed he was watching her, his blanked-out, black-swathed eyes were pointed in her direction and the corners of his lips were just twisted up in a smile or a sneer or a snarl, she couldn't tell.

She was coming on too heavy, *freaking out* as he'd put it, and over a few juvenile photos of young women in underwear. She stopped herself. At least he'd been straight about it, had told her where he'd got them as soon as she'd asked.

'Nicked them,' he'd said, blowing smoke at her and looking pleased with himself. 'Off Niamh's dresser where she left them. Silly cow.'

She had no idea what he was thinking now, no idea if her ridicule had sunk in or had slid straight off his trim duck's back.

* * *

'You should get something,' her friend Maeve had said to her in Dublin. 'Anna got the black French knickers, she was showing me, said it was like having a secret weapon on under her jeans, said she fancied everyone she met all day.'

'Anna must be made of money.'

'Twenty quid,' Maeve had said. 'The suspenders are ten. Trust you to worry about the money, Niamh, such a buzz, Anna said, cheap at the price.'

'If I want to feel sexy,' Niamh had said gravely, 'I don't wear any knickers at all.'

Maeve had giggled and rolled her eyes to heaven. 'God Niamh, you're such a puritan, what're we going to do with you at all? Here, take it anyway, have a look at it, something might rub off.'

And she had taken it, though she hadn't really understood why Maeve had called her a puritan. She had looked through it by the fire one night before Ciaran came, had even wondered briefly if black French knickers mightn't increase her chances.

I must have been mad, she thought now. Did I want to spend my whole life on my back?

Niamh stood by the fire after Hannie'd left, the cheap paper catalogue in her hand.

'Joss borrowed it,' Hannie had said. 'You should be careful, Niamh, young boys are suggestible. It's their age, they like erotic stimulation.' She had shrugged. Boys will be boys, the shrug had said.

'Borrowed it,' Niamh muttered indignantly to herself. What was it Mrs Coady had said to her only the other day? *If something goes missing, Niamh, ask yourself if it's something Joss might want?*

Stole it, more like. Then round comes Hannie, behaving as though I've given him pornography to read in bed.

Pornography, indeed. Naïveté. She might be a puritan but even she could see the silly straightforward innocence of the pictures. Fuck Hannie, she thought. And fuck Maeve for forcing it on her when she hadn't wanted it in the first place.

It was unbelievable – like church again – poor decent Adam, befuddled with sex, misled by evil Eve and her womanly wiles. *You should be careful, Niamh, young boys are suggestible.* Well, she would be careful all right. She dumped the catalogue into the fire and felt much better.

Then she stopped feeling better and remembered Ciaran. Draw the curtains, don't tempt the boy. That had been Ciaran's gist as well. The realisation was disquieting.

It never once occurred to her that Hannie might have been trying to warn her.

'The day after Stephen's day,' Niamh said in answer to Patrick's question about Ciaran's return. 'Or the day after that. Depending on how the lifts go. He may not make it down from Belfast in a day.' Niamh broke the thin ice on the puddle carefully with her wellington as she spoke. She liked doing this normally, the creaking sound that it made, the trapped air-bubbles coming free, but somehow today it didn't give her much satisfaction. Patrick was going himself in the morning. She wanted to ask his advice about Joss but she didn't know how.

And even if she'd known, she thought, it mightn't be any good. Patrick might react like Ciaran.

Ciaran was amused by Joss. He was a liar and a cheat, all right, but then who wasn't at Joss's age? Ciaran insisted that Joss was normal, that his behaviour was adolescent only and nothing to get excited about. And he'd gone on insisting, even after Joss had sat one night telling them his hopes and plans for the future. Life here was only a temporary arrangement, it seemed, Hannie was only looking around for something better, Hannie was a mover, she wouldn't stick this dump for long.

'Just wait till she finds something worth getting her claws into. Old Ned won't see her for dust.'

He seemed confident of Hannie's opportunism, proud of

it. He didn't seem to look on her as his mother, more as a partner or a stooge, one who was playing the cards for the moment, but always at his direction. Niamh was horrified but Ciaran had laughed at her, he'd said Joss was only a kid, didn't she know when a kid was boasting to keep himself up?

The truth was Niamh didn't want Joss visiting her any more but she didn't know how to stop him coming to the cottage when she'd been happy enough to have him hang around the last holidays. She had the feeling that calculations were happening in his head and she didn't trust those calculations. She knew now they might be in a language that she barely even knew existed.

'She says I'm not to leave Joss in charge of the puppy,' Niamh said suddenly. Patrick looked startled. 'She says he'll forget, he'll just go off somewhere with Pippa and come back without her.' She felt stupid saying this, it wasn't what she'd meant to say, it just came out in a rush.

'She being Hannie?' Patrick spoke as though she was a child being taught to refer to her nursery-school teacher by name. 'Well, she should know, shouldn't she. I thought Ciaran was going home with you, don't you want to be with him over Christmas?'

Niamh looked up at Patrick, at his bland, amiable, well-fed face, and she knew abruptly that it was no use trying to get through to him, he'd just say something easy to keep her happy, he'd pat her head and soothe her down, lest she disturb his ease.

'Not really,' she said. 'I asked him but I'm sort of glad he didn't want to, it was a terrible idea really.'

She swirled her wellington about with the slices of dirty ice in the muddy puddle. There was no one she could speak to, it was no use telling Ned of her disquiet, he wouldn't even know what she was talking about.

Hannie would though, suddenly she was certain that Hannie would. But somehow she just couldn't say it to Hannie.

∾ *Chapter 32* ∾

'*P*atrick said you fucked up, married the wrong man, you should have married Lannigan.'

'Lannigan?' Hannie nudged the iron into the shoulder of Ned's shirt. 'What are you talking about, Joss? I don't even know anyone called Lannigan.' Her voice was dead-pan, bored, but beneath the feigned indifference she was taut with shock.

'What are you talking about?' she asked him again. 'And who's this Lannigan that I don't even know?'

'The auctioneer. The one in Dungarvan. See – you *do* know him. Patrick said you backed the wrong horse, said you'd have done better marrying Lannigan. More money than old Ned, more future.'

It was Christmas Eve. Ciaran had gone and Patrick had gone, and this morning Niamh's brother Donal had come and taken her home. Hannie hoped these changes accounted for Joss's sudden hysteria. She assumed that it *was* hysteria. Hysteria, and rage at her refusal of his latest project. Joss had come to her that morning with some tale of Ciaran inviting him to Belfast. He wanted money for the trip, he said, he planned to go straight after Christmas.

Hannie set the iron carefully on its end and buttoned the shirt loosely. Then she spread it face down on the board and started to fold in the sides and sleeves. Joss watched her minutely. The only sign was the faintest of tremors in her hands. She was good, his mother, except for the hands you would never have known he'd scored. Serve her right for refusing him, he thought. He felt marginally less savage towards her.

'Joss, stop telling lies,' she said, not looking up from her folding. 'Or, if you *must* tell lies, at least tell lies that are credible. Never attribute a statement that's out of character. Never say someone said something that they wouldn't ever have said.'

'He did say it, he did, he did, he did!' Joss was furious again, his rage the wilder as he heard himself contradicting like a child. She was cheating, diverting, pretending to be instructing him. She just didn't want to face what she'd done: how she'd fucked up, messed up, screwed things up for him and for them both. She wouldn't admit it, wouldn't accept the truth though it stared her in the face. It was all right for her, but he had to take the consequences of her stupid, poxy mistakes.

'You say Patrick told you I should have married Lannigan.' She was speaking now in that calm, even voice, the one she used when she was trying to put him down, to make him feel like a fool.

'Well, Patrick might have thought it,' she said, 'Patrick might even have said it, but Patrick would never, ever have said it to *you*. Therefore Joss, either he didn't say it at all or he said it to someone else and you were just sneaking round, eavesdropping.'

'He told Ciaran, I heard him, the old gas-bag, I heard him tell Ciaran – and I was *not* sneaking around, I was in the room all the time, they knew I was there.' Joss was shaking with fury, oblivious to everything, needing above all else to shatter her calm, destroy her power. Because if he didn't she'd manipulate him, make him do what she wanted, then everyone would turn on him the way they always did and he'd be fucked.

And he could see it and hear it, just as it had happened. Patrick, man of the world, know-all, sitting by Niamh's fire telling Ciaran that Hannie had backed the wrong horse, not caring that he, Joss, was listening, that it was *his* mother he was rubbishing and slagging off.

'It's natural enough,' Patrick had said. 'She threw in her lot with Ned's class because she thought it was the safest, the best bet. But it isn't where the power or the money lies now. She'd have done better with the auctioneer in Dungarvan. Our lot are useless in this new state – useless, sidelined, unable to integrate.'

His favourite theme, the old windbag, he was never done going on about it. Ciaran was into all that too, he'd jaw on with Patrick for hours. Modern Ireland's Brave New World. Nepotism and Corruption and Plenty of Jobs for the Children of the Rich. Meet the New Boss same as the Old Boss. The Provisionals had the measure of them – the only way forward was a clean sweep.

Except he didn't say the last bit to Patrick, he saved it for Niamh and Joss when Patrick had gone.

And Joss had slipped out, unnoticed, sick to the core that his mother was so vulnerable, that she was all he had to depend on.

'Joss,' Hannie said carefully, 'you can't have the money, no matter what you do or say. Do you understand? I haven't got the money, but even if I had, I wouldn't give it to you to go to Belfast. And that wouldn't change, no matter who I was married to. Not Lannigan, not Ned, not Patrick, nor anyone else.'

'So Patrick's on the list, is he?' Joss was on to it like a ferret on a rat. 'Well, well, Mother, not bad. Better than present company, I'll say that.' Joss's pale small face sneered at her through the dusk that was thickening around them. Her heart hurt her with sudden pity for him.

'Canada, eh? Better than this dump, but that wouldn't be hard,' he continued. 'Better make sure Joss keeps quiet, though, Mother. Better pay him to keep the cat in the bag till she's good and ready to let it out, eh? Wouldn't want old Ned getting wind of this change of plan now, would we? Old Ned might just boot her out in the cold before it's properly hatched.'

'You're wrong there, Joss, completely wrong.' The door had swung quietly open; Ned spoke from his stance in its frame. 'Old Ned won't be booting her out, as you put it, whatever she says or does. Old Ned happens to be very glad she fucked up, very glad she married him.' His voice trembled slightly but his face in the half-light was expressionless. 'Very glad indeed.'

Then he turned on his heel and went back down the corridor the way he'd come.

Joss's white face was whiter. He stared at his mother. Hannie crossed to the door and closed it, pressing on the handle till she heard the latch click home. She switched on the light and the dusk at the window thickened abruptly into blackness. She took a pillow slip from the laundry basket and laid it on the ironing board. Then she picked up the iron and moved it backwards, forwards, backwards, forwards, her knuckles showing as white as the linen.

Joss extracted a cigarette from the packet she'd set on the mantelpiece. He lit it with her lighter and crossed to the window. He moved his shoulders once, compulsively, as though to loosen them. Then he picked up his old pose of indifference and swung it around himself like a cloak.

'What will you say?'

'Nothing. He won't ask.'

Joss stared out at the sudden night beyond the panes.

'So, Mother,' he said casually, 'I'm not the only one that goes sneaking around, eavesdropping.'

Hannie's mouth tightened but she didn't speak. The room they were in was at the end of the corridor; if Ned had wanted to find them he must come the way he had come, he had no other choice. But she didn't say it, she couldn't bring herself to defend him, she was far too threatened and angry for that.

How long had Ned been standing there, how much had he heard? That night she lay in the dark going over and over Joss's words, her own words, trying to remember exactly what they'd said. Had he heard the whole lot, or only from where Joss had jumped in with Patrick being 'on her list'? Bad as that was, it wasn't as bad as Joss's account of Patrick's words to Ciaran: his precious cousin not only understanding her motives in marrying him but sitting discussing the whole business quite casually with Niamh's boyfriend.

He couldn't have heard that, she decided. If he had he'd never have said what he'd finally said. She breathed deeply in relief.

But he'd said *fucked up*, he'd quoted Joss quoting Patrick's words. So he must have heard. Suddenly she was coldly certain he'd been standing there listening from the very start.

So why had he spoken out when he needn't have, when he could have just slipped away without ever revealing he'd heard their exchange? Why had he told Joss so firmly he wouldn't be throwing her out?

To subvert Joss's pathetic little blackmail attempt? To bolster her authority with her delinquent son?

She dismissed these thoughts. She wasn't used to magnanimity, she was used to self-interest, had no difficulty in accepting it as she'd accepted Ned's acquisition of her and her own self-interested compliance in the arrangement. Their marriage was a bargain which suited both of them and when it ceased to suit it would be broken or re-negotiated. That Ned should suddenly transcend the bargain was a possibility altogether beyond her experience.

Ned had said what he'd said on account of his own mistake in marrying her, she decided. Once done, he wouldn't disown his action, that would be a worse weakness than the first weakness. He'd done it and he would stand over it, that was Ned. Let Patrick think what he liked.

As for Patrick, she wasn't really surprised. Patrick would be mindful only for himself and his own comforts. That was why he wasn't married now, though he had been once, why he had no real roots or attachments. Too inconvenient, someone else. Patrick was as selfish as she was – one of her kind. No, not entirely one of her kind. She revised her self-judgement fractionally. She wasn't lazy, a love of ease had never marked her out. For a moment she hated Patrick, briefly and completely. Then she dismissed her hatred as she had already dismissed the man.

* * *

Hannie sat forward with her elbows on the pew in front of her and her face in her hands, a sort of leaning crouch that imitated Ned's. Christmas Day. The clergyman droned from the altar regions but she didn't mind him, he was easy to ignore. She didn't mind the crouch either, it was strange but not uncomfortable, and gave at least the illusion of privacy.

Her mind kept returning to Joss's words about Lannigan. She went over and over the conversation, trying to work out its consequences, trying to mediate her fury against Ned.

She couldn't understand herself why she was so angry with him. It wasn't a pretty conversation that he'd overheard, it had put Joss in a bad light and herself in a worse one, but essentially it was information that Ned already knew. Hearing Joss's speculations, having the reality of the way she lived her life spelled out like that might be distasteful, but it didn't actually change anything.

So why did she mind so much, why was she so angry?

It was being known, she realised. Being known and judged and pitied. It was unbearable to her that he should see what her life really consisted of: the narrowness of her options, the sordid smallness of her many shifts and prevarications.

And if it was shameful to her that he should see and know, it was unendurable that she should have to see her life reflected through his eyes, assessed and diminished by his upright unyielding values.

Old Ned happens to be very glad she fucked up. That's what he'd said to Joss. Old Ned was prepared to forgive her whatever she did.

Big deal. She didn't want to be forgiven, she wanted to be young again, young and free and strong. She wanted to live as life took her and to hell with the consequences, to hell with anyone who didn't like it, she wanted to laugh at them as she'd always done, to despise their cowardly, safe self-righteousness, to move on.

There was a peal of organ music from a hidden tape recorder and everyone abandoned their crouches and heaved themselves upright. The recorded carol began. Most people mouthed to it but a few sang defiantly, their voices quavering and rough against the effortless river of joy from the choir on the machine. The congregation was elderly and sparse and well wrapped up, though the church glowed with overhead heaters and was far too warm for these denizens of old and draughty houses. After the initial relief they shuffled uncomfortably and glanced with longing at the chilly mouldering aisles closed off by plate-glass partitions from the sealed box in the nave where they sat.

The church was decked for Christmas. There were great stands of vegetation: chrysanthemums and poinsettias, holly and bay. The brass memorials to dead soldiers on the walls shone with fresh polish, the sills of the narrow lancet windows were snowy with cotton wool, stubby red Christmas candles poked up through clustered holly and trailing green ivy.

Alison has been busy, Hannie thought sourly. It was years and years since she'd been in a church but she recognised an act of solidarity when she saw one: this was a small, carefully tended rock pool on the edge of a great surging sea of threatening otherness. She glanced at Ned's absorbed oblivious face and cursed her own stupidity in making this placatory gesture. It only made her feel more reckless and deepened her alienation from his world. Abruptly she gave up telling herself he'd done nothing wrong and let herself drift on a tide of anger and morose despair.

The rest of the day passed in an agony of slowness. Joss had stayed in bed and she was too relieved to be rid of him to nag about getting up. He came downstairs to eat Christmas dinner and was heading up to his room again directly the food was eaten. Ned called him back.

'Washing-up,' he said. 'I thought we could do it together. To thank your mother for the dinner she's just cooked. Then there's presents.'

Ned gave her two packages. The first held an ebony fan that had belonged to his mother, the second a sea-blue chiffon scarf with a border of pink and orange flowers. She liked the little blue scarf in spite of herself. She shook it out and knotted it round her neck. His mother's fan she would sell later.

Ned gave Joss a book on insects and Joss gave Ned a new clasp knife that she'd bought in a shop in Waterford Ned was always recommending. She gave Ned a pair of extra-thick wellington socks from the same shop. She'd thought badly of them at the time, it hadn't seemed much of a present, just picking out socks and putting them on the account, but what was the point of spending his money on something he mightn't like?

It felt different now. She nearly left them in the drawer and faced him empty-handed, even a pair of socks was more than she wanted to give him. For Joss there was an envelope which he was careful not to open in front of Ned. He needn't have bothered, she thought sourly, there wasn't much in it, Ned wouldn't have disapproved. But that too, was more than she wanted to give.

Ned suggested a walk and Hannie put on her coat and her boots and went through the motions. They tramped through the muddy half-light but she closed herself off and repelled his efforts at conversation. Ned didn't try very hard, he was relieved when he heard himself lapse into silence.

They went by the lower field to check on the sheep. A heron got up from a reedbed and drifted heavily across the fading sky. Bess rounded up wandering ewes and Ned stood counting while Hannie stared at the sheep and they stared back, black-faced, lop-eared their strange diamond-shaped eyes impenetrably blank and alien. The heron went flopping across again, it let out a short sharp shriek of protest at their prolonged intrusion. The rain came seeping out of the dusk.

Hannie thought of all the hot bright riotous Christmases she'd spent with people who longed for Christmases like this and wondered at their nostalgia.

∾ *Chapter 33* ∾

'God, what a disaster.' Niamh closed her eyes at the memory and spoke the words aloud to her empty kitchen. At least she hadn't insisted on taking Ciaran home with her. That was about the only redeeming feature of the last two days. She thought bitterly of her brothers and sisters.

'They just want me to look nice and wear pretty clothes and put everyone else's needs before my own,' she used to complain to Maeve. Well that wasn't true any more. Now they just wanted her to wear odd clothes and to say odd things and to go on being 'peculiar', the baby, their peculiar little Niamh.

So it wasn't even that they were incapable of changing, they were simply incapable of seeing her as she was.

Perhaps it was time for a total reassessment, she thought. Perhaps she should go back to Dublin and eat humble pie. Get hold of Maeve, tell her she'd been right all along, the country was a rotten idea and was there any chance of sharing a studio after all?

But then she'd have nothing to live on. Her father didn't want her in the city. He wouldn't give her even this one year to see what she could do.

Well, so what, she could sign on, couldn't she? She could stop being so bourgeois and spineless? Maeve did, and Ciaran did, and everyone did when they were trying to make it after the end of college and before they'd established themselves as working artists.

It wasn't a big deal or a public shame the way her father made it out to be.

Anyway, it was either that or teaching and once you started the teaching game it was only a matter of time before the work slipped altogether. She'd tried to explain that to her father, but he didn't understand. He asked her couldn't she paint at the weekends?

She'd said it wasn't something you could just turn on and off like a tap, you had to live it and breathe it, or it didn't grow out of you. She had blushed when she'd said this, she didn't know why because she'd meant every word of it, but suddenly she was as embarrassed as if she'd been standing there telling him about her sex life. And then when she looked at him she'd seen that he was embarrassed too. He wasn't looking at her, he was poking with his ash plant at a new rat-hole in among the nettles behind the old harrow. Poking and trying not to hear.

And then she'd felt miserable; miserable, and angry at herself and at her father because she couldn't stop minding what he thought enough to defy him. And after that he had talked to Ned, and he'd come home happy and full of his new arrangement and she'd let herself be manoeuvred.

Ned had continued to pester his friends for commissions. James stubbornly went deaf when he mentioned Jacko, but he'd got money up front from a Mrs Cardew for a view of her cottage garden, and there was a widow who'd sold her dead husband's crumbling birthright and now wanted a picture of it to hang in her bright new draught-free bungalow. Both had supplied photos.

Ned said he understood perfectly that she didn't want to paint people's houses or their pets. Such projects were simply earners, 'potboilers' that paid the bills, let you do what you really wanted to do, that was why you did them.

He had always taken on extra commissions himself, he said. Bits of data-collecting and map-making projects and statistical work. Dull, but necessary, and not a bad discipline. They taught you how to operate on two levels: to work on a pot-boiler lightly, keeping your passion for the real thing.

Niamh had paid the electricity with Mrs Cardew's advance and then started in on the painting of her garden. She'd blocked it in fairly easily and then put it briefly aside. The aside had been a mistake, she should have just finished it in the one go; in the interval she'd grown self-conscious and then stupidly she'd left it uncovered and Ciaran had seen it. After that it was hopeless, the more she tried the more she hated it. Worse, the hatred seemed to have spilled over into her real work. She'd been doing a painting from a papier-mâché bust she'd made, the head and shoulders of an androgynous figure just looking up as though it had caught some half-heard sound. The bust had been experimental but it had something, a peculiar quick attentiveness, and she'd wanted to see if she could take this further in a painting.

Some hope. She'd been making herself go on trying, but she couldn't get her confidence back, she couldn't put Ciaran's critical appraising glance out of her head. On a good day she dabbed miserably; on a bad day she just stood. She'd stopped believing in herself and it was nearly easier to struggle with flowerbeds and roof angles than to trust to her own fragile vision.

Ned was trying hard to help in his own way, Niamh knew this, but somehow it just made it all worse. Now she had him on her back as well as her father. Ciaran said she was out of her mind to be even thinking of potboilers, or whatever it was Ned called them. You had to do what you wanted to do and not deviate or compromise or you'd end up making crap work and not even knowing it. Niamh, stung, said she hadn't noticed him making any work at all, but he just grinned at her and said no work was better than crap work and the world could wait.

'I hope it's not holding its breath,' she'd said, and flounced off to stare hard at the garden-photos one more time.

Now she wandered into the little studio room and stood trying to look at her canvases with a cool and appraising eye. It was her own fault, she thought, it was no good blaming anyone else, she'd just have to take some decisions and act on them. First, the studio had to be made more habitable. The chimney smoked so badly that she'd long since given up lighting a fire in there. She wore three jumpers and fingerless gloves, and she was still frozen. Jackdaws, likely as not, Ciaran said. A nest in the chimney. She'd asked him to clear it out but he wouldn't.

'Would you wise up, I know sod-all about chimneys. Ask Ned – he's the landlord.'

He was right, but she didn't want to ask Ned, she paid so little rent and she didn't like to bother him. Well, that would have to change, she'd just have to bother him. She'd go straight up to the house now and tell Ned that she wasn't going to do Mrs Cardew's commission or the widow's commission, she wasn't going to do any commissions at all. And even if she wanted to, she couldn't because of the chimney.

'Of course she won't stick at it,' Hannie said, lifting rashers out of the pan and holding them there a moment for the fat to drip. 'All this talk of integrity and jackdaws is just noise. Noise and excuses. Because she is doing no work.' She laid the rashers in the serving dish and put it back into the Aga to keep warm. Joss sat at the kitchen table, waiting. Ned was striding around the room in his stockinged feet, worrying aloud about Niamh. He stopped pacing.

'She will, Hannie, she will,' he said. 'If she gets a bit of support, a bit of encouragement. When she sees money everything will change, when she realises she's making her own way, that she's independent.

'And she's right, she can't work when she's frozen. It'll be different when the chimney's cleaned, I wish she'd mentioned it before, I'll take the brushes down tomorrow, have it clear in a couple of hours.'

Hannie broke eggs into the sizzling fat. 'No,' she said with finality. 'You're wrong, she won't stick at it. She won't stick at it and you can't make her, no matter how hard you want it for her, no matter how many people you persuade into commissioning pictures that she doesn't want to paint.'

'I'm not making her do anything,' Ned protested. 'If she doesn't want commissions she doesn't have to take them. I'm only trying to help her do what she wants to do and become a professional artist. To hear you talk you'd think I was trying to make her do something she *doesn't* want to do.' Ned warmed to his subject, he was glad to see her belligerent, he found it easier than silent antagonism and less confusing. Neither of them had mentioned the overheard conversation, but it was there between them like the smell of decay. Communication, any communication was, to Ned's way of thinking, a definite advance.

'And what makes you so sure she won't stick?' he demanded. 'She got top marks at college. She's got talent, character . . .'

Hannie slid the fried eggs on to the dish and lifted two more from the rack. She cracked them into the pan without turning her head.

'It is not to do with talent,' she said. She flicked hot fat over the bubbling whites. 'Nor character either. It's the way she is bred.'

Ned waited. She didn't seem to be about to add to the statement.

'The way she is bred?'

'Like a Dutch *hausfrau* who knows what the future will hold.' Hannie bent for the dish again. 'Born to a hearth, to shined copper pans and her grandmother's linen. This is what she is, it doesn't matter what she wants to be.' Two more eggs left the pan and the dish was returned to the oven.

'That's nonsense, Hannie, that's got nothing to do with it, plenty of artists come from stable middle-class homes.'

'Male artists . . .'

'Male, female, what does it matter? You underestimate her, Hannie, she's more than that, she wants her life to be more than that.'

'I told you – it's not what she wants or what she thinks she wants, it's what she is, what she can't avoid. She'll marry – it's her nature's imperative – she'll have no choice. Then there'll be children and their care will come first because that's the way she is, and then it will be too late. All this talk of painting is only talk, Ned. I think already she knows this somewhere, and somewhere she accepts it.' She half-turned, saw Ned's face.

'Oh, not Ciaran, she won't marry Ciaran, he's only a passion, he isn't a marriage. And anyway he'll leave her, already he's bored.'

Hannie picked up the dish of bacon and eggs and carried it to the table where Joss waited. 'Perhaps it is *you* who wants her life to be more, Ned,' she said. 'Perhaps you should leave her alone.'

'That's ridiculous.' Ned was stung. 'Why should I care what her life is, so long as she's happy?'

'Oh, because in some way you identify. Your young self with the way she is now. And you don't like her young man, you don't want him to have her affection. But I think it's already too late, much too late –'

Late that night the phone rang and Joss answered it.

'Hey, Joss, how're ye doin', man? Niamh there?' Ciaran's voice was slurred, there were party noises in the background.

'I'll get her.'

'Wise up, would yous? Tell her I got held up, couldn't make it, say to expect me when she sees me, not before. Hell, Joss, say what you like, use your imagination, tell her I'm dyin' for her, tell her I ran out of money and got cut off . . .'

Then he talked for another ten minutes or so. Rabbiting on, this and that. Then he hung up.

Joss passed the message on to Niamh the next morning, putting in some stuff about Ciaran missing her, watching her face light, telling her no, Ciaran hadn't said why he'd got held up, maybe he needed a break?

Watching her face as it made itself go blank.

It was no fun, baiting Niamh. He wished Ciaran would come back. Niamh by herself was poor company.

∾ *Chapter 34* ∾

'– and then she told Ned he was jealous of Ciaran. And he just stood there, the dirty old git, never denied it, never said a word. So it must be true.' Joss was feeding Danno's sparrow hawk with titbits of badger entrail, speaking softly and evenly, not looking at the bird just as Danno had told him, not looking at Danno, either.

'Who'd have thought it, eh Danno? Old Ned fancying Niamh. Young enough to be his granddaughter. And her daddy all gratitude and can't do enough for him on account of his kindness to his little girl. Not half as kind as he'd like to be, eh Danno?' Joss chuckled.

'Ciaran won't be surprised when I tell him,' Joss continued. 'Ciaran was wise to him all along – said the *auld fella* was never done knocking the door mornings, keeping Miss Niamh standing on the step in her nightie, talking away.' Joss was getting into his stride now, relishing the words, mimicking Ciaran's Northern accent. 'And him only just through over-hauling her himself, lying out on the bed upstairs too knackered to move, listening to every word the old fool sez to her, laughing away.'

Danno's gaze was fixed on the back of the smooth yellow head, the smooth-packaged self. I'm like a rabbit watching a stoat weave, Danno thought, unable to stop himself. He was mesmerised and immobile, helpless before the undulating death-dance.

'That's something to put in your pipe and smoke, eh Danno? You wouldn't mind being kind to Niamh yourself now, would you, Danno? There's not many would mind, I'd say, and Joss wouldn't be the one to blame them, not a bit, he wouldn't. What's a little kindness between friends, eh Danno? If only Old Ned knew how kind Joss has been. How green he'd be; how – green – he – would – be.'

Joss spoke the last words separately and deliberately, as though he were remembering them to himself. Danno rose abruptly, breaking the spell. The sparrow hawk, startled into rage, scuttled sideways on the perch, jerking furiously at her jesses.

'Joss was here just now,' Danno said.

'I know.' Hannie flicked her cigarette into an empty tea mug. The hot ash fizzled a moment in the cold dregs. 'We are all visiting. Niamh will be the next. She has come rushing back from the bosom of her family, quivering with indignation and new resolutions.' Hannie was wearing an old jersey, full of holes, and a pair of baggy cord trousers stuck into wellingtons. Ned's clothes. Her step was springy, she seemed in good spirits, on the edge of being pleased with herself.

'You should build a barricade, Danno, a high thorn stockade as we do against wild beasts in Africa. But there must be a secret entrance, perhaps an underground tunnel, a souterrain, isn't that what such a passage is called here? Will you dig a souterrain, Danno? A fine one, just for me, so I can visit you while all the rest are held at bay?' She roamed restlessly round the room as she talked. 'Oh, don't look so dismayed, Danno, you can keep a pile of stones handy, lob them at me when you can't stand the thought of me, drive me off. I understand, really I do, there are plenty of times when I can't stand the thought of me myself. Besides, it's only right for people like you to throw stones at women like me, whatever your Jesus once said.' She shot a glance at him, but he was avoiding looking at her.

'You don't speak, Danno? Is it possible you don't believe me? That you don't believe there's ever a time that I can't stand the thought of myself?' She stopped pacing and stood staring at the darkness in the great black window. Half past five going on midnight. She needed something stronger than tea. 'But it's true,' she insisted, 'I assure you it's true.'

'What's the matter with Joss, Hannie?'

'The matter? Why? What's he done?' Her voice had changed, it was casual, non-committal, but underneath it was on guard. She didn't turn round, but he could see the alertness in the back of her shoulders. This was a question she'd been asked before.

'Nothing. He hasn't done anything.' Danno didn't have to look at her to catch her relief. 'But he was here, and he was talking.'

'Human beings do, it's one of the characteristics of the species, some say it's most of the problem –'

'He was talking about sex,' Danno said stubbornly. 'About sex and Niamh.'

'Oh? Was it interesting? What did he say?' She was lighting a cigarette, her back still turned.

'It wasn't so much what he said, more the tone of the saying.' Danno scraped carefully at the inside of the emptied badger's skin. He hoped she wouldn't make him spell it out, that he'd just have to warn her obliquely and she'd do something to keep Joss away from Niamh.

There was a moment's pause. 'What did he say, Danno?' she asked again, her tone quiet and relentless with an edge of contempt in it. She was bullying him, he realised, willing him to let it go. But he wouldn't. Danno braced himself.

'He thinks a lot of Ciaran,' he said, getting the words out quickly. She waited. He opened his mouth to say more but it didn't come.

'And not much of Ned?' she finished for him.

'And not much of Ned.'

'And you think that Ciaran is a bad influence and I shouldn't let Joss spend time with him, is that it?' Again she waited. 'OK, let's try again. You think that Joss is a bad influence on Ciaran and I should protect him from my delinquent son?'

'He – Joss – intimated at a certain ... physical intimacy with Niamh.' Danno got it out in an embarrassed gabble. Hannie was very still for a moment. Then she threw back her head and laughed with relief.

'And you believe *that* – it is *that* that has upset you so? Oh Danno, that's just boasting, wishful thinking, boy's fantasy. You remember boy's fantasies, surely? Masturbation, wet dreams, all that stuff?'

She stopped herself. 'On second thoughts, perhaps you don't. I bet you masturbated with a pin-up of a Labrador and had wet dreams about hawks,' she said nastily. 'What is it with you all? Niamh might as well be a bitch on heat for the effect she's having on you.'

But she'd misjudged him. Danno wasn't to be ridiculed into submission so easily.

'I may be inexperienced, Hannie, but I'm not the sort of prude you seem to think me. This was more than boy's fantasy, there was something twisted about it, something horrible.'

'You're getting this out of proportion, Danno. This is the spoiled priest in you talking.'

'Who told you that?'

'Mrs Coady.'

'Well, you tell Kathleen Coady I'm disappointed in her. Tell her I didn't think she'd be wasting her time on erroneous tittle-tattle, I'd thought more of her.'

'Erroneous?'

'That's what I said. But we're getting off the subject, which is Joss, not me. What's wrong with him, Hannie?'

'Wrong?' She left her stance by the window and coasted around the room again, trying to find the words that would put him off. This was a new side of Danno, she wasn't prepared for his determination.

'Nothing's wrong,' she said coldly. 'He's just not very well-adjusted. A bit odd, if you really want to know. But not schizophrenic or psychotic,' she added bitterly, 'they all seem to agree on that.'

'You've had him tested?'

'Oh, he's been tested,' Hannie said evasively. 'He's had all the tests.'

She got up, strolled over to the window, pausing to look straight into the yellow eyes of the sparrow hawk in a way she knew would anger Danno. Then she stood with her back to him, smoking and staring out at the darkness. Why not tell him about Joss, she thought suddenly, it might be a relief, she'd never just said it out, she was always so locked into trying to prove the opposite. That black was white, that Joss wasn't as she knew he was. And Danno saw no one, it didn't matter what he said or thought, talking to him was scarcely more indiscreet than talking to herself.

'Joss is odd,' she said quietly. 'Not normal. But in a way that doesn't show up on tests.'

'Autistic?'

'No, not autistic.' There was a pause. 'Corrupt.'

'Corrupt?'

'Corrupt,' Hannie agreed. 'That was the word I used, Danno. Sometimes you sound like a bloody parrot.'

Danno laid down the skin he was cleaning. His questions weren't idly curious, he had asked about Joss because he was anxious for Niamh. But he wasn't that anxious, he didn't want to hear what he was learning now, he realised, he didn't want Hannie's confidence, he wanted to tell her the problem and have her take it away.

And she was doing the opposite. He was too private, too unused to human intercourse to accept her secrets lightly. He'd made a mistake in pressing her, had uncovered far more than he wanted to know. So he swivelled on his tatty revolving chair and sat loosely and quietly, his grey eyes averted behind their spectacles and vaguely focused on the floor.

'It's his nature,' Hannie said finally, still not turning. 'That bird there – she's a killer, you can't blame her, it's her nature. Well, Joss is corrupt – you can't blame him, it's his nature.'

There was another silence.

'Hannie, that hawk is a raptor, a bird of prey,' Danno said carefully. 'It's an evolved killer, has spent thousands of years honing itself into what it is. Joss is a human being, not a raptor, it's not his destiny to be corrupt, you can't compare the two.'

'Can't I?' Hannie said, her voice low and stubborn. 'Who says I can't? You, Danno? What do you know? Joss likes corruption. He likes hurting, spoiling, dirtying. Going the crooked way.' She spoke so quietly now that Danno had to strain to catch her words.

'Did something happen?'

No answer from Hannie. She was staring at the great black curtainless window, unredeemed by moonlight or stars. She blew out smoke so it rolled and billowed defiantly across its darkness.

'Was he born like that?'

'Was he born like that, did he get like that? Who knows? What made you the way you are, an old woman fussing away at these horrible birds? Because you were born like that or because they wouldn't have you as a priest?'

Danno gave an almost imperceptible start and straightened very slightly in his chair. 'Is that what Kathleen told you?' he asked quietly.

'She said they wouldn't have you because you're illegitimate. She said that's how things were when you were young.'

'She's got it wrong, I never asked them, I didn't want to go.'

Hannie looked at him, at the stubborn, closed hurt in his face. He'd wanted to all right. It was as Kathleen had said, he just wouldn't give them the satisfaction of turning him down. She crossed to the window seat and picked up her coat.

She stepped out into a darkness that crept and clung at her neck, her face, her hands. The cold had softened a little, cloud

hid the stars. She'd left her torch behind at Danno's, could see nothing, her feet found the puddled track and followed it haltingly. She wondered at the black closeness of this darkness that moved and breathed like an intimate against her skin. There was nothing else beside it, nothing in the world but the stones under her feet and the moist black night.

She'd seen his face as she left, the ill-concealed hurt reflecting her over-stepped mark. She'd been almost pleased at the time, she was sick of being patronised, of being the problem, the one always in the wrong. She was a problem and Joss was a problem, but the lives all around her weren't so perfect either, they were just better camouflaged here where they belonged. Sometimes they needed reminding of this. And sometimes it helped your own pain to take a swipe at someone else, even if that someone else came close to being your only friend.

She tramped on. Already the strength she felt from her deliberate little cruelty had all but leached away, leaving nothing but self-disgust in its place. She felt rudderless and directionless, like the dead sheep the November rains had carried down the river. Day after day it had drifted up and down, up and down, moving swiftly away with the pull of the sea's ebbing tide, pushing back again as it rose. Bloated, a perch for the gulls. Till it snagged on some drowned tree and left off its journeying.

❧ *Chapter 35* ❧

*I*t was that dark, dank time that stretched and sagged like a bit of old rope between Christmas and the New Year. It was hard for Hannie to pull herself out of despondency, harder still to stay that way. The tentative easing and harmonising of her relationship with Ned had disintegrated like old silk suddenly restored to light, now parting at the lightest touch. There seemed little to be gained in trying to darn it together again, only to watch it open somewhere else under the strain of the new stitches.

Besides, she had the measure of the life here and of the people who lived it alongside her and she expected little from either. Nothing was going to change, so what was the point of trying? She almost let herself decide against the effort.

Ned's relations came from Galway the next day and saved her. They arrived without writing or phoning, a car drew up and a man got out, walked over the thin gravel, hesitated in ▮▮▮▮ the heavy iron knocker. Hannie heard and watched discreetly from an upstairs window. When the knocker thumped the first time she made no move to answer it. It pounded again and she went slowly downstairs, leaving whoever it was plenty of time to give up and go back to wherever he'd come from.

He went on knocking. She undid the snib but the heavy door, swollen with winter damp, stuck fast near the top. She heaved and pulled, calling to the man on the other side to put his shoulder to it. The door gave suddenly under their combined efforts, it burst open and he stumbled in after it. He gathered himself. His name was Andrew Clarke, he explained,

he was a great-nephew of Ned's by marriage, now come with his wife to visit because they were in the area and didn't want to pass Ned's door.

'It's only a call on the off-chance. I haven't seen Ned since I was a boy, I doubt he'd even remember me.'

Hannie let him run out of words and stand awkwardly. 'Ned's gone to Waterford,' she said, which was true. 'I don't know when he'll be back,' she added, which wasn't. 'You can wait if you want.' Her tone was utterly discouraging.

The man, relieved, started backing out. On the far edge of her vision Hannie glimpsed a movement which she knew was Joss, sidling off behind a door.

'You must come in and wait,' she said, changing her mind abruptly. 'Ned will want to see you – he won't be long now – come in, make yourselves at home, stay for dinner.'

'We wouldn't want to put you to any trouble.' Andrew Clarke looked confused. 'We'll call again some other time.'

'It's no trouble and you can't go now, you've only just come. What will Ned say if he gets back and finds I haven't held on to you?'

Hannie's voice was false and almost arch. Alarm flickered across Andrew's face, he went on trying to refuse but she wouldn't listen. Then he gave in abruptly, looking embarrassed and muttering about having a word with Nora.

Hannie stood and watched him cross the patchy gravel and bend to talk to his wife through the wound-down window of the car. She knew that this great-nephew of Ned's hadn't any idea who she was, nor what was the set-up. He had plainly expected the elderly bachelor Ned, perhaps a housekeeper, certainly not a wife. She knew from the set of his back that the woman in the car didn't want to come in and he was telling her they had to, they couldn't get out of it now. She was arguing, but not very hard, she'd give in soon because he was asking her to.

Hannie didn't care, let them go or stay, it was all one to her. And Ned wouldn't want to see them, she knew that, Ned had had enough of other people's company for the time being. Yet it would be better than nothing, better than sitting silently with Ned by the fire, Joss in Niamh's cottage, she wondering should she go over there or let him alone.

A slim woman, dark-haired and pretty, got slowly out of the car and came with her husband to where Hannie was standing waiting. Hannie put out her hand.

'I'm Ned's wife, Hannie,' she said easily, catching the shock on the man's face. The woman was blank. Either she was better at concealment or simply too preoccupied with her own reluctance.

'Nora,' the woman introduced herself shyly. 'But really we can't put you to this trouble, it was only a whim of Andrew's, we were passing so near to you . . .' She flushed and the words ran out. Hannie took her by the arm and drew her in through the door.

'It's no trouble,' she said again, 'it's a pleasure. You'll stay the night.'

It wasn't a question. Andrew had no choice but to follow.

When Ned came back they were drinking gin by the drawing room fire, Hannie playing the hostess in a dark dress, her hair smoothed and restrained, her manner similar. She said they were staying over and they didn't contradict her. Surprising himself, Ned was pleased.

He hardly knew Andrew, a grandson of one of his dead wife's many brothers, and remembered him only dimly as a lanky youth who had blushed and mumbled when spoken to except when asked about rugby which it seemed he played with flair and talent. He didn't look like an athlete now. Ned saw a big, loose-boned, good-humoured, peace-loving man in his late thirties, the powerful body running a little to fat.

Rugby? Andrew laughed quietly. Those days were long gone, he was his own man now, an auctioneer in a biggish town outside of Galway, his business secure, his peers suggesting to him that he think of standing in the next election.

He hadn't decided yet, he said, he was still turning it over, taking soundings. Of course it was harder for a Protestant to get elected, but Nora was Catholic and her family was long-term Fine Gael; that would help him with the nomination.

He spoke with so natural a modesty, so simple and serious a belief in his life, that Ned could not but listen and warm to him.

He liked Nora too, but he couldn't get her to relax. She was shy and she wanted to stop being shy and open to them, but she wasn't at ease. She was unsure how to behave with her husband's relatives, and over-anxious to deliver whatever it was they expected of her.

Nora was the daughter of a strong farmer on the Offaly-Galway border, one of many children, used to company and noise and laughter, to warmth and work and family. She knew that as a young man Andrew had hero-worshipped his great-uncle and she wanted to do well so he'd be proud of her. But she felt more out of place here than she'd expected to and she wasn't used to such self-consciousness. Everything – her voice, her attitudes, her clothes – seemed suddenly somehow different and open to question.

She had a six-year-old son, she told Hannie, a girl of four and another of eighteen months. A sister of hers was visiting over Christmas and they'd taken this chance to go away together. It was Andrew's idea, for herself she thought Christmas so precious a time that she wanted to be with the children, but still it was only a couple of days, a business visit in Youghal, an overnight in a quiet hotel, a little driving around to show her where his father's family had come from. It was clear that she missed her home and her children and yearned to get back to them.

She was pleased when she discovered Joss. She liked teenage boys, she said, following Hannie out to the kitchen and settling in beside him at the kitchen table, happy to leave the grown-ups to her husband. Hannie fed Joss baked beans and fried eggs while she cooked dinner for the rest of them and Nora did her best at conversation. She made little headway. Joss ate fast, then rose to go.

'I'll be at Niamh's,' he told his mother. He didn't even glance at Nora.

'You feel for them so at this age, don't you?' Nora said, as the back door shut behind him. 'I always remember what it was like – the wanting to join in and not knowing how, it must be harder for an only –' She stopped herself. 'Or maybe it's easier. No competition, no thinking the others are prettier or cleverer or stronger.' She finished with a small, embarrassed laugh. Hannie said nothing. She was thinking that for once Joss had a point.

They had dinner in the dining room. Ned was glad of Joss's absence, he was still recovering from his discovery of the depths of Joss's alienation and the strange complicitous relationship between the boy and his mother. Besides he was tired of making an effort, tired of Joss's odd disruptive presence, tired of his own face reflecting from the mirrors of his stepson's shuttered eyes. He wanted to sit quietly and talk.

Ned saw the ease with which Andrew moved through his life and he guessed that much of this ease must have come through Nora. He plainly liked his relations through marriage, liked the influence of her big noisy family, liked having a foot in both religious camps and feeling neither disloyalty nor any need to convert. For him there was to be no self-imposed silence, no holding a little apart from the daily life of community or state. He and Nora loved and understood each other: life was for rearing your children, making your way, earning the respect of your friends and your community. It was all simple and healthy and straightforward.

Andrew was confused by Ned. He had been in awe of his legend since childhood, and their few meetings had deepened his sense that here was someone different and extraordinary. Now he looked at his great-uncle and wondered what all that adventuring had been about. He saw an old man with an odd wife and a strange stepson, trying to run a bit of a farm and

knowing less about it than one of Nora's half-grown brothers. He felt pity for Ned because he hadn't stayed at home and done something with his life, but had frittered it away, travelling with nomadic peoples in forgotten places.

He said all this to Nora in bed that night and she listened and held his hand while he talked. He said he wondered now why he had romanticised Ned, why his life had once seemed so special to him. His own immaturity, perhaps? He saw Ned's travelling now for what it was: a refusal to accept the changing world; ultimately probably an inability to grow up and adapt and take on responsibility.

He didn't know what to make of Hannie, nor why Ned had married her. Could it be that Ned was in love with her?

Nora said she thought Ned had married Hannie because he was lonely. It was a shame he'd had no children of his own, he'd have been a wonderful father, it made sense of life if you had children . . .

The next day they were easier in themselves and not so inclined to be overawed. Ned saw that he had been judged and found wanting, and he saw that Hannie saw it as well. He smiled at her ruefully across the kitchen and she grinned back at him. They were companionable in their outsiderliness.

Ned took Andrew off about the place but Nora stayed with Hannie, insisting that they do the washing up together. Hannie looked at her mutely and handed over the gloves and the mop. Nora could wash up if she wanted, but she could do it alone. She filled a mug with hot water and put a plastic bottle of ear-mite drops into it to warm. Then she knelt on the kitchen floor, clamped the wriggling puppy between her knees, lifted each ear in turn and squeezed in the drops. Joss came downstairs. He ignored Nora and stood watching her.

'Ciaran's come back, Niamh's creaming herself.'

'Niamh that you were round with last night?' Nora asked from the sink.

Hannie released Pippa and got up off her knees. 'Ned's tenant,' she said. 'She's a painter. Ciaran's the boyfriend.'

At once Nora wanted to meet her. It seemed she had a young cousin who might go to art school.

'Joss, take Nora round to Niamh's and introduce her. Tell Niamh to show Nora her paintings.'

'She'll love that.'

Even Nora heard the sarcasm in his voice.

'She doesn't have to if she doesn't want to, it must be so hard to believe in yourself when you're only beginning.'

Joss threw a Who's-This-Moron? look at Hannie. Then he ushered her through the door and followed after her.

Ciaran and Niamh would still be in bed, of course. Hannie hoped Nora would be shocked. Perhaps she'd tell her husband that Ned was allowing all sorts of carryings-on on his property.

Joss seemed to like her, despite the looks he was throwing around; Hannie watched them talking as they walked together across the yard. The damp was on Nora's dark curly hair, there was a glow on her fair skin, she was enjoying herself. Joss looked easy and young and almost animated. Hannie curdled with jealousy.

They were away longer than expected. It seemed Ciaran and Niamh had indeed been in bed and Nora hadn't been shocked at all, she'd lit the fire and put on the kettle and when they'd come down she'd eaten a second breakfast with them.

Ned came back with Andrew and they had lunch. Nora was animated, she tried to draw Hannie into household conversations but Hannie wouldn't have it. She tried again, but Hannie kept on thwarting her so she gave up and talked about her youngest brother who was Joss's age. Hannie caught Ned's eye on her during one of these attempts and she saw to her surprise that he didn't mind that she was stonewalling Nora. Hannie was good at the house, Ned knew that, but there it ended. She wouldn't discuss recipes or getting stains off polished furniture or the perfect kitchen floor.

They ate everything she put on the table and sat over coffee and Nora wanted to help wash up again, but Hannie was firm as a rock. When they finally got into the car to drive away the blue-grey twilight was with them like a witness. Ned and Hannie stood together, hearing the sound of the engine fade off into the distance, feeling the damp silence flow back over them and close them off again in their hidden, frosty world.

Hannie bent to snap a cluster of blackened hips from a long, thorned spike on the Frensham rose. 'Do you think Joss would be more normal if I was?' she asked into the silence.

'You mean if he had Nora for a mother?'

She nodded, her face averted.

'If Nora was his mother he wouldn't be Joss,' Ned said quietly. 'It's a meaningless question.'

She snapped off another cluster of hips. 'Niamh thinks Joss is all my fault,' she said.

'Do you?'

She thought for a minute and then shook her head. 'Not all. Joss is Joss, he was born Joss. But I think I've made him worse.'

She had dropped the shrivelled hips on to the ground and was drawing patterns in the gravel with her shoe. 'Then again, there are times when I think I'm all his fault.' She looked up at Ned, a sad, tired look. 'Nothing is as simple as Niamh believes.'

'When you're young you think that way,' Ned said gently. 'Don't you remember? You think everything could be put right if only people went about things differently. You think there is choice. In twenty years' time she'll be astonished that she thought these things at all.'

'She won't remember,' Hannie said bitterly. 'Niamh will always be sure that she's right.'

Ned smiled and shook his head, but he didn't speak.

That night Ned came to Hannie's bed and tried to please her more than himself. It was a failure. For the first time he knew himself to be hopelessly clumsy and incompetent. He wanted to ask her to help him learn, but he knew he couldn't ever get the words out and if he did it would only make it worse. He saw himself through her eyes and knew himself already far too old and inexperienced. He wished he had known her over years, then at least there would have been the tenderness of friendship to lean on. As it was, she was merely fulfilling the terms of their contract. She would service him efficiently and without resentment, but she expected nothing. He wondered if she thought of old loves, or of nothing at all.

He wanted to stay with her for the rest of the night but he didn't want to impose on her more than he already had. He took himself off to his own room and lay a long time looking into the darkness and thinking about the day. Andrew and Nora's visit had thrown them together, had shown them as misfits, almost outcasts, in this intensely settled and familial society. He wondered if she felt like this all the time, and if it made her lonely. He wondered if it was why she'd taken to Danno.

It was the first time she'd referred, even indirectly, to the scene he'd witnessed on Christmas Eve, the first time she'd spoken of Joss and of his strangeness. He suffered for her now when he saw her trapped or hopeless. He wondered if this suffering was a form of love.

worse. He saw himself through her eyes and knew himself already far too old and inexperienced. He wished he had known her over years, then at least there would have been the tenderness of friendship to lean on. As it was, she was merely fulfilling the terms of their contract. She would service him efficiently and without resentment, but she expected nothing. He wondered if she thought of old loves, or of nothing at all.

He wanted to stay with her for the rest of the night but he didn't want to impose on her more than he already had. He took himself off to his own room and lay a long time looking into the darkness and thinking about the day. Andrew and Nora's visit had thrown them together, had shown them as misfits, almost outcasts, in this intensely settled and familial society. He wondered if she felt like this all the time, and if it made her lonely. He wondered if it was why she'd taken to Danno.

It was the first time she'd referred, even indirectly, to the scene he'd witnessed on Christmas Eve, the first time she'd spoken of Joss and of his strangeness. He suffered for her now when he saw her trapped or hopeless. He wondered if this suffering was a form of love.

as a rock. When they finally got into the car to drive away the blue-grey twilight was with them like a witness. Ned and Hannie stood together, hearing the sound of the engine fade off into the distance, feeling the damp silence flow back over them and close them off again in their hidden, frosty world.

Hannie bent to snap a cluster of blackened hips from a long, thorned spike on the Frensham rose. 'Do you think Joss would be more normal if I was?' she asked into the silence.

'You mean if he had Nora for a mother?'

She nodded, her face averted.

'If Nora was his mother he wouldn't be Joss,' Ned said quietly. 'It's a meaningless question.'

She snapped off another cluster of hips. 'Niamh thinks Joss is all my fault,' she said.

'Do you?'

She thought for a minute and then shook her head. 'Not all. Joss is Joss, he was born Joss. But I think I've made him worse.'

She had dropped the shrivelled hips on to the ground and was drawing patterns in the gravel with her shoe. 'Then again, there are times when I think I'm all his fault.' She looked up at Ned, a sad, tired look. 'Nothing is as simple as Niamh believes.'

'When you're young you think that way,' Ned said gently. 'Don't you remember? You think everything could be put right if only people went about things differently. You think there is choice. In twenty years' time she'll be astonished that she thought these things at all.'

'She won't remember,' Hannie said bitterly. 'Niamh will always be sure that she's right.'

Ned smiled and shook his head, but he didn't speak.

That night Ned came to Hannie's bed and tried to please her more than himself. It was a failure. For the first time he knew himself to be hopelessly clumsy and incompetent. He wanted to ask her to help him learn, but he knew he couldn't ever get the words out and if he did it would only make it

∾ *Chapter 36* ∾

Nora phoned while they were eating. She thanked them for their hospitality and spoke convincingly of how much they'd both enjoyed their visit. She said she'd mislaid a small gold bracelet, she didn't know where. Stupid of her, perhaps they would keep an eye out for it and give her a ring if it turned up? Hannie put the phone down and passed on the message, her voice neutral and indifferent. Later she went through Joss's drawers carefully but the bracelet wasn't there. She searched in the most obvious places but all she found was a woman's high-heeled court shoe under the bed. Probably Nora's, though she hadn't mentioned shoes. No sign of its twin. Perhaps Joss had only wanted the one.

She took it away but said nothing. He'd discover the loss: she wanted him to know she knew.

'Garth Brookes?' Ciaran drawled. 'Bit close to Country-with-its-tongue-*not*-in-its-cheek for my taste. You know the style – sleeve notes all about God and the wife. Songs about men in bars hitting each other . . .'

Joss smirked appreciatively. Niamh, sprawled in the lumpy armchair by the fire, stirred irritably but kept her thoughts to herself. She wished Ciaran would stop showing off for Joss. She'd told him as much only two days ago and he'd said she was jealous.

She'd been dumbstruck. Jealous? The injustice of the word! How did he figure that one?

He'd said it was obvious. They were into stuff she wasn't into, so she felt left out and jealous.

Everything she said about Joss after that came out as though to confirm his verdict, so she avoided saying anything. She'd begun to avoid any subject that might annoy Ciaran, she noticed. She was ashamed of her behaviour, but more ashamed of the besottedness that induced it.

She didn't know how Ciaran felt about her; often she wondered if he even liked her. He wanted her, that was plain enough; he reached for her, unable not to reach, already bored by the imperatives of his body. She was as bad, she knew that, and she wasn't yet remotely bored. More like obsessed. Did she love him? She really had no idea. She'd stopped telling him she did when she noticed that he never said the words himself, only nodded vaguely as if in agreement. She glanced across at him now and decided that he despised her. Well, that was all right, she despised him back.

He seemed always detached and sarcastic with her. With her, but also with the rest of them. Except for Hannie. Hannie took no notice of Ciaran, hardly ever addressed him unless it was a request or an enquiry: he was Niamh's boyfriend, that was all, she was formal with him. With Hannie Ciaran watched, he didn't speak. He spoke disparagingly of her, called her The Hag, but there was a tension in him when she appeared, an alertness.

Ciaran had nicknames for everyone, he called Joss The Spook, he rubbished him, but he didn't seem too unhappy with his company. Unless he wanted to go back to bed with her, but even that wasn't really a problem, Joss seemed to know when they wanted him gone. 'I'll be off then,' he'd say, sliding his blank black gaze across her face, the corners of his mouth turned upwards in a smirk. She thought The Smirk would have been a better name than The Spook, but she kept the thought to herself. Ned was A. R. for Anal Retentive. She'd laughed, despite herself; Ned was so stiff and private.

She sighed now and settled herself deeper in the lumpy armchair and tried to let go of her thoughts and get back into her book. The chair was too small, her long limbs stuck out

'Anita Brookner,' Niamh addressed Hannie seriously, looking up at her from her open book. 'She writes about women by themselves.'

'Spinster moralist,' Ciaran drawled from the table. 'Writes about people too scared to live.'

'How would you know? You've never read her.'

'Have so,' Ciaran said casually. 'Great stylist. Still crap. You should try her, Hannie, put some courage into you. Read two of them books in a row and you'll run out the door and burn the world down just to stop yourself from suffocating in fucking moderation.'

'Hannie doesn't read books.'

'Yes she does.'

'No she doesn't.'

'Yes she does. Tell you what, let's ask her.' He swung fully round in his chair and gave Hannie all his attention. Joss watched from somewhere a long way off. 'D'you read books, Hannie?'

'Not very often,' Hannie said indifferently. She was propped against the dresser, smoking a cigarette.

'D' you think auld Brookner's right?'

'About what?'

'Low moral standards and loads of friends?'

'Of course.' Hannie spoke as though it was too obvious to need stating. She took a drag at her cigarette. She looked thoughtful.

'You think I need courage?' she challenged Ciaran suddenly.

'Courage?' He was puzzled.

'You said it would put courage in me?'

Ciaran hesitated. 'I think maybe you're in the doldrums,' he said slowly. 'Temporary-like. Nothing to write home about.'

A curious atmosphere had sprung up between them, an intimacy that was tangible. Hannie's expression didn't change but she stood waiting, as though she hadn't heard his words. Joss stayed very still, but his right hand came forward as though it was separate and autonomous. It picked up his dark beyond its confines, but she didn't want to move because the puppy was asleep on her stomach and she liked stroking the soft hairless belly as she read.

'It says here that people with low moral standards have more friends than people with high ones.' She spoke the words aloud before she knew she had intended to; she heard them with a vague surprise.

'Why d'you read that crap?'

''Tisn't crap. She won the Booker Prize.'

'Still crap.' Ciaran extracted a card from his hand and laid it on the table. He threw a quick glance at Joss.

'She says it's because they're easier to be with.'

'Who are?'

'People with low moral standards.'

'Which would be why I'd have a whole lot more friends than you do,' Ciaran said. Joss laid a card on to Ciaran's and took the trick. A little pulse showed for a moment at the corner of Ciaran's mouth.

'More acquaintances,' Niamh said, looking at him, her brown eyes level and steady. 'I have more friends.'

Ciaran shrugged. His lazy voice belied the pulse. 'Have it yer own way,' he said. He was waiting for Joss to lead, watching the back of his cards as though he could read through them. Joss's dark glasses lay on the table beside him. His face looked curiously empty without them, almost bereft, the skin round his eyes very white, the rest of his face still holding the mark of the African sun, his flaxen brows and lashes accentuating both the colour and the absence of it.

'Who is this crappy author that you're reading?' Hannie asked from across the room. She was roaming around with a glass in her hand, picking up objects, putting them down again. She'd come over from the house with a bottle of vodka, ostensibly to return past hospitality, in reality to check on Joss and the chemistry between him and Ciaran. She'd dismissed Danno's words to his face, but nonetheless she was alert to them.

glasses and settled them on to his nose again. Niamh grabbed at the puppy, pulling the little body close and rubbing her cheek against the soft fur. Only Ciaran seemed unaware.

At last Hannie moved. She tossed her cigarette into the fire and looked straight at Ciaran.

'The doldrums,' she said thoughtfully. 'Becalmed, no wind in the sails, nothing to blow you this way or that.' She laughed, a low easy laugh that was utterly surprising. 'Perhaps it's the right place for me,' she said, still speaking to him and to no one else. 'Now that I'm almost an old woman. The doldrums. Respectable. Safe.'

'Would you wise up, Hannie?' Ciaran said. His voice had a harsh authority. 'You're never going to be respectable. And you're never going to be safe, neither. Face facts, stop dreaming dreams. It's not the world that'll stop you – it's yourself.' He stared at her furiously, consumed in the intensity of the drama between them. Then, with a hard effort, he broke her gaze and threw a card down on the table. With a toss of the head he challenged Joss to follow his lead. 'And leave off the fucking glasses, dickhead! You want to play – you play straight. Or as straight as your twisted wee soul can allow for. I want to see your eyes, an' that means no glasses.'

Joss didn't answer. He removed the dark glasses and glanced at his hand. Casually, he laid a low card of a different suit over Ciaran's queen. Ciaran looked at him, wanting to know the catch, then took the trick, sweeping the cards towards him without lifting them off the table so that Joss wouldn't see his hand trembling. Joss saw. He didn't know what had happened but he knew that Ciaran had unnerved himself and he knew his mother was the cause of it.

He'd let Ciaran win the next few tricks, then he'd change the suit with a trump and take the game.

❧ *Chapter 37* ❧

*H*annie walked back over the yard, the moist black air eddying about her, fine needles of rain showing in the halo around the yardlight. The temperature had changed, it was much milder; she'd rather the frost with its quickness, she felt that the sky had moved down and was pressing in round her. The sky, or was it the sea? She might shipwreck in these waters, she might drown. And she longed for a continent under her feet, for the great empty emanations of a continent, not this small dense island which was like living confined in a single room.

She knew that Ciaran had connected with her and in doing so had shocked himself. A connection of that intensity had always a sexual charge to it, a charge that had passed far beyond flirtation to enter the starker realms of recognition. Sexual recognition, but also psychic recognition. They were two of a kind, she and Ciaran, both physically and psychically, and the strength of this mutual revelation had momentarily bridged the chasm of age.

Hannie hadn't seen it coming: she, too, was caught off-guard, but she knew enough to know what it was when it came. That she'd been unprepared was odd in itself: usually she knew precisely when she had caught a man's attention, knew it long before he did. Then, even to herself, she seemed to forget it. But underneath, she still knew. Her unpreparedness, she decided, was his age. Ciaran was only a boy to her, she had never considered him either sexually or otherwise, unless with a voyeur's detachment, watching Niamh embroiled in her infatuation.

She pushed open the back door and went in. Perhaps she'd